naked
sleeper

Also by Sigrid Nunez

A Feather on the Breath of God

naked
sleeper

a novel

SIGRID NUNEZ

HarperPerennial
A Division of HarperCollinsPublishers

The author is grateful to the Corporation of Yaddo, the MacDowell Colony, Blue Mountain Center, and the Mrs. Giles Whiting Foundation for their generous support.

A hardcover edition of this book was published in 1996 by HarperCollins Publishers.

HarperCollins books may be purchased for educational, business, or sales promotional use. For information please write: Special Markets Department, HarperCollins Publishers, Inc., 10 East 53rd Street, New York, NY 10022.

First HarperPerennial edition published 1997.

Designed by Nancy Singer

The Library of Congress has catalogued the hardcover edition as follows:

Nunez, Sigrid
    Naked sleeper : a novel / by Sigrid Nunez.
      p. cm.
    ISBN 0-06-017276-2
    1. Married Women—Psychology—Fiction. 2. Women—Family relationships—Fiction. 3. Women biographers—Fiction. I. Title
PS3564.U475N35   1996
813'.54—dc20   96-16819

ISBN 0-06-092861-1 (pbk.)

97 98 99 00 01 ❖/RRD 10 9 8 7 6 5 4 3 2 1

Background is important. Things happen in the country that would never happen in the city. Things happen to people in strange places that would not happen to them at home. It isn't true that people who cross the sea change their skies but not their natures. We are different, depending on where we are. What kind of room we are in can be critical. Even how it is furnished. And the view. And the light. Landscape matters. A lot can depend on the season, the weather, the time of day. ("How much a small moon can do.") People do not want to believe this. It is like not wanting to believe, as Einstein said he could not, that God plays dice with the universe.

chapter
one

First, this letter.

Dear Nona,

It is very late. I mean, it is very early. It is almost morning. I have not slept. I have been up all night, packing. Are you asleep? I hope so. Did you take a pill? I worry about you. You say the effects of insomnia are far worse than the side effects of the pills, but still, I worry. I love you. There I go again. You have told me I mustn't, but I must, and I do, again and again. Forgive me. It is wrong, I know, and yes, yes, yes, you are right, dear Nona. It is not possible for me to be as in love with you as I am, or (I hear you correcting) as I *think* I am. It's just this place, being away from home, things will look completely different once you are out of my sight—hear me repeat (for the thousandth time) all the reasonable things you tried telling me last night. And the whole time you were speaking all I wanted was to take your hands, to pull you to me and kiss your eyes and drink from your mouth— There I go again. Okay, okay. I will get up and go out now. I will take a quick walk around the house and pull myself together.

Back. The sun came up while I was out. Another
glorious day. What a month this has been! But what
does it mean to me now? The sun beams upon this
page only to illuminate my foolishness, and the birds
are jeering at me. I am babbling, forgive me. It is
fatigue—nerves—the horror of leaving you. Let me
come at last to the point. You will not see me at breakfast. In a few minutes I will take my bags and go very
quietly downstairs to wait for the taxi I arranged last
night to pick me up. You will not see me again. I know
I promised that I would be at breakfast, to say good-
bye to you and the others, but I cannot do it. I cannot
bear to say good-bye to you, especially not with the
others around. And so this letter. First, I want to tell
you that you are wrong to believe that I will forget you
when I go home. I don't dare say that you have broken
my heart, but you have changed my life, and I could
never forget you. Second, I want to ask your forgive-
ness for all the trouble I've caused. I have brought
inconvenience and anxiety and confusion into your
life—I have behaved with perfect selfishness—and you
have been kind and respectful and gentle with me, and
I am grateful to you. I have no right to ask for anything
more, but please, one thing: may I write to you? And
will you write me back? It is this hope that makes it
possible for me to leave you now: the hope that I might
somehow go on knowing you, if only on paper.

(The taxi driver just honked his horn, though I
specifically told him last night not to! Let's hope he
didn't wake you.)

When I was out, I picked a rose. Now, before I leave,
I will go to your room and slip the rose and this letter
under your door. Don't worry: the sun stealing through
your window will not be more quiet than I. Sleep on,
as I stand outside your door and picture your room:

first light, the curves of your body under the blanket (stay warm, my dear; it's chilly this morning), your books and your papers, your kimono lying across the chair. And as so many times before, I will summon all my strength to stop myself from opening that door and going to your bed—

Lyle

Nona wrote the answer to Lyle's letter in her office, between classes. She put down the red pen with which she had been correcting homework and she took up a blue pen and she wrote:

I am home now. It has been two days. It is very strange to be back—I am sure it's the same for you. I was sorry that you decided not to come to breakfast that last morning. Everyone missed you. I read your letter, of course. I don't know what to say. If you want to write to me, of course you may, and of course I will write you back. I would write more to you now except that I am very busy—work and so on—and my mother is coming day after tomorrow, and her visits always send me into a bit of a tailspin. I miss you, of course. Thank you for the flower. I hope you are well.

She sealed the letter and laid it aside. Then she picked up her red pen again and went on correcting homework.

NONA'S MOTHER, ROSALIND, had been thirty years old when she had Nona. Seventy now, she lived alone in Los Angeles and seldom came East to visit her only child. She would not have come now, except that an old friend had died, and the funeral was in Riverdale. Nona did not get to visit her mother very often, either. She was grateful that her mother had four sisters living in or near Los Angeles, which is where they were all originally from. Another blessing to be counted was that Rosalind was unusually self-reliant. She enjoyed living alone. She knew how to keep herself busy and fit. She swam every morning, she still had the stamina to shop all day, and she loved to read. She read every night in bed, her book supported on a tray to which was attached one of those tiny lamps intended to allow reading without disturbing a partner, though there had been no partner to disturb in Rosalind's life for many years. She could have left all the lights in the house burning, if she'd wanted. Her happiest times were when she began a book and was so drawn into it that she would stay up all night long until she had finished it. Then she would get up and fix herself a sandwich and have it with a glass of milk out on the patio; after that she'd go back to bed and sleep like a log. She said she was sure she got as much out of such nights as others did out of nights on the town. Her daughter's insomnia bemused her. Why didn't Nona just stay up and read? (Because she had to work the next day, Nona reminded her.)

Rosalind didn't watch television, and like a lot of people who don't watch television, she couldn't resist throwing this up to others. She was forever quoting Frank Lloyd Wright's definition: chewing gum for the eyes. She'd had a television long ago, but after it broke and she never got around to having it fixed, she realized that she didn't miss it. When Rosalind came to stay with Nona and Nona's husband, Roy, though, watching television was one of her pleasures. She watched with the fascination of an alien. The commercials especially transfixed her. Every few minutes she let another exclamation escape. "Incredible!" "What a culture!" "It all goes by so fast!" "I had no idea!" "I'm still in the Stone Age!" And she laughed and she laughed.

Watching her mother before the television set, Nona remembered how, as a child, she would try to get Rosalind to watch TV with her, because that would have been something they could do together, while her mother's reading shut Nona out. Every book her mother read was like another brick in a wall. When she was a little older, Nona had tried to get her mother to share the books. But: Too old for you, Rosalind would say, taking the book out of Nona's hands. Then, as now, the best-seller list was Rosalind's guide, and so, though she read a lot of bad books, she read a lot of good ones, too. Still, they were not the kind of books that Nona, once she was old enough to read whatever she wanted, would have read.

Next to reading, Rosalind's favorite pastime had always been shopping, and here again Nona found herself facing a wall, for be it for clothes or housewares or Christmas presents, shopping was an activity Nona loathed and always tried to avoid. All the years she had lived at home, and even after she had gone away to college, Nona had let her mother do her shopping for her. Might as well have had a son, Rosalind complained.

Nona never saw her mother for the first time in a while without experiencing a small thrill that had everything to do with Rosalind's looks, which were neither youthful nor beauti-ful but undeniably striking. Unlike most people her age, Rosalind looked as if she was in command of her appearance. This had to do with certain decisions she had made years before: To wear only bold colors, usually red and black. To have her hair dyed, and to ignore her hairdresser's advice to leave a streak or two of gray for a more natural look. For that was just the point: a good instinct had told Rosalind that, after a certain age, what would work best for her was a look that was honestly artificial. That many people thought she was wearing a wig was fine with her. And it was not that she was ashamed of her gray hair, she wanted you to know, but the truth was, very few complexions went well with gray hair and hers was not one of them. Black as licorice her hair was now. Sometimes she hid it all up under a turban. She made up her face: dark lipstick and powder and rouge, all applied with a heavy hand—no, not because her eyesight was failing. She wore bright red nail polish. Perfume, always, and sometimes false eyelashes. Her favorite fabric was silk. She wore jewelry: large, plain, geometric pieces. The painted face, the red and the black, the turban, the silk, the Euclidean shapes—there was something mystic and ceremonial about her, Nona always thought: like a shamaness. (Roy's first impression was of a deck of cards.)

Background is important. When Nona went to California and saw her mother against the palm trees and low roofs of West Hollywood or in her own airy, light-filled house, Rosalind always looked taller, younger, and even more vivid than Nona remembered, with a touch of the glamour, perhaps, of one of those aging stars who lived in the hills nearby. In New York Rosalind seemed somewhat diminished, like a bright potted plant that has been brought into the shade. Smaller, muted, less substantial in some way—it may have had something to do with her sleeping in the living room. Background is always important.

Many people who saw Rosalind for the first time now imagined that, in her youth, she had been quite a vamp. Her son-in-law had made this mistake. But Nona knew that her mother had been a demure girl, a good Catholic girl in a good Catholic boarding school; a soft, shy girl in a white night shift, sleeping on a hard narrow bed; and when she slept on her left side she dreamed of entering a convent, and when she slept on her right side she dreamed of love. And for this Rosalind of so long ago, and so different from the later Rosalind, Nona felt an unnameable emotion that had all the tug of nostalgia, though Nona did not see how you could feel nostalgia for something you had never known. But if she were given the proverbial three wishes, one, at least, would be to go back in time and make friends with that tender stranger.

The devil asks us: if you could choose your family as you do your friends, would you choose your own? In the years when Nona had found her mother most maddening and herself least up to coping with her, she had been struck one day by the thought that if Rosalind were not her mother, and if by chance she were to meet this vibrant, independent woman, she would like her very much; she would want to know her better. And constantly reminding herself of this had become part of Nona's way of dealing with Rosalind, and of remaining fair. To judge one's parents solely by how they had treated oneself was not just. Simple, obvious, it seemed to Nona now, but the path to that understanding had been long and steep. And that understanding, along with the understanding that her mother had suffered in life, had made relations with Rosalind finally bearable.

Rosalind, who had once lived in New York, hated that city, and it wasn't just because the life she had lived there had ended unhappily. It was for all the usual reasons, too: the dirt, the curtness of the people, the Augusts and the Februaries, the tall buildings cutting off the sun. When she came it was never for long. This time it was for just four days. Those four days she would not go out much. She had old friends in New York, quite a few of them, but none that she particularly wanted to see. There would be one major shopping spree and a visit with her daughter to an exhibition of Impressionist paintings. There would be dinner at an old neighborhood restaurant that she liked and that Nona and Roy always took her to. And there was the funeral, of course, which was held the day after she arrived.

That evening they had dinner at home. They had planned to eat outside, in the small backyard of Nona and Roy's Village apartment, but it was September now, and the day had turned cool.

"Move to California, children," Rosalind said, "and you can practically live outdoors. Doesn't that sound good? And the food is so much fresher, too," she added, poking at her salad.

"How was the funeral?" Roy asked, with a little frown that showed that he knew this might be a difficult question.

"Oh, funerals." Rosalind shrugged. "They're all the same.

Weddings, funerals, they're all so boring, so—*unnecessary*, I think." (Just because she was always dressed for one didn't mean that Rosalind liked ceremonies.) "If Nona didn't live here, I wouldn't have come at all. I haven't seen Muriel for— what? Twenty years? Do you think she would have cared? Muriel wouldn't have given a damn how many people came to her funeral."

A mistake the living often make about the dead.

Rosalind turned to her daughter then and said, "So, did you have a good time, wherever you were? On your—retreat?"

Nona laughed. "I wouldn't call it a retreat."

"Where were you, exactly?"

"I told you. I was at Phoebe's. She's turned the estate into a kind of conference center. People go there all year for different events, but in the summer there's usually some time when nothing is scheduled and the place is free and Phoebe invites people to come up and work or rest—and to keep her company, I guess. It's pretty lonely up there. It was very nice of her to ask me. She said to give you her love, by the way."

"Who?"

Rosalind's blank look brought Nona a pang. Her mother really was getting old. "Phoebe," she said. "Benedict's daughter."

"Oh! That's right, that's right. You told me that. Well, you know, I barely remember them. I don't think I'd recognize Phoebe if I ran into her on the street! So, did you have a good time?"

"I had a wonderful time. You can't imagine how nice it was to get out of the city for a whole month. And I got a lot of work done."

There was a pause. They had come to a subject far more chilling than the funeral: Nona was writing a book about her father.

"A whole month," Rosalind said, deftly paddling away from the whirlpool. "You must have missed Roy."

"Yes, of course."

"And how is the teaching?" Rosalind rushed on, a little breathless, paddling harder. "I tell everyone back home all those funny stories, and they just love them. Oh, tell me more."

And so, for the next several minutes, Nona entertained her mother with quotes from the foreign students whom she taught English. "My neighbor is Grecian, he has a beauty saloon." "I take the fourth or fifth train to Brooklyn." "A piano is heavy, I cannot heave it." "We could not sleep last night because a dog was barfing." "I wear the short skirt to please my thick boss." "He was beside himself with rape." "Bensonhurst is an Italian aria." "The American writer Mark Taiwan." "The American novel *Passing Wind*." "The favorite thing of my wife is to hang and kiss her baby." "In America is many foods, but here is eat only hen, is no eat cock."

The fish was okay, Roy told himself. He had been worried that he had overcooked it. All in all, he was satisfied with the way dinner had turned out. A very light meal of fish, rice, and salad. Nona had asked him please to cook lighter meals for now; she had put on seven pounds while she was away.

Roy laid down his knife and fork and felt that familiar craving that he supposed would never go away entirely: he had felt it after every meal since he quit smoking ten years before. Resting his elbows on the table and his chin on his hands, he sat silently watching. Before him was a tableau of no small wonder: the woman he loved and her mother. Mystery and the Mother of Mystery.

Around Rosalind Roy was never really himself. She was one of those women who burn with a low but steady flame of resentment toward men, and in her presence Roy was aware of certain changes in his manner: speaking in a voice lower than usual; pretending to know less than he did, to be less capable and confident and sophisticated than he was; slouching (but careful not to appear too at ease), and practicing what is known to religious as custody of the eyes.

Roy spoke to his mother-in-law pretty much only when spoken to, and that was not often. Rosalind seldom asked him how he was or what he was doing. She was one of the only people he'd ever met who showed absolutely no curiosity about his profession. It was doubtful that she could have told you much about where Roy was from or about his family, though of course she had been told these things. He had no idea (and neither had Nona) what Rosalind really thought of him. But he was used to her distance, and he did not really mind it. Things could have been worse. She could have lived in New York. She could have come to dinner once a week and been openly hostile. It was enough for Roy that she was civil to him. Besides, Roy liked Rosalind.

"Oh, Nona, why do you have to do this? Why do you want to write this thing?"

Having steered clear of the whirlpool and left it far behind, Rosalind now turned around, paddled back, and dove straight into it. No one was surprised. It was her character.

For Roy, this was a cue. He did what he knew Nona would have wished him to do. He got up and cleared the table. In the kitchen he set water to boil for coffee. He brought out cups and dessert plates and the lemon pound cake he had baked that morning. Coming and going, he caught bits of a familiar argument. *Privacy. In bad taste. All Sasha's idea. Nobody's business.* Both women kept their voices calm, but now and then Rosalind let out a laugh in which anyone could have heard the scorn—and sharper listeners the anguish as well.

When the coffee was ready and Roy had sat down again, he saw that his wife had taken her mother's hand.

"I told you, Rosalind," Nona was saying. "Anything you don't want in that book won't be in it. Anything you don't like will be taken out."

Even as she said it Nona was wondering how on earth she was going to keep such a promise.

"That's impossible," Rosalind said, freeing her hand so that she could pick up her cup.

"Why?"

"Because I won't read it."

IF SHE WOKE UP DURING the night, as she often did, Nona would not look at the clock. Partly superstition, perhaps, though Nona was not superstitious. She was afraid that if she saw how late it was, she would have even more trouble falling back to sleep. It was the same when she was trying to get to sleep for the first time. She would know that it was getting later and later but would refuse to look at the clock to confirm this. That way she might be able to trick herself. The next day, if she did not know for sure how much sleep she had gotten, she could pretend that it had been enough. These were old stratagems for Nona, who had followed them ever since her sleeping troubles began several years ago. Sometimes it got to be so late that the day broke, and then, of course, the game was up.

And so, waking now, Nona did not know and did not look to find out that it was four o'clock.

Her first feeling was regret for not having taken a pill. If she had, she would probably still be asleep. But she had drunk wine with dinner, and she had been very drowsy when she got into bed. She had not been worried about sleep then. Now she knew instantly what she was in for. She was as wide awake as it was possible to be. Beside her, Roy slept—soundly, as always, in accord with what seems to be a rule governing the spouses of insomniacs. He was snoring. Nona could hear the faint, comical sawing noise through her earplugs. She had started wearing earplugs only recently—not because of Roy's snoring, but because there was so much construction going on in the Village these days, and some of it went on at night.

Nona had an early class the next morning. She would be miserable all day if she didn't get more sleep. Then, tomorrow night, she would go to bed exhausted, but even so she would have the same trouble falling asleep. She knew from experience that it could take weeks to break this pattern.

If she wanted a pill, she would have to get up and go into the bathroom. Another stratagem: Nona did not keep the sleeping pills by the bed. This was to help her resist, to prevent her from reaching for them too soon. They had to be a last resort, those pills. She and her doctor had worked it out. The dosage of each pill was low; it was important not to take more than one or two pills more than two or three times a week. If she took one now, she could expect to be asleep within fifteen minutes. (There had been a few exceptions to this rule, and those were nights Nona had done her best to forget.)

She got up and put on her bathrobe. It was not a kimono, as Lyle had called it, just a blue-and-white cotton flannel robe with rather wide sleeves. In the bathroom she took the bottle of pills from the medicine cabinet, opened it, and shook one out, all without turning on the light. She swallowed the pill with a little water cupped in her palm. Earlier, her mother had taken a bath, and the air was still moist and tinged with the scent of patchouli from the soap that Rosalind never traveled without.

Back in bed, Nona relaxed. It was a help already just knowing that she would not have to suffer; the pill would mend her broken night. She curled against her husband, slipping an arm around his waist. Good, warm, solid Roy. What a relief it had been to get home to him. How changed everything can seem when you are in a strange place. She had promised herself that when she got back she would try to sort out the events that had happened while she was away. But so far she had not even begun to do this, and now was no time to try. Her breathing had slowed, her body felt increasingly light, but her mind was racing. Thoughts and images spun through her brain and as the drug took hold became both more vivid and more fragmented. It was like the earth-falling-away sensation and kaleidoscopic view of a Ferris-wheel ride. Nona saw her mother at table, the fish bones on her plate, her red fingernails. Roy standing by with a knife in his hand, and a grave, closed expression on his face as he cut the cake. What day was it? Was tomorrow Tuesday? A little jolt of anxiety, and Nona's eyes snapped open. Her teaching schedule was different each day. Tuesday, yes. First class at nine. Another jolt. Had she corrected the homework? Oh, here they all were before her: a double row of foreign faces, staring uncomprehendingly at her and waiting for that miracle that they never quite stopped believing in: if they spoke to her often enough in their native tongue, one day she would speak it back. Now all the faces changed, becoming unmistakably American. Phoebe was laughing, looking as she did so exactly like her father, Benedict. The bright waters of the lake ringing around them— a dozen people fitting miraculously into one rowboat—and the sound of Phoebe laughing became the sound of lapping water. Across the lake rose the mountain—and who had blown the giant smoke ring that had snagged on its top? Excuse me, Nona said, getting up, for she had remembered something urgent. She stepped out of the boat and into the woods. Ahead, crossing her path with slow, stately steps, was a deer. It turned its head toward her and Nona saw Lyle's eyes staring imploringly across the wide dinner table. *Patchouli,* she said helplessly. But Lyle was already gone; he had entered the cave, parting the beaded curtain of the waterfall. *Rat-a-tat, rat-a-tat*—what a sound, what a dreadful sound that was. Rosalind's hand shook as she lifted the cup and saucer. The coffee spilled a map upon the tablecloth. *Why, oh, why do you have to do this thing? No harm done,* said Benedict, who was dead. It was absurd for Roy to be outside in the backyard at this moment sawing down that tree, but he was her husband. What? A party at this hour? Were her neighbors mad? She would have to go speak to them. She got up and put on her best red-and-black kimono. Upstairs, the apartment door stood open. Now, who would have guessed their small building contained so huge an apartment? The ballroom was packed with dancing couples. As she stepped inside, someone stole up behind her, a large hand in a white glove lowered itself over her eyes, and she saw that all the dancers were naked. Another hand pressed her breast. She leaned back, a word was whispered into her ear, a magic word, a potent word, never to be repeated. She knew the incantation, but the poisoned wine had numbed her lips. It didn't matter. It was over now. The lid of the sarcophagus was coming down. Her body went slack. She slept.

AFTER ROSALIND HAD GONE back to California and the living room was their own again, Roy and Nona sat on the couch, talking about her.

"Well," said Roy, "at least this time she didn't say, Why don't you wait till I'm dead." And Nona laughed in spite of herself. Rosalind had sunk this very barb into her daughter's flesh more than once. But Rosalind had said good-bye with a typical gesture. Having noticed that the upholstery of the living-room couch was a bit worse for wear, she had forced a large check on them. "You deserve a new one, children." It was all the more generous, because Roy and Nona were not particularly hard up right now, and Rosalind was not rich. Her income came from money that had been set aside by her father after her divorce. He had seen—accurately and with blood in his eye—that Shep Shelton could not be depended on to meet alimony payments, and that Rosalind was likely to outlive him by many years (also accurate). That grim old Irishman, who had worked his way up from laborer to boss of his own water-supply company, had greeted the news of his son-in-law's death with cheer. "So, I'm not to be deprived of the pleasure of living out my days knowing that bastard is burning in Hell."

Whenever the subject of Nona's book came up, her mother would say, "But it wasn't even your idea." For some reason Rosalind was stuck on this, that the whole business was something Nona had been *put up to* by an outsider. Nona thought it must have galled her mother even more that the instigator had been Sasha Becker, no outsider at all, but the child of a friend of Rosalind and Shep's, one of the old crowd (now mostly dead). Nona and Sasha had played together as children, but they had been out of touch for years, and so Sasha's call that day had come out of the blue. Sasha had an idea for a book: a collection of essays by people whose parents were artists. To Nona, it had sounded far-fetched. But *Children of Psychiatrists* had done well, she was told; and someone was working on *Children of Convicts*. "Children of Anyone is a hot issue now," Sasha said. Besides, she had a contract.

When the book came out, Rosalind read it all in one night and concluded that the best thing in it was Sasha's own essay, which was about her mother, who had killed herself when Sasha was thirteen. ("I cried and cried, remembering that crazy bitch.") She had not found much to upset her in her own daughter's essay (the shortest in the book), because it dealt mostly with Nona's impressions of her father when she was very young, and how only gradually—and reluctantly—she had come to understand that he was just a painter, and not the mysterious color-mixing sorcerer she had imagined him. She had said little about his personal life, and not one word about sex. But when Nona saw herself in print, she covered her face with her hands. It was the most peculiar form of betrayal—for who had betrayed her? Neither Sasha nor the editor had changed a line. No, these were her words, all right: every one of them bad or wrong. The entire essay cried out to be rewritten. And this was what, that same sleepless night, Nona sat down to do: rewrite the essay about her father. When she looked up again, a year had passed.

Two things about writing had especially surprised Nona: how hard it was and how much it engaged her. And this had made her think (though not for the first time) that, so far in life, she had not been adequately challenged. She had not been one of those lucky people who find just the career to suit their needs and talents. There were not many such people, she knew, but they were the ones she envied most. She had never been a very good student, and it had not been at all clear to her, once school was behind her, what she should do with her education (she had majored in classics); how she should get on with her life. And though she was not lazy or unambitious, there had been long periods when just getting by had been job enough, a day-to-day struggle exhausting all her resources.

If Nona had a special gift, it was her voice. She had known early on that she could have made a career of singing, and there had been people—one high school teacher in particular—who had tried to push her in this direction. But, much as Nona loved to sing, she hated to perform. In fact, she was so sure of her unsuitability for a performing career that she had never had any doubts or regrets about having avoided one. It had taken her months to feel comfortable just standing in front of a classroom.

Six years ago, a funny thing happened. We are speaking now of a very low period in Nona's life. She was living alone, she was unemployed, paying her bills with money sent by Rosalind. She could not work. She could not think. She could barely move. She was caught on the flypaper of depression. And suddenly, as she later described it, it was as if she had been possessed by the spirit of a songbird. A hundred times a day music welled in her. Wherever she was, whatever she was doing, Nona had the urge to sing. She had never experienced anything like it before. At night she woke from dreams in which she had been singing. It was bizarre, a kind of disorder, almost; at times an embarrassment. (Sometimes the urge seized her in public, and she was not always able to suppress it.) She had not sung in a long time, and the sound of her voice was new to her. Age had mellowed and colored it; it seemed at least a size larger than she remembered. When she mentioned to her mother that she was thinking of taking a class, just for fun,

Rosalind could not have been more enthusiastic—"a great idea, just what you need, get you out of the house, how expensive can it be?"—and sent her a bigger check that month than usual.

The class, at the New School, turned out to be just that: a great idea, just what Nona needed. The teacher was good: articulate, patient, and respectful of amateurs, and Nona quickly took to him and to the five other students. They met twice a week, and Nona looked forward to those evenings as to nothing else. She enjoyed them so much, she had to wonder why she had been denying herself all this time. How could she have forgotten how much fun it was to make music with other people? She had forgotten, too, the keen physical pleasure to be got from singing: the flood of sensation in the chest, throat, and mouth; the warm vibration spreading through the entire body; that sense of fulfillment and release, oh so like that other pleasure, the pursuit of which was so much more complicated.

One evening on her way to class, Nona ran into one of her neighbors. When she told him where she was headed, he said, "Oh. You look so pretty I thought you were going on a date." Pondering this remark as she went on her way, and remembering how carefully she had dressed and put on her makeup before leaving her apartment, Nona acknowledged a certain troubling suspicion. That suspicion was confirmed when she arrived and saw the note on the classroom door. Class was canceled. The teacher was ill.

The crushing force of her disappointment. The rocketing of her pulse at the word *ill*.

Later, in the full flush of their romance, Nona and Roy liked to joke that it was for this that the gods had sent the spirit of a lark to possess her.

It was just before they got married, fourteen months later, that they found the one-bedroom apartment where they now lived. It was much too expensive. It was a little too small. But there was a fireplace. There was the backyard. They took it on the spot.

Roy no longer taught at the New School. He worked mostly with professionals now, in a studio near Lincoln Center. He also taught one semester a year at a college in Connecticut. Nona had continued at the New School for a while after Roy left, taking workshops in a cappella and in lieder, but her life was changing, and she found less and less time for music. She was no longer single and living alone. She had her own classes to teach, and her book to write, and if she sang now it was at home, with Roy accompanying her on the upright. They still kept up with some of the students from Nona's first class, and occasionally they all got together at someone's place, and when they got together they usually sang. But if weeks went by without any singing now, Nona found that she did not really miss it.

The narrow desk where Nona worked was in the bedroom, facing the window. Her favorite time to write was in the mornings, on those mornings when she did not have to teach. She usually had the apartment to herself then, and it was very quiet. The window faced the backyard. She had seen the seasons change from that desk: snow falling, and the tulips Roy had planted coming up, and the hibachi used for barbecues standing under the plane tree. Now the leaves were turning. Time passing, herself working, lifting her eyes now and then to the view—those hours at her desk were like a thread that bound her days one to another. Concentrating, trying to pin down a thought, Nona would hold her breath for a hushed moment, sensing—what? A message being beamed at her; a mystery about to be revealed—not just about her father or her own little life but about everyone and all of life. Nine times out of ten it turned out to be an illusion. There was nothing behind the dark veil. Sometimes there wasn't even a veil. But she had had her share of tiny epiphanies, sitting at that desk. At times she was aware of being watched: an older woman, looking back at her from the other side of that window and remembering: *I was happy then.*

chapter
two

Dear Nona,

Here I am, without you. There is no truer way of saying how I see myself now. You cannot know how much I think of you and long to see you again. To cure myself of this infatuation (your word), this is the lance I use: She is married. She is twenty-five hundred miles away, she is fully engaged in her own full life. She is married. She gets up, eats, works, plays, sleeps—all very well without you. She is married. . . .

A coincidence: I met Charlotte the same year that you met Roy. Had you realized that? Whenever I think of you and him, I am jealous. It is not just a sexual jealousy (though, of course, there is plenty of *that*). It's details like this that get to me: the two of you having your morning coffee together, sharing meals, you cooking and him cleaning up afterward, discussing what movie to see or where to go on vacation—that sort of thing. The appalling state of my own marriage is no secret to you. My being away for a month changed nothing. Nothing has changed since my return. I want to leave, she wants me to stay. Back and forth we go. It is torture. Needless to say, she knows nothing about you. I must spare her that extra grief, I suppose. A typical argument goes like this: Me: I'm unhappy, you're unhappy. She: But we're happier than most couples. Me: I can't stand the fights anymore. She: But we don't fight as much as other couples. And so on. She is a good woman. She has tried her best, and she wants to keep on trying. But I am miserable. I am no longer interested in working things out. I want to flee. I want to flee to the woman I love.

Oh, Nona, it is good of you to let me write to you. If I am writing things you don't want to hear, you must tell me, you must stop me, I cannot stop myself. I realize what a fool I must sound to you, but please bear with me. I know that in time these feelings must pass (though of course there is that part of me that does not want them to pass; being with you has made me remember what it was like to be alive, a feeling I want to hold on to forever), but for now I ask you, please, don't make me go through it alone. I need you. You have no idea how lonely I am. Bear with me, and I promise to try not to burden you too much.

You say that you are back at work now. Where is your school? Do you take the subway? Do you teach every day? Do you like your students? They like you— that much I don't have to ask. But I confess it's a little hard for me to imagine you teaching. I know how anxious you are when you have to get up in front of other people. Easier for me to picture you alone, at a desk, bent over a page—in profile. (You have such a lovely profile.) Perhaps it's because that is how I saw you the very first time: I came round the corner of the house and there you were, sitting on the porch, reading. In a flood of sunlight, appropriately. *You.* (Have you any idea what color your hair is in such light? I can think of nothing to compare it to.) But of course when I think of you, you are alone. "To the lover the beloved is always solitary" (Walter Benjamin). Uh-oh: time to apply the lance again: *She is not solitary. She is not the Lady of Shalott yearning at her casement for you. She is married. Happily so, remember?*

About me (which I dare to hope you are thinking and will want to hear): I am back to teaching now, too. I suppose it is fair to say that my students speak a little better English than yours. Last semester, on their final exam, they were asked to define "animism." "Animism is when" every answer began. "Animism is when people attribute humanist qualities to wild animals." (Look—there goes another Renaissance elephant!) This is university, mind you. When I asked this budding scholar for an example of what she could possibly mean, she gulped and said, "Uh—the unicorn?" They say over sixty percent of adults in this country do not read books. The real horror is, this includes people in college.

So, what the hell am I doing here? Well, Tucson is a great city, I have to say. And I'm lucky to have found this job. But sometimes—often—I think how I would like to give up teaching, tenure be damned, and open a little bookstore. Customers would have to don gloves before they touched any of my books. I'd ask every one to say what was the last book he or she read, and I wouldn't sell them a new one unless I approved.

And how is your book coming along? I often think now of that night in the library, when you read to us. Myself, I can't imagine wanting to spend all that time thinking about my parents, but if I had to I could say everything in very few words. My mother will always be that witch, my father the poor weak fool in the witch's thrall. Whenever I try to be objective I feel again the sudden swift kick in the butt, and I think,

What kind of woman attacks a child from behind? Abuse doesn't make you tough, as some people think. It makes you craven, cowardly. It coats you with a scent that leads the bullies straight to you. (You have no idea how often I was beaten up in school as a child.) And, much as I may pity him, I know I'll never be able to forgive my father for not protecting us. After all, we were just kids, but he was a man—a big man, in fact. I'll say this for Charlotte: she's a fine mother, and her children adore her. (I've met the father, too, a few times, and he's not a bad guy, either, except when he's drinking.) It was part of the big attraction, initially, seeing Charlotte with the kids: pretty, loving, single mom, coping like a champ. I think we were both happier when the kids were around. Even now, we seem to get along better when they're home from school.

I try to imagine you all the time, where you might be and what you might be doing at any given moment. Here of course it is three hours earlier, so when I am sitting down to dinner sometimes I think: She must be getting ready for bed. Or: She is already asleep. And wherever she is, whatever she is doing, bless her.

Write to me, tell me about your days, your routine, give me details, long lists of details, so that I can imagine you more fully. And would it be too much to ask you to send me a picture?

Oh, Nona, I am not a monster or a fool. I know the implications of my behavior toward you, and that grave responsibilities are involved. But what I don't know and what I need to know is how you feel about all this. How do you see me in your future? Is there a place for me in your life? Or have you already forgotten me? (That last thought is death to me: the lance dipped in poison.)

When I am not trying to imagine what you are

doing, I am trying to imagine how I could possibly arrange to see you again. I want to call you but I don't, because I'm afraid it might cause you problems. Likewise, if you are going to call me, it would be better if you used the office number I gave you.

Write to me, dear one. I'll be living to hear from you.

Lyle

P.S. Got it: *daylilies*. The color of your hair in bright sunlight.

Before Nona had a chance to answer this letter, another one arrived. ("Forgive me, but I cannot keep away.") The next day came yet another. The following day there were two. ("What have you done to me?" the first one began. "What's to become of me?" ended the other.)

The mail usually came between ten and eleven. On those mornings when she was home and trying to work, Nona found it hard to concentrate. She was waiting for the mailman and that day's letter. After her letter arrived, she would read it over several times and put it aside. But when she tried to get back to work, she could think of nothing but what Lyle had written. The trouble concentrating spilled over into the rest of her day. In one of her classes she had two Polish sisters. Correcting their homework, Nona had changed an error on one sister's homework but missed the very same error on the other's. When the women pointed this out in class, Nona was humiliated. Apologizing, she said, "Your teacher is a little—" and she twirled her hands about either side of her head to indicate a fuddled state of mind. The students giggled. "Maybe in love?"

All this Nona included in the letter that she finally sat down to write at the end of that week. With this letter she enclosed two photographs. "It was hard for me to decide which ones to send to you. Almost all of the photos I have seem to be from at least five years ago. In them I look younger and prettier than I do now, and I didn't want you to have a photo in which I looked better than you remembered me."

She had obeyed Lyle's request for humble details. She worked Monday through Friday, her school was downtown, near Wall Street, and though she usually took the subway, some days, when the weather was fine, she walked. "I like teaching because I find that it brings out the very qualities I am usually in shortest supply of: patience and tolerance. In general, my students are respectful and hardworking—not at all like college students."

She told him about the efforts of a group of her fellow teachers to organize a union, and about the carping director with whom she did not get along.

"You don't sound very happy, Lyle, and I am sorry for you. The situation with Charlotte does sound enormously difficult, and I wish I could help you. I know how hard it is when a relationship is failing; there is nothing more depressing. I will not depress you further by offering banalities. But I do want to say that, given your emotional state, now might not be the best time to make any major decisions. After all, you've only been home a few weeks.

"About my feelings for you I am not sure what to say. That I miss you very much and think of you very often. That not to be able to go on knowing you strikes me as an intolerable possibility. That I understand all too well what you mean by having had certain feelings wakened in you that you can't bear to see die. That I wait for your letters and tear them open with a pounding heart. That my feelings for you do not change my feelings for Roy by a jot, and that, for me, this has been the most curious and unexpected feeling of all."

She finished by saying that she hoped he liked the photographs, and would he please send one of himself?

The day Nona mailed her letter to Lyle it was raining. The sky was pewter-colored, but the rain was gentle and even, and it was not cold. She had written the letter the night before. She could have waited and mailed it on her way to work, but instead she went out right after breakfast.

In the rain, the edges of things were blurred and colors were muted. It was a nice street they lived on: brownstones, tree plots, a minimum of litter and graffiti, thanks to a conscientious block association. And, at the corner, a café that served as good café au lait as Nona, at least, had tasted anywhere in Paris.

Slowly walking back home under her umbrella, Nona wondered at the fullness of her feelings. Why this surge of tenderness for her street, her neighborhood, her café, as if she were about to leave them forever?

Back home, two hours later, the mail arrived. Only a few lines this time, evidently scrawled in haste. "It's all over. Charlotte and I stayed up till dawn, talking, screaming, weeping. And finally agreeing. I'll be moving out at once. I'll send you the address as soon as I have it. Forgive me for not writing more now, but I am drained. I love you, Nona. I know it's impossible, but there it is: I love you."

She would not have to wait for a photograph. Lyle had enclosed one with his note, though he made no mention of it. Nona stared at the photograph for a full minute. She stared at it until she could no longer see it. Then she placed it facedown on her desk and went to the back door. She opened the door and stepped outside, where she was protected from the rain by a small awning. The rain fell steadily, as it had all morning and as it would all day long.

Looking into her heart, Nona saw a darkness like that in the sky, and in the midst of that darkness she thought she saw the shadow of an old demon, mocking her.

Hadn't someone written a story that began like this? Some French writer, or some Russian, wasn't it? A story that ended with something about a long, long road ahead, and the hardest part only just now beginning?

chapter
three

"... Tall and thin and quite good-looking. Fifty—my age exactly. We were at Chicago together. Smart, interesting, a bit broody. Difficult at times—he can be very critical. In a bad way at the moment because his marriage is coming apart. What else. . . ."

This was Phoebe speaking. She had picked Nona up at the train station, and on the drive to the house in Timber Lake she was describing the other guests whom Nona would soon be meeting. It was a radiant August day, and Nona was listening with only one ear, distracted by views of some of the most beautiful country she had ever seen.

"And which one is he again?"

"Lyle Cook. He came a couple of days ago. He was tight as a fist when he arrived, but now he's beginning to relax. Although there does seem to be some tension between him and this woman Rita."

"Who's Rita?"

"The ex-girlfriend of another old friend of mine from Chicago. She's only here for another few days. Thirty-two, very pretty, and very much *defined* by that, you know, as happens to women. I don't know her that well, but I've always sort of liked her. She's aggressive, the type that really goes after what she wants, if you know what I mean. Like calling me, even though we hadn't spoken for ages, and asking to be invited up here. She'd been working on this screenplay and she was running out of money and couldn't find a job. And so I said, sure, why not? But when she got here I was a little worried. She was so *wired*. She reminds me of a horse: always dancing around and tossing her head and taking up so much space. I thought she might have some problems with the others, and that's just what's happened."

"Like what problems?"

"Well, like, the other women hate her. No, wait: that's too harsh. Let's just say they're wary of her. I'm not sure whether it's jealousy or good old-fashioned American puritanism, or what, but whatever it is I'm not free of it, either. There's a part of me that really admires her for being the way she is, and a part of me that can't help disapproving."

"Disapproving of what, exactly?"

"Oh—you'll see. I shouldn't—I've said too much already. Anyway, to be honest, I'm glad she's leaving. She's one of those people who's really easier to deal with one-on-one. She's not good in a group, she stirs up too many feelings. Or, as someone else put it, she upsets the group dynamic." Nona winced: it was the kind of language that made her wince. "But the funny thing is, the one person I thought she'd really hit it off with here was Lyle."

"Oh, Phoebe!"

"What?"

"Look!" They were passing over a gorge. To left and right the earth fell away, and directly ahead was a waterfall.

"Ah, yes, I forgot. You've never been here before. Now, aren't you glad you came? Really, Nona, it's been way too long. The last time I saw you was at your wedding, for God's sake. We have a lot of catching up to do."

This was not the first time Phoebe had invited Nona to visit, but Nona had always made excuses before. First of all, she did not travel easily, not even for short distances, and she had always disliked being away from home. And though she knew she would enjoy Phoebe's company, she was not so sure about the others. Nona was timid in groups, and she knew that Phoebe saw to it that the house was always full. But this summer things had been different. For one thing, Nona had come to a point in her book where she thought she could benefit from a period of solid concentration, and Phoebe's suggestion that she come up for a couple of weeks and work in peace was an irresistible one. And then Phoebe, who had been born and raised in New York, had all but stopped coming to the city in recent years. If she was not in Timber Lake or visiting her one son, who lived with his Italian wife in Rome, she was visiting her other son and his wife in Austin, or staying in another house that she owned, in Seattle, a city she much preferred to her hometown. And Nona missed Phoebe. Theirs was an old and special tie. Nona's earliest memory of her friend was of a leggy girl with a blond flip and braces, painting her toenails in front of the television: the baby-sitter. Phoebe's father, Benedict, had been Nona's father's mentor and great friend. Benedict had had the kind of success that most painters can only dream of and that Shep himself would never know. But Shep had been heard to say that, whatever success he had, he owed mostly to Benedict. It was odd for Nona to think that there had been years in which Phoebe had seen more of Shep than she had, and Shep himself had visited Timber Lake as a guest.

Benedict had been married twice, the second time to a woman from a very wealthy family. It was she—Phoebe's mother—who had owned the estate where the family spent their summers. After her parents died—both, as it happened, in the same year—Phoebe did not know what to do with the property, except that she would not sell it. Some of her happiest memories were tied to it, and she still wished to spend as much time there as possible. By now she was in her forties, she had been married and divorced, her children were grown and off on their own. There was the possibility of turning the house into a business, but the idea of being an innkeeper, or any kind of entrepreneur, made Phoebe shudder. More in keeping with her principles was a nonprofit center dedicated to helping bring about a better world, and this was what the house had become: a meeting ground for people active in Phoebe's causes: feminism, human rights, literacy, the environment.

"I'm the one who gets the most out of it," Phoebe said. "I get a steady stream of interesting people passing through here. I am never bored." With a twinge she acknowledged that her mother might have been appalled to see some of the people who now muddied the carpets of those cherished rooms. But the axiom about pleasing everyone applies also to the dead, and Phoebe, who had adored her mother, liked to think that had she lived she might have evolved into the kind of person who approved of what Phoebe was doing. Nona, who had a strong memory of that marmoreal woman, doubted this.

Whenever the house was not booked for a particular event, Phoebe threw open the doors to her friends. At the same time that she had invited Nona she had also invited Roy. But though Nona was entitled to a leave of absence from work, Roy would not have been able to get away just then. Besides, he was no lover of the country; he had spent too much time there already, growing up. And so Nona, who did not want to go without him, had been on the verge of letting her old friend know that, once again, she would have to decline. It was then that the school where Nona taught, and which was dependent on government grants, had announced that, owing to a lack of funds, it would have to close down for the summer. Like it or not, Nona was on vacation.

Later, at different times and in very different moods, Nona would reflect on this: how close she had come to not going to Timber Lake; how many things had to conspire to get her there at that particular time; how all that happens in our lives, even the biggest things, might just as easily, by the smallest of chances, never have happened at all.

As they turned onto the road that led to the house, Phoebe said, "I saved the nicest room for you—I hope you like it. And remember, you're here to do as you please. Don't feel that you have to socialize if you don't want to. I know you came up here to work. But there are some nice people here, and I think you'll enjoy them."

"How many people are here now?" Nona asked, with an effort to keep the anxiety out of her voice.

"Not including myself and staff, eight. But as I said, Rita's leaving. Speak of the devil."

They had reached the house. Beyond the house, farther on down the road, a woman could be seen retreating: the kind of shapely, promising back that made men rush ahead and pass, so as to get a look at the front.

"Where's she going?"

"I don't know. For a walk, I guess. Plenty of good hikes around here."

After Phoebe had shown Nona to her room, Nona spent the next hour settling in. The windows were open, and as she unpacked she could hear occasional sounds drifting up from the lake: voices, laughter, splashing water. When she had finished unpacking and had showered and dressed, Nona went downstairs and made her way to the dock. The lake was about a mile wide at this point, and about a third of the way across were two people in a canoe. They were paddling back toward the dock and, as she stood watching, Nona thought perhaps because of the bright sun reflecting off the water her eyes were playing tricks on her. But it was not so. In the back of the canoe sat a man, and in the front was a woman. The woman was kneeling, and her breasts were bare. As the canoe drew nearer, Nona saw that the man looked to be in his mid-twenties, and she thought he might be Phoebe's son from Austin, who she knew was also visiting at this time. Rita (for it was she) had blond hair that fell straight to her shoulders, a long neck, a round face, and large round breasts.

The lake encircled by mountains in full summer bloom. The boat gliding evenly toward the land. The woman kneeling with her naked breasts. Nona felt a current pass through her, as if she were in the presence of something uncanny. *The fall of Troy. Menelaus seeks out his treacherous wife, to kill her. When he raises his sword above her head, Helen bares her breasts. At which sight Menelaus cannot kill her.*

When they had reached the dock and climbed out of the boat, Nona learned that the young man was not Phoebe's son, but her office assistant, Sandy. He excused himself immediately after introductions, saying that he had to get back to work. Nona thought maybe he was embarrassed, having to stand there with a stranger and Rita wearing nothing but her bikini bottom. But, judging by Rita's tan, this was not the first day she had gone about topless.

"Didn't you bring a bathing suit?" asked Rita. Something slightly flouting in the question—a light slap of the glove—as if it were not the woman but her bare, high-held bosom speaking. Nona was dismayed at her response: pained and baffled emotions taking her all the way back to grade school. She had always wanted the pretty girls to like her.

"Yes, but I just got here," Nona said, "and I just wanted to come down and take a look. I've never been here before. I had no idea it was so beautiful."

Rita did not appear to be listening. She was watching Sandy as he went up the path to the house. "He's cute, isn't he?" she said, and Nona smiled: they had graduated from elementary to high school. "I know you just got here. Phoebe told us you were coming. I'm in the room below you. But not for long. I'm leaving Tuesday." And she added, with unmistakable bitterness, "I've worn out my welcome."

With a spasm of irritation, Nona thought, What does she expect me to say to that?

"I'd never been here before, either," Rita went on. "I'm always amazed at how rich people live, aren't you? Some house, huh?" Gazing narrowly toward it. "Lyle calls it Versailles in Knotty Pine." And she laughed, unpleasantly. "It's too hot. I'm going in."

Everything she said, regardless of meaning, was tossed out like a challenge. But there was an undertone that came through just as clearly: wounded feelings, wounded pride.

To Nona's relief, Rita dove into the lake. Nona watched her swim for a moment but then turned around and left the dock. She did not want to be there when Rita came out of the water.

Halfway up the path Nona ran into a woman who introduced herself good-humoredly as "Phoebe's old auntie Josie." Nona knew that this was her friend's favorite relative. She had a high prominent nose and a wreath of short gray curls and, with a large white towel draped over one shoulder and sandals on her feet, looked very much like a Roman senator. Peering down toward the lake, she said, "Oh, dear. Is *she* down there prancing around naked again?" Nona turned and, as she saw Rita emerge, sleek and glistening, like something born of the water, she felt an impulse to defend her. But then Josie said, "Oh, well. Do your own thing, eh? See you at dinner," and went on down toward the lake.

When she reached the house, Nona sat down on the porch and picked up a magazine from a small round wicker table. It was at this moment that Lyle, who was just returning from a trip to town, came around the corner and saw her. Nona did not see him until he was right upon her.

"Welcome," he said. "I'm Lyle, and you must be Nona." They shook hands. He went into the house, leaving Nona with only a fleeting impression of height and attractiveness and trying to remember which one he was and what she had been told about him.

Too many people, she thought, getting to her feet. She had been up since before dawn and she was very tired. Climbing the stairs to her room, she felt resistance at each step, as if she were wearing a gown with a heavy train.

She lay down on the bed and closed her eyes. She would not take a nap, as people who have trouble sleeping at night are advised never to nap, though no one could stop her from savoring at least for a moment the delicious feeling of drowsiness creeping over her.

She awoke to the loud bonging of a bell.

Ten minutes later she went downstairs, the last one to arrive at the dinner table.

* * *

Dearest Roy,

Well, I am settled in now, and I have met everyone, and it is all still a little strange, but I am happy here. Phoebe has done everything to make me comfortable. I have a room on the top floor of the house, on the southeast corner, with big windows and a huge oak roll-top desk and the most beautiful antique quilt on the bed. I can see the lake from here. The air is clean and the water is clean, and at night I can see stars and hear the owls calling. (Nature is a place I have visited so seldom I forget that such things as stars and owls exist.) There are places to climb to around here from where you can see for miles, and all you can see is mountains and lakes. Up there I feel that for the first time in my life I know what it means to breathe. Now that I know what it is like I am sorry I put off coming for so long and even sorrier that you are not here to share it. Phoebe doesn't live in the main house, but in a cottage about half a mile into the woods, which is where some of the servants used to live. She spends most of her time in the office, though, which is downstairs in the back of the house, working with her assistant, Sandy. She hasn't changed at all since you met her at the wedding. When I was a kid, I always thought she looked like a Breck girl, and she still has that wholesome, soap-and-water freshness, even without the blond flip. She's still as slim as she ever was, too. Speaking of which, I was embarrassed when I went in swimming for the first time yesterday. It's been a while since I wore this old bathing suit, and it's now a little too tight and quite unflattering. (There is a woman here who goes about topless, if you can believe it, but she has a body to die for.)

Phoebe's younger son and his wife are here, and so is her charming aunt, Josie. Then there's another old woman, whom I don't like at all. Imperious, crabby, very busy nostrils—the kind of woman who loves to tear the wings off young girls. A real dragon. "I knew your father," she says to me, in a way that I felt was intended to make me squirm. She used to own a gallery and was a good friend of Benedict's, but she hated Shep's work. You should see her around this woman Rita! It seems Rita's penchant for semi-nudity is more than she can bear. She keeps complaining to poor Phoebe, who has to deal with complaints also from the local women who do the cooking and cleaning, and who, it must be said, despise Rita. Phoebe has tried to explain to them all that it is not for her to tell another grown woman—and her guest at that—how to dress. Rita herself keeps harping on this new state law, according to which it is now legal for women to go about shirtless anywhere men do. (Had you heard about this?) At any rate, I gather everyone, including Phoebe, is relieved that Rita has decided to leave day after tomorrow, albeit in a huff.

As for the other guests, there is a journalist visiting from England and an English professor from Arizona and a woman who is one-third of a performance artist group called the Ugly Stepsisters (the others are expected in a week or so). I like everyone except the dragon, but so far I've been keeping pretty much to myself. The food is good, though of course not as good as yours, and I am happy to report that I have not been having any trouble sleeping—no pills! If you were here with me now, everything would be perfect. I miss you more than I can say. Love from Phoebe, and a thousand kisses from your

Nona

P.S. My computer arrived the day before I did, safe and sound, thanks to your careful packing.

One evening toward the end of that first week, Nona sat next to the journalist, who had been a guest all that summer. His name was Ralph and he was from London: a large, handsome but beset-looking man in his forties, whose eyes drooped at the outer corners, like a hound's. As she spoke with him— this was the first time they had sat together, their first real conversation—Nona was distracted by Rita, who was sitting directly across the table, between Lyle and Sandy. Phoebe was right: Rita was about as easy to ignore as a filly dining with them. Watching her, Nona found herself wondering: How conscious was she of her behavior and its effect on other people? How much of it was done on purpose, and to what end? What emotions was she trying to inspire in the people around that table: jealousy? anger? love? What did Rita want?

Meanwhile, Ralph was telling a remarkable story. It was a personal story, an emotional story, but he was telling it in a quiet, clinical way. His work as a journalist had taken him to hot spots all over the globe. He had been in Africa and in Southeast Asia and in the Middle East. He had been wounded a few times, he had been arrested, and once, in Angola, he was held hostage for several days. It was his job, and he loved it, and he was not afraid. His wife, on the other hand, lived in a state of constant fear. ("You know how it's much worse, sometimes, to be sitting at home worrying than to be right in the thick of things.") They had been married for ten years and they had two sons. Recently, his wife had given him an ultimatum. He could find other work, or she would take the children and leave him.

Nona was grasping for something intelligent to say when Rita sang out, "Ralph will miss me, won't you, Ralph?"

"Oh, my, yes," Ralph said. "The view around here will be quite diminished after you've gone." The gallant words were tinged with mockery, but there was no malice in them. Rita beamed. It was a nice moment of triumph for her. As she blew Ralph a kiss, the others around that table whose conversations had been interrupted rolled or averted their eyes, and the dragon squeezed hers shut, as if against an unbearable light.

One of the big complaints against Rita, Nona had learned, was that she paid attention only to the men, and this if nothing else would have been enough to damn her in the eyes of those women. But to Nona Rita had seemed like someone hungry for female company, and so far Rita had made several attempts to befriend her. Nona had discovered also that Rita was fair game among the women. Even Josie, though she herself did not speak ill of Rita, kept silent when the others did. Everyone knew that Rita was sleeping with Sandy, and for this she was roundly denounced, though opinions of Sandy—generally approved of as a fine young man—did not change. It was this unfairness, this spiteful, punishing attitude toward certain women, that had always exasperated Nona about her own sex. The contempt of women for women.

Nona never did think of anything intelligent to say to Ralph about his predicament—nor did she have to, thanks to Rita's outburst, after which he changed the subject.

After dinner, Rita and Nona went for a walk together, as they had planned earlier that day. These summer twilights in the mountains were pure magic, when the sky was colored rosy blue and the lake was bluish rose and the birdsong took on a jewel-like clarity. From time to time, a breeze set all the tall trees swooning with a wild, rushing sound, which Nona always heard as an expression of yearning.

"So, how do you like Ralph?" Rita asked.

"Very much," said Nona, thinking of his British accent, his heroic profession, and his face of an intelligent hound.

"Did he tell you what was happening with his wife?"

"Yes. Awful. But he seemed very calm about it."

"Well, in fact, he isn't calm. Underneath, believe me, he is furious. And, speaking of furious, did you see the look on the dragon lady's face when he was talking to me?" (It had been their first bond: the discovery that they both privately called her that.) "I read something somewhere, about older women— that, as women get older and stop having sex, they become sadistic. I think it's been proved. I think it was Freud who—"

"I don't think it's quite that clear-cut," Nona said, at the same time sending up a silent prayer of thanks that no one else had been there to hear this comment.

"Hey, we're being watched."

They had come, as they came every day at that hour, to graze near the fence that protected the vegetable garden. They followed the humans' movements with stares eerie in their intensity, until the largest stamped its hoof twice on the ground, and fled. All the rest then turned as one and went bounding away through the pinkish haze.

Nona said, "I am such a city person, the first time I looked out the window here and saw a deer on the lawn, I thought, oh, there's a Great Dane."

"Oh, that's wild," said Rita, laughing. "I'm a city person, too." Like Nona, she was from New York. "And to tell you the truth, nice as it is here, I'm not sorry to be leaving." (This was her last day.) "I've had enough fresh air. I want to go out to lunch! Besides, things are getting too complicated."

Knowing what Rita was referring to, Nona thought it appropriate to say, "Do you think you two will ever see each other again?"

Rita shook her head. "I've been in this situation before. It's one thing, having an affair when you're away from home, on vacation or whatever, and a whole other thing when you get back to real life. Might as well be four different people, if you know what I'm saying."

There was something Nona had been meaning to ask Rita, and now seemed the right time.

"Phoebe told me there was some trouble between you and Lyle before. But you two seem to be getting along just fine now." In fact, Nona had seen little evidence of the tension Phoebe had spoken of. He had looked quite smitten, sitting next to Rita at the dinner table.

"I won him over," Rita said. And the way she said it—disdainfully, with a grimace that tightened her fine features and made her look hard—almost took Nona's breath away. "I don't find him that attractive," she went on. "He's too old—I prefer younger men. But he's in terrific shape, I'll admit that. I don't like academics, though. And I *really* don't like people who go around correcting other people's grammar." (It was Lyle's bad habit, Nona had to admit.) "I think it's just a sign of his own insecurity, you know? Because he comes from a white-trash family, and now he's an English professor—big deal!" She did not like him, he was not her type, but still she had to win him over. What a burden such women bore, Nona thought, and she was reminded of something she had once read: that thirst to be beautiful and to be desired that Jean Rhys called the real curse of Eve.

They had entered a path in the woods some time ago. Now Nona said, "It's getting dark. We should turn around." They had not brought flashlights.

On the way back Rita asked Nona if she was getting a lot of work done, and when Nona said that she was, Rita said:

"That must be very interesting, writing a whole book about your father. I don't know enough about my father to write one page."

Even before she had been told the facts—Rita's father had died in a car crash when she was a baby (drunk, definitely; a suicide, maybe), after which there had been a tacit agreement among the grown-ups never to speak of him to the children again—Nona had guessed something like this about Rita. She could always tell about women who had grown up without fathers. In her imagination they were identified with one of those cursed, wandering female bands of mythology who are one day turned by some pitying god into birds or fish or a grove of trees.

Just before they reached the house, Rita said, "You should call me when you get back to town. We'll get together, have a drink or dinner or something, okay?" And she added, "Maybe I'll have finished my screenplay by then. Maybe I'll have sold it for a whole lot of money, and there'll be something to celebrate," in the voice of one who has had nothing to celebrate in a long time.

Back in her room, Nona worked at her computer for about an hour, then got into bed and read until she fell asleep. Deer passed through her dreamscape, leaping over subway turnstiles until one of them fell and lay panting and moaning, moaning.

Nona listened to the sounds coming through the floor from Rita's room below. Displeased as she was at having been wakened, she found herself smiling in the dark at the joke: while Sandy lay sleeping alone in another part of the house, that was Ralph down there, getting even with his wife.

chapter four

For the first ten days in Timber Lake—one day after another hot, bright, and blue—Nona followed the same routine. She got up at six every morning and went straight out for a walk. She kept the walk short, between ten and twenty minutes, as invisible hands gently plucked off the mist in which each new day came wrapped. She came back into the house through one of the back doors, which led to the kitchen. Moving quickly, she made coffee and poured it into a thermos to take up to her room. This early, there were usually few people about, but if she did run into someone, Nona was careful not to let herself get drawn into conversation.

She drank the coffee while she was working, not leaving her room again until eleven-thirty, when she returned to the kitchen and fixed herself a sandwich, which she also carried upstairs to eat in her room. In this way she managed to avoid people until late afternoon, when she went down to the lake for a swim. This was her favorite event of the day. She had learned to swim only recently. Roy had been appalled to discover that she could not swim at all and had nagged her until she joined the Y and learned. She still felt like a child in the water, shy and overexcited and a little afraid. And the lake was so cold!

With Rita gone, the mood of the house had changed. Everyone seemed more relaxed, and Nona thought maybe it was true: maybe Rita really had upset the group dynamic. For a day or so after she'd gone, a certain kind of comment continued to be heard. If Ralph was present (people bit their tongues in front of Sandy), he would remain silent, his face betraying nothing, and Nona felt a touch of—what? Disappointment? Resentment? He might have said something, she thought. Toward the end of the week Ralph received a letter from Rita. Phoebe brought it out to him where he sat on the porch, and Nona, sitting nearby, had watched him open it and skim it with the same inscrutable expression on his face.

Of course she was sorry that Rita had had a bad visit, Phoebe told Nona. But, she added, "I was also quite fed up with her. I don't like bad girls, you know? I just don't have any patience with them. I don't like people who are always wanting to shock and to get other people to look at them and trying to arouse strong feelings, sexual or otherwise, in everybody they meet. It's greedy, and it's adolescent, and it's boring."

"And that," said the dragon, coming up behind the two women on the dock where they lay, "is precisely what is wrong with ninety-nine percent of the art that you see today: 'I don't have anything to say, but I'm going to scream it anyway, and you're going to listen.'" It was a point she had made at least a dozen times, the topic with which she had dominated several dinner conversations already. They all knew her story. How she, who had opened her gallery in the early fifties, had abandoned it a decade later, in disgust and despair, and until such time (which of course never came) when artists began doing work worth showing again. A more truthful version of this story would have included some mention of her partner (her husband) and the series of bad calls and disastrous investments she made after his death had left her to manage on her own.

Although she still got on Nona's nerves, Nona no longer felt quite so hostile toward this woman, who had softened considerably since Rita's departure. Reduced to human scale, what was she but a disappointed old lady, a widow of thirty years, with a mind and body that were failing—and when Nona saw her with crumbs sticking to her mustache, or slack-jawed and listing in a chair before the fire, unable to stay awake past nine, she understood those ancient tyrants who never let themselves be seen eating or sleeping.

Saying good-bye to Nona, Rita had predicted: "I guess they'll be talking about me for a long time after I'm gone." But Phoebe's words turned out to be the last anyone spoke of her, and Nona imagined how irked Rita would have been to find herself sunk to the bottom of everyone's thoughts, as if she had slipped into the lake and the waters had closed over her head.

By the end of her second week, Nona found herself craving distraction. She began spending less time in her room, she lingered in the kitchen with her morning coffee, and in the dining room with her after-dinner coffee, and she no longer minded when someone tried to draw her into conversation, or asked her to go for a canoe ride or a hike.

Two new guests had arrived. These were the missing Ugly Stepsisters, and with the group all together now, the house livened up. They stayed up till all hours watching videos and drinking bourbon and practicing a new piece that they called "The Vagina Dentata Cantata." Upstairs, alone in her room, Nona would hear music and great whoops of laughter coming from other parts of the house, and she would experience again a tumult of schoolgirl emotions; she had always wanted the cliques to accept her. But when she joined the women she found that they were too much for her. They were jokers, relentless kidders, they loved to rag each other and everyone else, and their attitude toward Nona was belittling. They teased her about her trouble sleeping ("Oh, did you forget your vibrator?"), about her fear of the water and her self-consciousness in her ill-fitting suit ("We hate to tell you, but nobody's looking"). They were fun, they were entertaining, but they *were* a clique, and they did not accept her.

Although he might be somewhat lacking in chivalry, Nona liked Ralph very much. He, too, would soon be leaving, and she would miss him. She enjoyed listening to him talk. He talked about politics, mostly, and he had a way of describing world events so that they became not just the horrifying mishmash that she got from the news, but realities that might be understood and for which solutions might even be found. Phoebe shared this interest in politics, and whenever Nona listened to the two of them talk, she had the satisfying sense of her vision of the world being enlarged. But when Lyle was present, it seemed to Nona that a different note crept into the discussion. Less informed than Ralph, Lyle would nevertheless often challenge things that he said, pointing out weaknesses or contradictions in his arguments. Ralph's equable response was part of his charm. "I don't have all the answers, of course," he would say, gently throwing up his hands. Or: "I'm not recommending any particular system." Now and then things might heat up and the talk degenerate into a debate in which both men seemed concerned mainly with scoring points. It amused Nona to hear how at these times Lyle would begin clipping his words and exaggerating his diction, as if he feared that the prize would go to the best British accent. But the men were friends. They often sat together at meals, went off on day-long hikes together, and in the evenings sometimes they went to a bar in town, without inviting anyone else.

They had their similarities, Ralph and Lyle. They were both attractive. But, for Nona, Lyle was more so. He had a dark, ascetic face, long and smooth and lean, with a light sheen to his skin, like a polished wood carving. His gray hair had a strong, even wave—it looked almost marcelled, which gave his appearance a quaint element. He had a small, hard-looking brown mouth; you never saw his teeth. He looked younger than fifty, and he had the kind of body that announced that it had never been out of shape. Good carriage—something equestrian about the way he bore himself. Nona liked his deep voice, and everyone liked his sense of humor, but there was often something acrid about his humor (*he* had no trouble holding his own with the Stepsisters), as there was something sullen about his melancholy. Broody, Phoebe had called him. Someone else would have said morose. Like Ralph, Lyle was there partly as a respite from domestic strife, and Nona assumed that this was another thing that had strengthened the bond between the two men: both marriages were doomed.

Nona had winced when, speaking of Lyle, Rita had used the words *white trash*. But it turned out Rita had gotten them from Lyle himself. "I come from white trash," he said. (Sometimes, for a joke, he said "trash blanc.") He said, "My parents could barely read and write." Nona, too, now heard the story, told with what struck her as heartbreaking raillery, about the chicken farm where, one summer, the temperature in the coops soared so high, all the birds suffocated to death. The reek of the coops hung over the place long after the carcasses had been removed. ("I swear it's there still.") There had been a sister who died of meningitis; a brother, badly deformed by polio. At night, after his parents had drunk themselves to blackout, Lyle lay awake, listening to the screams of raccoons that his neighbors had trapped and were torturing. "They didn't have TV, you see, they had to entertain themselves somehow." From this hell he was rescued by an ardent young schoolteacher, who took him to live with her own family. "She must have had a strong stomach. When she got me"—*got me,* he said, as if he had been a dog—"I had ringworm, impetigo, and lice." Although she let the teacher take him without hesitation, Lyle's mother never forgave him for going. The scholarships to schools far from home, the good education, the respectable career: "She never forgave me any of that." His first year at the University of Chicago he brought Phoebe back home with him for a visit. By then both brother and father had died. His mother sat with one leg on either side of a kitchen stool, her beer-bloated stomach straining against her filthy housedress, and harangued about "the niggers who are destroying this country." Phoebe, who understood that she had been invited along more as witness than as guest, said, "It was the only time in my life, and I'm ashamed to admit it, that I felt my gorge rise at the sight of a fellow human being." She was dead now, too, the mother. They were all dead—"'and I only am left alone to tell thee.'"

It made him more interesting, this story. Hillbilly boy to college professor: it was the kind of fairy tale people loved. The wry, unself-pitying tone in which he told the story ("chicken shit: that's *my* madeleine") helped, too. Also: the way he wasn't ashamed to be ashamed. There was a coolness about him, a stoicism, a knowingness—all this made him more interesting, more attractive. He was respected. He was liked. Phoebe, who had been his witness, had remained his loyal friend all these years. The dragon adored him. All the women liked him, and this surprised Nona, whose instinct told her that he was no feminist.

He was canny, though; he knew how to lull suspicion, what not to say. And it was this canniness that gave Nona pause. People who begin with an idea of how they want to be perceived and then calculate every word, every gesture . . . Lack of spontaneity usually put Nona off. And she did not like the way he used "white trash." So glib, so cold, so . . . *gloating.*

She ran into him on one of her early-morning walks. A surprise: Lyle was never up before ten.

He was standing on the dock with his back to her, and he did not see her approaching. Another minute or so and the sun would appear across the lake, in the bowl between two peaks.

Background is important. This was how she would see him often later: a tall lean lone dark figure with the mist-covered lake and the mountains behind him: a Caspar David Friedrich to hang in her memory.

He heard her footsteps on the dock and turned. The sun

brimmed in the bowl between the two peaks. It would be another fine blue day.

They took out one of the canoes, gliding almost noiselessly over the water. There was no wind. When they reached the middle of the lake, they stopped paddling and let the boat drift. It was the kind of hush one hesitates to break, even by a whisper.

A loon bobbed nearby, its stiff, dark little head sticking up like an umbrella handle. Almost too quick to be seen, except as a flash of silver, a fish leaped into the air.

"Your hair," said Lyle, "is the most marvelous color. I've never seen quite that shade before. Is that what they call titian?"

He was flirting with her. He was taking a chance—a chance she did not think he would have taken with any of the other women. That was no surprise. Men risked behavior with her that they would not have risked with other women. Only for a short time, when she was very young, had Nona believed that the boldness with which men came on to her was not unusual.

Titian was blonder, she told him.

It was awkward, talking, because of their positions in the boat. Being the lighter, she had sat in the bow, and she had to talk over her shoulder. When she mentioned this, Lyle said, "Yes, but I get a great view of your profile."

I will not be alone with him again, she told herself, and a sense of desolation came over her. She was not young, she was not inexperienced, and she knew that alone with a man she gave off signs that only one in a thousand—and a child could see that Lyle was not that one—would have ignored. She knew; she had been told, though she had not needed to be told. It had been so since schooldays. She had always wanted the boys to want her.

I will avoid him now, she told herself, and her desolation grew and grew. Gentle, courtly, innocent as this flirtation was, it pierced her like a violation.

Another quicksilver fish-flash, this one very close to the

boat. She stirred the icy water with one hand. The loon disappeared, resurfacing several seconds later, a remarkable distance away. Such a distance, indeed, that Nona could hardly believe it was the same bird.

"You've got a secret, haven't you, dear?"

Once, when she was still in school, a famous professor, a poet, had embraced Nona in his office. She had thought that he would kiss her, but instead he stuck his tongue into her ear, into her mouth, into her other ear, as if she were nothing but so many orifices to be poked, and grunted, "Oh, why is the opposite sex so attractive?" Her friends had been incredulous when she told them. "That was his *line?*"

Now she said, "'Everyone has a secret that would make him hateful to all others if it became known.'"

"Who said that?"

She shrugged. She didn't remember. She had read it somewhere a long time ago and written it down. Lyle said, "I'd guess dead, European, and male."

Oh, she was not young, she was not inexperienced, and she knew that when Lyle said that, about her having a secret, it did not mean that he had fathomed something deep in her; it meant only that he knew her weakness, as men always knew, and as she pulled her numb hand from the water and wiped it on her jeans, she told herself to be clear about this, to remember this, and not to mistake it for anything else.

And if she could manage all that, no harm would come to her.

Heading back to the dock, Nona began to sing. Out on the water her voice rang out very big and very clear. ("Fill the sky," Roy would say. "Fill the great big sky. After that the concert hall will be easy." "Don't think silver," he said. "Go for silver and you get tinsel. You want a richer tone. Think gold.")

"I am a poor wayfaring stranger—"

The mist had all been plucked away. The sun was warm. The sky was that tender newborn blue.

"A-wandering through this world of woe—"

Helping her out of the boat, he pulled her to him, and they kissed and kissed. Her closed eyes filled with tears, and when he felt the trembling of her mouth he pressed her harder, made the trembling stop. They kissed, and Nona shut her eyes more tightly against her tears, against the vision of her life in ruins, her peace and all her happiness destroyed. They kissed and kissed, and from somewhere on high came the loon's maniacal laughing-wailing cry, appropriate fanfare for the birth of a calamity.

When they broke apart, he said, in the deep voice that she loved, "You've bewitched me."

They walked back to the house in silence, their arms at their sides.

AVOIDING LYLE TURNED out to be easy for Nona. He made it easy for her. He did not try to get her alone again. He followed her only with his eyes, with a look that was questioning, at times imploring, but never insistent. She knew what he was waiting for, but she was able to ignore this. He grew quieter, kept more to himself, aloof from the others. Everyone attributed his subdued behavior to Ralph's leaving. But Phoebe said she had seen him often like this. "I told you: he gets broody." As for Nona, her sense of desolation lifted. She was like a child dreading punishment who has just learned that she is forgiven. She was not lost, her life was not ruined. Her heart was light, she was bursting with gratitude and energy and the will to be good. She sat down at her desk every morning and worked better than ever.

"I WANT TO PAINT YOU," Josie said. "That hair! Whistler would have loved you."

Nona agreed to sit for her portrait every afternoon, sometime in the hours after her swim and before dinner.

Josie called herself a Sunday painter, a hobbyist, as if going out of her way to show that she was not competing with her famous brother. ("I'm no Benedict. But everyone in our family could draw.") She had set up a studio in the unused half of an old storage building. Nona had agreed to sit for her reluctantly, only because she had not known how to say no to this nice old woman. But the sittings turned out to be a pleasure. Why not while away the afternoon on an old wicker chaise longue with a cup of tea and nothing to do but relax and chat? The west wall of the studio had a sliding door that Josie kept wide open to the mellow, late-day light. Some days they were joined by one of the caretaker's cats who had discovered, in the clever way of cats, that here was sun and quiet and a still, soft lap.

Nona had noticed how the others often grew impatient with Josie, who talked on and on, mostly about herself—as people do when, like Josie, they are mostly alone. But Nona found Josie's talk interesting. She enjoyed listening to people talk about their pasts, in sympathy with that urgent need to keep memory alive. She had noticed, too, that it was often those whose memories were saddest who seemed most passionate about preserving them. Someone like Roy, who had had a rare happy childhood, was completely free of that deep, mordant nostalgia that Nona saw in herself and in many other people.

There are those who are capable of replacing one great love with another—one after another, if it comes to that—and those who fall in love only once and for all time. Josie belonged to the second group, and hers was one of those stories, of the one great love for whom she had sacrificed everything. And so, as Josie painted, Nona was busy, too: erasing pounds and pouches, smoothing lines, and inking hair, until it stood restored: Portrait of Josie as Lovestruck Young Girl.

He had been an adventurer, a wanderer, to romantic eyes, but to the eyes of Josie's family a drifter. A bum. Well, okay, then, a dharma bum, Josie conceded. And she had been a child, a flower child, born before her time. She had followed him to California, to Mexico, to Paris, Berlin, Morocco, and at last Tibet. Her parents' letters had pursued her, scolding, entreating, predicting the worst. And of course they had been right. He had not loved her. He had betrayed her. Josie's voice grew fainter as she spoke of it.

He was a gambler, a daredevil. He crashed the small plane he had been learning to fly.

"And, of course, that was it for me," said Josie, suspending her brush and turning up her eyes as if acknowledging at once the beauty, the folly, and the inevitability of it all. "I knew I would survive, but I would never love again." So she would grow old alone, cherishing in her unkissed, unsuckled spinster breast memories of rapture in Paris and Marrakesh.

This story got to Nona. It brought back her feeling of desolation. It made her want to open up, to tell stories of her own. Of course she and Josie talked about the other guests—gossiped about them—and there had been a dreadful moment when Josie said, "You know, I think Lyle was head over heels with Rita. If she hadn't already been with Sandy . . ." And Nona had had to struggle to keep her feelings out of her face. She had a great urge, a need to talk, but she stopped herself, as Lyle's mouth had stopped hers from trembling. With nervous hands she stroked the cat, her unmade confession blocking her throat.

Almost every afternoon, Phoebe stopped by for a few minutes on a break from her work. She would bring homemade cookies from the kitchen, and the women would have tea together. She was very busy now, preparing for the alternate-energy conference that was scheduled to begin next month.

"I'm going to hate seeing everyone go," Phoebe said. But all the rooms would be needed for the conference. "Nona, I wanted to ask you, would you like to read to us sometime? I was hoping you would. You see how it is here in the evenings. It's nice to have something for us to do all together. We could do it after dinner, in the library, light a fire, have wine."

Nona hesitated, and Josie said, "Oh, yes, please say yes," and so Nona did.

Nona was doing her laundry. Waiting for the clothes to dry, she sat on the grass outside the laundry room, writing post-cards.

"This is the life. I write, I read, I sit for my portrait, I hike and swim and canoe. But in spite of all this physical activity I do not lose weight. The food here is plentiful, my appetite enormous."

"I have begun to do yoga. A woman here who used to teach yoga for a living has been giving us classes."

Very tall, very slender, and five months' pregnant, Phoebe's daughter-in-law was amazing to watch, gliding through Sun Salutation "like a boa that swallowed a turkey" (Lyle).

"I feel as though I'd been away for ages. Yes, I will be back at school next month now that classes are starting up again. In fact, I'm looking forward to it."

"My work continues to go well. Sometimes I feel almost as if the book were writing itself. At long last I can see it: The End."

"The days are passing so quickly now. By the time you get this I'll soon be home."

"In a moment of confidence I agreed to read after dinner next Wednesday, but now I am having second thoughts."

Overnight, the weather changed. The temperature dropped fifteen degrees, it was no longer comfortable to swim, and the nights turned chilly. Threads of bold yellow and red appeared on the green slopes, and the air was tinged with the smell of wood smoke and apples ripening.

It began to rain. It rained for three days, pouring steadily from a livid sky. And with this change in weather came a change in mood, a darkening, a chilling among the guests.

Every group has its differences, and there had been com-plaints within this one from the start. There were those who

did not think the smokers should be allowed to smoke anywhere in the house, not even in their own rooms. (Get real,
you fascists, snapped the chain-smoking Stepsisters.) Some
guests complained that the cleaning women used too much
Lysol, and the cleaning women complained that the guests
were lazy slobs who would not pick up after themselves. And
now, with the weather keeping everyone mostly indoors, and
probably also because they had all had enough of one another,
the complaints blew up into squabbles.

Eva the cook was a stout Austrian woman with a massive
square face and upper arms like the baked hams she served on
Sundays. "Don't they just make you terrified to imagine the
thighs?" said wicked Lyle, who was nevertheless Eva's favorite.
He often hung around the kitchen when she was there, joking
and flirting and sometimes lending a hand, and he had the
kind of huge, omnivorous appetite that Eva loved. Nona, who
had never learned to cook, was always so relieved and grateful
to have food placed in front of her, she could not imagine
complaining about what it was. But those baked hams of
Eva's, the rump roasts and stuffed chickens and the legs of
lamb that were her pride, were the despair of the vegetarians.
Why not just eat the vegetables? Nona suggested. What vegetables? they said. The spinach was frozen; the corn, canned.
And both have been prepared with animal products, sighed
Phoebe's daughter-in-law, pushing her plate away. The purest
of the purists, this woman had not eaten any animal products
or refined sugar in ten years. Chemically speaking, most
processed stuff was closer to petroleum than to food, she said.
Eva, who had a degree in dietetics and many years of experience on hospital staffs, took accusations that her cooking was
unhealthful very much to heart. Passing by the kitchen in the
late afternoon, you could hear her banging her pots and pans.
If you had the nerve to enter, you would be greeted with a
scowl so fierce it made you believe in the old saying that every
cook hides a murderer.

Bickering over cards, bickering over what to watch on television, what movie videotape to rent.

"I think it's a good thing we are all going home," Nona wrote Roy. She wanted to go home. She was not feeling well. She was fretful, logy, and glum: her period was coming.

One night, late, Nona was wakened by frightful cries. Outside, not far off, a predator had attacked; some poor creature was being killed and eaten. It dragged on for an unbearably long time. Nona had never heard anything like it. Now it occurred to her that of course this kind of thing went on all the time in what she had been thinking of as those peaceable woods. She lay awake after the cries had died, absurdly oppressed by this thought. Outside it was quiet again, except for an owl wondering *What to do—do—do?*

She decided against taking a pill, and this would turn out to have been a mistake. She stayed up all the rest of that night; and every night after, until she went home, she would be forced to take at least one pill to get to sleep.

The next day Nona learned that everyone else had slept through the commotion. The Stepsisters teased her about hearing things, and Lyle said, "You know, those animals were probably just fucking." In a flash Nona realized that he was right. For some reason this infuriated her.

Although she still tried to work in the mornings, Nona no longer felt rested, and she had trouble concentrating. It was almost a relief when her computer broke. Booting up one day, she found that the bottom half of the screen was pinstriped.

"Broken screen cable," the technician diagnosed over the phone. Sandy helped Nona pack the computer and ship it to the factory service center for repair.

It was like a sign, Nona thought. It really was time to go home.

chapter
five

After the rain, the sun reappeared one morning brighter than ever, as if its vacation had done it good. But that afternoon thunderclouds massed all along the horizon; on its way was one of the worst storms of the year. A sharp wind blew up, a wind like an axe, hurtling through the woods, hacking limbs, felling trees.

This was Wednesday, the day Nona was supposed to read. It was after dinner and she was in her room, looking over her manuscript, when there came a thunderclap so loud she cried out and covered her ears like a child.

The room went black.

Nona groped along the wall to the bookcase, seeking the candle that she knew was there. As her fingers touched it, she remembered that she had no matches.

From all parts of the house came sounds: doors opening and closing, bumps and scrapes, voices, laughter. "Downstairs!" "Downstairs!"

Nona left her room and crept along the hall to the staircase. She had never been in darkness so complete; it poured into her eyes like ink. She had reached the second-floor landing. Leaning over the banister, she saw a fiendish sight: disembodied hands bearing lights moving hither thither across a black pit.

"Who's that?" she said to the one approaching behind her. For some foolish reason her heart was charging.

"It's only me," said Lyle, who had stopped.

She could feel him only inches away, but she could not see him. "You don't have a flashlight, either?"

"No, but I have great night vision." She could feel his breath on her hair when he spoke. She could tell that he was grinning. "Come." He fished for her hand. She let him lead her down the last flight of stairs.

In the dining room, candles had been placed in a single row down the center of the long mahogany table. Most of the others were already there. The emergency had sparked a festive mood. Like children, they seemed to be enjoying the surprise and the spookiness of it. "Let's have a séance," one voice suggested. But another voice warned: "Don't mess with the Yonder unless you know what you're doing." The spirit of camaraderie that had not been much in evidence lately had been revived. They drew their chairs close to one another. Someone lit a cigarette and no one complained. In the light and shadow thrown by the candles, faces were transformed. They all looked made up for something, Nona thought. Glancing at Lyle, she thought of a monk.

Rain ran down the windows so hard it looked as if they were being hosed from outside. In the crescendo and decrescendo of the wind Nona heard an echo of the ghastly howls of some nights before.

Footsteps on the porch. The door flew open and there stood Phoebe, holding in one hand an enormous flashlight and in the other a bottle of whiskey. So much water dripped from the hem of her parka she might have been just dragged from the lake. But beating her way from her house through the storm had exalted her. "Nature doing it up big-time out there!" She set the bottle on the table and asked Sandy to fetch some glasses.

When she had taken off her parka and sat down, Phoebe

said, "I was in Manhattan during the big blackout, the summer of seventy-seven. Do you remember that, Nona? Nine months later there was a mini baby boom."

"I don't get it," said Sandy, returning with the glasses. "You mean, people got romantic because it was dark?"

"Well, they couldn't watch TV that night, so everyone went to bed early and had sex."

Sniggers and groans. "Nothing better to do." "Oh, how depressing." But one person laughed and said, "Then it's a really great thing people watch so much TV, eh? Keeps the population down."

Nona noticed that everyone had accepted a glass of Scotch, even people who did not usually drink. She of all people should not drink, as those who have trouble sleeping are warned never to drink, especially near bedtime.

It was Phoebe's son who started it—over protests of "I'm a wuss!" and "I'll never get to sleep!"—with an old-fashioned campfire story that had the refrain: "It's the Ha-Ha-Hatchet Man."

But most of the stories told that night—the scariest ones— were true.

It had happened right there in town, and not that long ago. Haunted by nightmares about a head buried beneath an outhouse, a woman consulted a psychiatrist. Under hypnosis she gave the details that led to the bones that led to the arrest of her mother, who had hacked up the woman's father two decades before.

In high school, Sandy had dated a foreign-exchange student from Spain. One day she told him her secret. Her father had strangled her mother. But, because he had caught his wife with a lover, the man was acquitted and allowed to go home and raise his daughter.

There were the twins who went trick-or-treating on Halloween 1984, and were never seen again.

There was the college girl who woke up in a pool of blood

on her dorm-room floor, and who learned only later that she had been raped.

A baby-sitter—

Oh, enough already! voices begged.

The bottle of Scotch was all gone. You could hear how much people had drunk in their speech. Nona, who had drunk too fast, had the sensation—odd but not unpleasant—of being unmoored. The hand that reached for her glass, and the hand under the table, holding Lyle's, felt disembodied, like the ones she had watched from the stairs.

There was a new face at the table: an environmentalist who had arrived just that morning, early for the energy conference. "When I was twelve," he said, "I came home from school one day and found my mother crying. She said one of my friends had died. He'd been playing and accidentally hanged himself from his bunk bed with his belt."

"That sounds like one of those suicides no one is willing to call by its real name," said Josie.

"Yeah," said Sandy. "Like all those people who clean their guns with their tongues."

"This is getting too morbid," Phoebe said, and her daughter-in-law pleaded: "Can't we talk about something else?"

Lyle said, "Sounds like a case of autoeroticism to me."

A few people needed enlightenment here. Josie remained incredulous. "Are you being serious or is this another crazy story?"

"Oh, perfectly serious. It happens all the time. Supposedly, it's the most amazing orgasm. Some people use poppers when they do it, to get a better rush." ("*Peppers*?" Josie said, incredulous again, and again Lyle had to enlighten her.) "A lot of accidental asphyxiations happen that way. We've had two cases at the university. Sometimes it looks like suicide, and some families prefer to believe that that's what happened, for all the obvious reasons."

"Well, well, well . . ." marveled Josie.

Then a sly voice asked, "Has anyone ever tried it?" and was slyly answered, "What—suicide or autoeroticism?"

"Can't we please talk about something else?" Phoebe's daughter-in-law whined again, but at that moment the dragon leaned forward and spoke. With the candlelight exaggerating her facial folds and her thick-lidded eyes, she looked grim as a gargoyle.

"My father committed suicide. I was just a child. He shut himself into the garage and turned on his car. My mother never admitted it was suicide. Her whole life she stuck to the story that it was an accident. She told me that I had done it. I didn't know that he was in there, she said, and I shut the garage door on him by mistake."

She leaned back in her chair again, back into the darkness and, in the silence that followed, the storm could be heard still raging—or was it a mob of bogeymen coming to get them?

They went to bed shortly after, out of Scotch and stories and humor.

Lyle was staying on the second floor of the house, but he walked Nona up to her room on the third. At her door they embraced, carefully holding the candles at arm's length. The force of his kiss threw her off balance. He looped a leg around her legs to brace her. He dug his free hand down the front of her pants and, when he found out what he wanted to know, made a low, exultant sound deep in his throat. Her fingers groped for him, as they had groped for the candle on the bookshelf, and as she touched him he said, "You're drunk," and his voice was wistful. He said goodnight, kissing her where her hair was parted, as one kisses a child.

She fell asleep right away but woke three hours later—in a panic. She could see nothing, it was so black, but the wind and the rain had stopped, and the silence was utter, like the dark.

What was the reason for her panic? There was none, and she knew it, but knowing did not help her. She took two pills at once.

* * *

The storm had blown over by morning, but the power would not be restored until midday. Outside, there was that subdued aura that often follows a bad storm, like sheepishness after a tantrum. Later that day Nona sat for Josie. Whenever she looked at the painting-in-progress, Nona felt prickly with self-consciousness, as when she had to look at photographs of herself. Too much gold in her hair, too much pink in her skin, altogether too too—she thought of Renoir, one of her least favorite painters. The more the painting progressed the less she liked it; now that it was almost done she could hardly bear to look at it. And something else struck Nona about that painting. It had to do with the stories Josie told while she worked. It made Nona recall what has often been said, that every portrait is really a self-portrait. "My, my," said Lyle, when he dropped by one day to see it. "Don't you look like the woman who's just lost her only true love."

Phoebe liked the painting so much she had already asked Josie if she could hang it in the library.

When she returned to her room that day, Nona was surprised to see loose sheets of paper lying in the middle of her bed. She could not remember having left them there. With a flare of anger she realized that someone had come into her room while she was with Josie. She picked up the pages and, as she looked them over, her anger turned to chagrin.

They were poems. Each one was dated: so she could see that he had begun writing them only days after her arrival. Poems to her and about her. Nona read them with the same cringing embarrassment she felt when she looked at Josie's painting. What he wanted to do to her. What he would do to her if he could. What he did to himself, thinking about what he would do to her if he could. The language of romance borrowing from the language of pornography. (What's the difference between pornography and erotica? went the Stepsisters' joke. Erotica is pornography for people who don't want to get their hands dirty.)

Nona dropped the pages back onto the bed. Though she had only skimmed them, she knew she would not look at them again. She was struggling with an emotion she had trouble persuading herself was not contempt. She had thought that Lyle was smarter than this.

Downstairs, in an old broom closet that had been converted into a telephone booth, Nona called her husband.

Her tone gave her away.

"You're getting your period, aren't you."

She could see him as clearly as if it were a videophone: the short curls of his dark brown hair, his glasses that always needed cleaning, his high round cheeks, his stubble (he hated shaving). He was her husband, her worthy husband, patient, loving, and true. She loved him for his steadiness, his strong nerves—he took almost everything in his stride.

It happens to hypochondriacs: no one believes them when they are really ill, and nervous people are in the same fix. How was Roy supposed to know when Nona was having a real problem and when she was just getting herself worked up over nothing? Whenever they fought, which was thankfully seldom, this was almost sure to be at the bottom of it.

"Have you been taking pills?" was the first thing Roy wanted to know.

"I couldn't get to sleep without them."

"That's not good—but let's not worry about it now. We'll wait till you get home and you can detox then." The danger, as she did not need to be told, was not just addiction but the dreaded side effects: anxiety and depression. "What about alcohol?"

Nona told him about the night before.

"Now, that's something you don't want to repeat." There was no reproach, not even a hint of criticism in his speech. When she told him about Lyle, he said, "He sounds like a jerk. Just stay away from him. Tell him you don't want his smutty poems." Nona burst out laughing. Then she began to cry.

"Listen to me, Nona. You're away from home for weeks, this guy is attractive, he's giving you signs, and you're tempted. It's not for me to tell you what to do, but you have to use your head. You have to ask yourself how you're going to feel about it later, how you're going to feel about yourself."

Curly hair, round cheeks, glasses, stubble—the beloved face floated before her as she listened to the beloved voice. She had heard him use almost this same tone before, in response to calls from jittery singers on the eve of an audition or a performance. He was her husband, her merciful, long-suffering husband. It was because of him that they would survive. Like a genie from a lamp, the spirit of love streamed from the receiver, and Nona bowed her head, down, down, under the weight of her own unworthiness.

"Please, please, Nona. For God's sake, you're coming home in two days, remember?" Two days! Nona wiped her nose on her sleeve. "Surely you can hang on that long?"

They talked for about twenty minutes more, turning to other matters: what their friends were up to, what mail had come for Nona, and so on. By the time they hung up she was feeling much brighter.

But, not an hour later, Nona's heart was flooded with darkness again. She was back upstairs, and it was as if that peaceful room had been invaded by snakes. Rage and contempt had sunk their fangs in to the root. And hatred—for Lyle, for her husband—a wild, raving feeling, terrible in its force and unreason.

Overwhelmed by the desire for oblivion, she set her alarm clock for dinnertime, took a pill, and went to sleep.

FOR NONA'S READING IN the library Phoebe had rearranged the chairs, got a nice fire going, and set out bottles of soda and wine. Nona read sitting on a high stool near the window, the pages rustling in her nervous hands.

It is strange to claim nostalgia for times and places one has never known, but I am not sure what else to call this feeling of mine for the New York of before I was born, the world of my newlywed parents. Unlike me, neither of my parents was born there. My mother was from Los Angeles, my father from Philadelphia, and it was in San Francisco that they met. That was the last year of World War Two. My father had been sent by the Navy to the West Coast, from where he would soon be leaving for the Pacific. My mother happened to be visiting her San Francisco cousins at the time. They gave a tea dance, and among those invited was a shipmate of my father's, who brought him along. Later, my mother would say that she started to fall in love right then, dancing to Marlene Dietrich, but forced herself to keep her emotions in check. After all, this was a man going to war. But why else should she have been so thrilled to learn that Shep Shelton was a Catholic? That he hadn't been to Mass in years did not trouble her overmuch; something could be done about that later. (Later, later: they would see each other only a handful of times before my father shipped out, yet she often caught herself assuming a common future.)

How young they were. First kiss: *later* my father would mortify my mother by acting out for others her flapping consternation when he put his tongue into her mouth. ("The nuns must've told her you could get pregnant that way.") Such an innocent was Rosalind. She had tender, blue-gray eyes and wore her long, sweet-smelling hair in a pageboy. My father, more experienced at kissing, perhaps, but green-looking as a Boy Scout in those old photographs. It was partly the sailor's uniform, of course (which, when you think about it, was surely designed by a lover of boys?).

Courtship: the coy song and dance of those days. He

arrives at her doorstep with his Dietrich and Ella Fitzgerald records, bottles of sherry, and huge bouquets of roses that drive her father gasping and sneezing from the parlor. ("He was clever, your father.") He never said anything about wanting to be a painter then. "*Then* it was poetry he got all hopped up about." He gave my mother books of poems by Robert Frost and T. S. Eliot and promises that he, too, someday—

And wasn't there a poem or two enclosed with the letters that he sent from the South Pacific? Rosalind couldn't remember for sure. What she did remember was the criticism in those letters—harsh criticism, of the Navy, and of the American military in general—and how that incensed her father, who had fought in the previous war and was head of the local chapter of Catholic Veterans. So early on, already it was clear that these two men, who had not liked each other when they met, would always be at odds. (But did anyone back then imagine how bad things would get? Had anyone foreseen my grandfather ranting and swearing that he'd sooner one of his girls had married a colored, and that my mother would be better off dead?)

Before my father left, there had been talk about marriage but no official engagement.

There was the possibility (never voiced) that Shep would not come back, and against this possibility my mother prayed to the Mother of God daily. There was the possibility that he'd come back, but by that time would have forgotten her. There was the possibility that he'd come back and would not have forgotten her, but, when they met again, would change his mind about marrying her. Or: he would come back and still want to get married, but her father would forbid it.

My mother's nights were long and dark with such speculations.

He came back. He had not forgotten. He sought her out at once and proposed to her, thumbing his nose at her father.

He must have had a bad time in the Navy, everyone always said. It was the one part of his life that he never talked about, and there was not a single friend or acquaintance from that time that he kept in touch with. People remembered that he returned from the war more serious and more mature and sure of himself. He had plans, he knew what he wanted, and he would have it. "Oh, he was cocky" (Aunt Peg). During the war he had seen this difference between himself and the other men: from all he could tell, his shipmates did not spend much time worrying about dying, whereas he could think of nothing else. Fear of dying would mark him all his life. Dying—especially dying young, before one's time—had no touch of beauty or romance for him. Rather, it was an outrage. (That was how he saw the death of his mother, of cancer, at twenty-three.) I have grieved at descriptions of my father crying in his beer, babbling over and over: "And if I were to die tonight, what would I have accomplished?" Fear of dying and fear of failure were like twin goblins escorting Shep through life. All this might give the impression that he was chronically gloomy, and that would be wrong. Constant awareness of death might keep contentment and peace of mind beyond reach, but Shep believed that it also gave life savor and intensity.

"He was envious of people who didn't share his thing about death," said his friend Benedict Stone. "But he was also mighty contemptuous of them."

The war appeared to have sharpened both his appetite for life and his sense of life's precariousness.

A civilian once more, his own man again, and the world had never looked so lovely. A ravening hunger, a greed for adventure and pleasure seized him. People who knew him then admired his energy, his easy laugh, and what a lot of people have described to me as his "animal vitality." Always up for a good time, always ready to play all night long, he was also hardworking; ambitious. By now he had decided that he wanted to paint, but that didn't mean he was giving up poetry. He would do both. He would paint, write, study on the GI Bill, get married, have kids—he would have it all, and why not? The war was won, he and freedom had survived, anything was possible.

To top it all off, he was in love.

Project Number One: Get Rosalind away from that oppressive household—six meek little women under the fist of one stiff-necked old soldier.

So, instead of Rosalind leading her new husband back to the fold, it was he who lured her away from it.

"He was just so down on the Church at that time," she told me. "He talked a lot about the collaboration of the Vatican with the Fascists. He told me how, when the German Church protested Nazi euthanasia policies, those policies were changed, and for him this proved that strong Christian protest could have helped save the Jews. And he was livid about American Catholic support for Franco. There was a fight like you would not believe between him and Dad at dinner one night. It still gives me the chills to remember the hate they spat at each other over the pot roast, and my mother in tears. And I remember what struck me most was that Shep wasn't afraid of Dad, which really set him apart from everyone else. He always got the better of Dad, no matter what the argument; he knew what he was talking about, and he was very agile and clever. Anyway, I trusted him; I believed everything he said. I would have converted to Gnosticism if he'd asked me to." And whether he wrote poetry or painted pictures was all the same to Rosalind, too.

By all accounts, they were a good match. Friends on both sides predicted happiness.

A crystal perfume flask; a white cashmere sweater with mother-of-pearl buttons and a bright red butterfly embroidered on the back; a fan made of peacock feathers; an antique locket to replace the crucifix he didn't want her to wear—these early gifts from Shep to Rosalind were the hallowed objects of my childhood. (*Shep, Rosalind*: I have called my parents by their given names for so long, I cannot remember ever calling them anything else.) And let me not forget the cigarette holder: that long slender tube, carved from the horn or tusk of some wild beast (they said), with its permanent dark lipstick stain. Glamorous toy: I flourished it, balanced it between my fingers, my lips. They both smoked cigarettes. No way I wouldn't one day, too.

Shep must have had enormous power over Rosalind to be able to convince her to leave not only Church but home and family and move all the way to New York, where neither of them knew a soul, and where they had no clear prospects. A cold-water walk-up on Lexington Avenue, a cracked windowpane that the landlord refused to fix, roaches that managed to infiltrate even the icebox; on one side a neighbor who lived alone yet talked nonstop, on the other a couple who slept all day and vacuumed at midnight. In letters home my mother wrote loyally: "Of course, there is nowhere else in the world I'd rather be."

They began by finding odd jobs to make ends meet. "Odd's the word," Rosalind said. Twice a day Shep went out to run a woman who was an exercise fanatic but happened to be blind around and around Madison Square Park. They both worked for a time for an agency whose clients were looking for names for new products. "They paid us something like a dime for each name they chose to present to the client, and a lot more if the client actually accepted one of them, which never seemed to happen. We would sit up late into the night drinking and brainstorming, covering pages and pages of yellow lined paper. The only one I can remember after all these years is Snow Kisses, for some kind of melt-in-your-mouth candy. Sometimes we got really silly. We didn't make any money, but we did have fun."

My mother finally signed up with a temp agency that gave her low-paying but steady work typing. My father got a job in the garment district, selling cloth samples door-to-door. On weekends sometimes he helped out a superintendent he'd gotten to know on the block. (It was this man who would give them their first taste of pot.) By this time Shep had narrowed things down: painting was not one of many things but the only thing he wanted to do with his life. Poetry was of course still to be read and revered and learned by heart; it wasn't Frost and Eliot now, but W. H. Auden and Frank O'Hara.

Shep turned out to be right again. There really was nowhere more exciting to be in those postwar years than New York. They went out every night. They went to see ballet and to hear music and poetry, they went to jazz clubs and to dance clubs—the rumba and the mambo were all the rage then. Some of their haunts, like Chumley's or John's, are places I could go to myself today, but of course most of their New York has been torn down. They spent a lot of time at the movies, often seeing two double features in one day. Every Saturday afternoon they went to Fourth Avenue, browsing from bookstore to bookstore that used to be there.

New York was a place where people moved a lot; people were forever packing up their things and moving to a new apartment, a new neighborhood, making a fresh start. Their first five years in the city, my parents moved six times. In memoirs of that era, comparisons to Paris after the First World War keep coming up, along with words like *romantic*, *freedom*, and *possibility*. Old-time New Yorkers will tell you that those were the best years of the city's life, and I have always believed them.

The spirit of that time is midnight-blue, has the voice of a saxophone, and blows smoke rings like the old Camel billboard that used to loom over Times Square. A sexy era, it seems to us now. No one ever got tired, no one ever slept. Everyone smoked and drank. An innocent time, when "you were not faced with a moral dilemma every time you put something into your mouth." If you ate a big steak for dinner and washed it down with whiskey and smoked all through the meal, you might not think you had done something good for yourself, but neither did you think you had done something depraved. Shep's drink was bourbon, Rosalind's was gin. Marijuana was around, especially at parties. There were other drugs, too. Benzedrine to go up and Miltowns to go down. And there was heroin. (It was strange, being a child of the sixties with parents who had done drugs before I was born.)

"When I think of all I would have missed if I had never met Shep . . ." I don't think my mother ever lost her feeling of gratitude toward Shep for opening up the world to her. If not for him, she said, she probably would never have seen a foreign film or eaten Japanese food or heard Charlie Parker live or learned Latin dancing. "Here we are, living la vie de bohème," she wrote her sisters. But was it any life in which to bring up a child? My parents had agreed on the importance of putting off starting a family. The first real trouble between them began when Rosalind understood that Shep would put it off forever if he could.

One steamy August night, they left the window on the fire escape open, and a burglar came in while they slept. "He took everything, went through every drawer and closet of every room—even the bedroom!—without waking us. He ate the leftovers from supper and drank a beer." Another night they were mugged right on their doorstep by a man with a knife. As the mugger was strutting away, laughing, and my mother was trying to drag Shep into the building, Shep suddenly shook himself as if he'd been asleep, and took off after him. He was gone for the longest ten minutes of Rosalind's life. He came back with his wallet in one hand and the knife in the other. My mother always liked telling this story. Even after everything had gone wrong, she told it. He was a man then, she would say. A real man.

By the beginning of the fifties, they had moved to Morton Street, in the Village. Thanks to the super who'd become their friend, and who now worked in that building, they got an excellent deal on a basement apartment. Shep could walk to the studio he had found on Broadway. It was now that he met Benedict Stone, who had a studio in a building a few doors down.

Benedict Stone died in nineteen-ninety-two. He was in the hospital when he heard that I was writing about Shep, and he made a tape and sent it to me.

"I liked the man and I liked the work from the start. He was doing something completely different from me, but so what. I wasn't one of those people who believed that if it wasn't abstract it couldn't be interesting. If the work *had* been abstract, though, I probably could have helped him a lot more than I was able to. By the time he did move in that direction, it was way too late. That was a bad mistake, and he paid for it—people were very scornful of him. But a lot of artists take detours like that. I always thought he would have redeemed himself if he'd had the chance. The terrible thing about his dying when he did was that it happened at a time when he was so alone. People—including most of his friends—were down on his work then, and he was very hurt by that. So he got in a huff and just shut everyone out. Then he died so suddenly—no time at all for explanations or making amends or—it was very cruel."

As with other artists of the time, when he first came to New York, what cried out to Shep to be painted was New York itself: the bridges, the El, the taxis and the Automats and the theater marquees. He loved Coney Island and Times Square. Benedict said he had never known anyone so intoxicated with a place. "I mean, we were all big on New York, capital of the twentieth century and all that, but Shep was even more extreme than that." He did not like to leave town even for short periods of time. When Rosalind went back West to visit her family, she had to go by herself. The one time he accepted an invitation for a weekend in the Hamptons he made an excuse and left early. The first thing he did when he got off the train was to buy a pretzel; then he headed for one of the penny arcades on Forty-second Street.

"Those early paintings of his were all done in that jagged expressionist style—the same style he would use in the portraits once he started on them. The line was very jazzy and free, but the palette was somber—lots of mauves and grays and browns. Not too many figures in the beginning. Then came *Blind Newsboy* and *G-Men* and *Execution on Broadway*." (This last painting, of a man being gunned down by mobsters in the street, was based on a true crime of the day which Shep himself witnessed.) "He started the *Shoeshine Triptych* on New Year's Day, nineteen-fifty-five." In what would become Shep's best-known work, three men are having their shoes shined. They are sitting on one of the pewlike structures that used to be a lot more common in men's rooms and terminals and building lobbies than they are today. Two of the men are talking together and the third is reading a book.

"I remember it well because we'd stayed up all the night before, celebrating at a party on Cliff Street. Shep went straight from the party to the studio. That wasn't really so unusual for him—he slept less than anyone I ever met. Of course, he was drunk. He drank as much as the rest of us in those days—maybe a little more—so what. At least he wasn't a brawler. He might get a little maudlin at times but he never got mean. I watched the progress of that painting and I thought it was hilarious. Still do. The figure in the middle is sitting a little higher than the other two, and he's got his fedora pushed back on his head (that was when everyone wore a hat, remember), so the brim reads like a halo, and then you've got the shoeshine boys kneeling near the bottom of the frame—like the donors in the old altarpieces. Hah!"

The triptych might live to be the best known of Shep's paintings, but in Benedict's opinion the best work lay some years ahead.

"How did he first get interested in boxers? I don't remember now. It must have been someone he met at the gym. He had taken up bodybuilding—a pretty unusual thing to do back then, by the way, not like today. He was going every day to this place on Fourteenth Street—a real dive, as I recall, with a lot of tough characters. Then he started going to the fights, and to other gyms, places like Gleason's, where boxers trained. He'd go there and he'd sketch, and then he'd go back to the studio and work from the sketches. He was already doing portraits then, and he got some of the boxers to sit for him. I found the whole *Gladiator* series just amazing. Those monumental heads! Some of them you couldn't look at without wincing or touching your own nose or mouth. And it was strange, because they looked so menacing, these guys, like if you leaned too close they'd bite your face off, and at the same time so vulnerable, because of the swellings and bruises. And of course you couldn't say for sure which facial distortions were the models' and which were the painter's. They got a very good response, those portraits. Boxers had taken on a kind of aura that they didn't have before. A lot of people—I mean artists and intellectuals—people who would probably never have paid any attention to prizefighting before—were suddenly paying attention. The reason was Cassius Clay."

Shep often acknowledged the good that came to him through his friendship with Benedict Stone. But Benedict spoke of a way in which he believed their friendship was bad for Shep.

"He used to say to me: I want to be famous. Those were some of the first words I ever heard out of his mouth. Oh, he was charming when he said it, you know: head to one side, big grin. Drunk, maybe—probably. But he was serious. He said, I want to walk into the Carnegie Deli and have people go, Ooh, look, there's Shep Shelton, with the little hairs standing up on their arms. He'd be laughing when he said it, of course, but he was dead serious. Now, my own success came early and, as things go, pretty easy. I always thought that this gave Shep the wrong idea. If the same thing

wasn't happening to him, he must be doing something
wrong. Or something wrong was being done to him.
That was his attitude. He'd be angry at the world for not
giving him enough attention, and then he'd turn all that
anger in and flagellate himself for not doing everything
he thought he should be doing. Well, of course that was
just nonsense. All he had to do was take a good look
around at all the other guys out there struggling. I was
the exception, not the rule. Not to mention I didn't
have to work, my wife supported us. That made a hell
of a difference, too.

"Sometimes the desire for success can help drive the
work and other times it can just take all the joy out of
it and make you crazy. I never met anyone so terrified
of failure as Shep. Even when things started working
out for him, he didn't dare call it success. It was never
enough for him, it was all just like a tease to him—
every show, every sale—because it was never the big
time that he really wanted.

"Of course, it was a little hard for me to talk to him
about this—with things moving so fast for me, and my
shows selling out, and my rich wife to top it all off.
The rumors are true: the last year or so, our friendship
had pretty much gone to pieces. What do you expect?
The few times I saw him I was always struck by how
nervous and run-down he seemed. The marriage was
over. So was his relationship with his gallery—They
dropped me like a hot turd, he said—and there was no
one taking care of him. He was drinking more and
more, and he always had a cold or a rash or something.
And he was very unhappy. I will be honest: I didn't
have that much sympathy for him. As I said, we
weren't getting along at the time. But I wasn't that
worried about it. I thought things would change again.
I thought we had all the time in the world. When I

think how I used to laugh at him for being afraid he was going to kick the bucket. Hell, he was ten years younger than me. Forty-three: what kind of age is that for a man to die?"

Nona said, "I think I'll stop there."

chapter
six

"She didn't like homosexuals."

An hour after the reading, Nona was still in the library. She had moved from the stool to a more comfortable chair, near the fire. When the others had gone to bed, she, Lyle, Phoebe, and the dragon had stayed up talking.

The dragon had a name, of course, and the name was Pearl Verga. It was past her bedtime, and she was tired. She did not like to be read to, but it had intrigued her to hear about these people she had known. The Sheltons she had not known well. The daughter, Nona, looked like the father. Pearl had not really seen it until tonight, and with the recognition had come a little heave of distaste. She had never liked the father— a mediocrity, a climber, she thought; she had never understood his appeal to Benedict. Now, Benedict Pearl had known well, and him she had loved. It was strange to hear his words, which Nona had read lightly mimicking—perhaps unconsciously—his southeastern Florida accent. At one point Pearl had turned in her chair to glance at Phoebe sitting behind her. Pearl wanted to see what effect the reading was having on Phoebe, who appeared to be calm, a faraway but rapt expression on her face: a woman dreaming with her eyes open.

As for Pearl, she had felt the throb of multiple old wounds.

Handsome, brilliant Benedict Stone. Few women who met him had not, to some degree at least, fallen for him.

Now Pearl slumped in her armchair. She had lapsed into a fantasy of a kind she had not had in years and years; it brought heat to the surface of her skin and moistness to her eyes. Then a log shifted in the grate, and she was back, the conversation from which she had faded suddenly loud in her ears, as if someone had opened a door on it.

They were talking about the wife now. Pearl remembered a pretty little woman, quite ordinary, something of a goody-goody. "She didn't like homosexuals," she said aloud, and then, because everyone was momentarily silent, added, "You would expect that, of course. She came from a strict Catholic background."

"So do a lot of homosexuals," murmured Lyle.

Phoebe said, "Nona, have you talked to Tim Banister yet?"

"I tried," said Nona. "I called him once about a year ago and told him I wanted to talk to him. He was very short with me. He said, I'm sorry, I'd love to help, but I'm just too busy burying my friends these days. I didn't know what to say. I couldn't bring myself to call him again after that."

"Well, I think you should try again. After all, he was closer than anyone to Shep at the end."

Now Lyle asked the question he had been about to ask Nona when Pearl interrupted. "Did your father come right out and tell your mother the truth?"

Nona shook her head. "I always heard that a friend told her."

"Friend!" Pearl threw back her head and opened her mouth wide; but the laugh the others expected never came out. "It was Monica Becker who told her." As Nona already knew. Monica Becker: poet, mother of Sasha, editor of *Children of Artists*. Monica Becker who had hanged herself. "Oh, I knew Monica very, very well, and let me tell you she was an impossible creature who was never a friend to anyone, least of all herself." Pearl used her elbows to prop herself higher in her chair, back in the conversation with a vengeance now.

"Everybody knew that Shep had a double life—he wasn't the only one, either. And there were a lot of people who thought that what he was doing was very shoddy, but they weren't about to say anything. After all, it wasn't as if everyone else's apron was so clean. Anyway, Rosalind got on Monica's nerves. Monica thought Rosalind was a goody-goody. And Monica, well, she was a type, you know—gutter mouth, unfiltered cigarettes, drink the boys under the table, three square fucks a day—reminded me of that woman, what was her name?—the one who was here—oh, never mind. Monica used to make fun of Rosalind. She used to say that nobody had a right to be that naive. And it *was* a little hard to believe, I should say, because Shep was never especially discreet. We all kept waiting for Rosalind to wise up, but it was years and years, and I guess Monica got impatient."

"Dad told me Monica was drunk when she called Rosalind that day," Phoebe said. "And her own marriage had just broken up—that may have had something to do with it. Who knows: maybe she really thought she was doing the right thing."

"She was a troublemaker," Pearl said. "And when wasn't she drunk? Anyway, Rosalind hung up on her. Rosalind told her she had a dirty mind (that was the kind of thing Rosalind would say), and hung up. And Monica called her right back and said, Well, if you don't believe me, go see for yourself. I don't know if Monica actually knew that Shep was with someone right then, or if she was just guessing."

The story was familiar to Nona, she had heard it more than once, but she listened carefully, as she always did, in case there was some new detail. She had been told that, after hearing Monica out, Rosalind had taken her, Nona, and walked the few blocks to the studio where she found Shep with a man who was never to be identified beyond "someone from the gym" (Benedict). But Nona had no memory of this visit to the studio. This was something that had always puzzled her. Later she discovered that if she wanted to put her mother in a foul mood, all she had to do was ask her about it.

"How do you expect me to remember that?" Rosalind would say, voice screwed to the pitch of frustration. "I was a little upset at the time." Bitterest sarcasm.

The waters had grown even murkier when her mother's eldest sister, Peg, who was hardly less testy when questioned than Rosalind, said: "Don't be absurd. Of course you weren't there. Do you think your mother would have taken you along?" But if not, where was she? Nona would not have been old enough then to be left by herself. "School, maybe." It would, over time, become bloated with significance for Nona: at this critical moment, no one seemed to remember where she was.

One thing needed no clarification: the three of them never slept under the same roof again. In a matter of days, Rosalind would have returned to Los Angeles with Nona. In the meantime, Shep went to stay with the Stones.

After Pearl had gone to bed, Phoebe poured out the last of the wine, and Lyle built up the fire. They watched without speaking until the wood caught and then Phoebe said: "It was spring break, so I happened to be home. I was too old not to guess a lot of what was happening, but Mother let me believe that it was another woman. Shep was around a lot when I was growing up, so I was used to him. I'd had a little crush on him when I was in eighth grade. He had these huge dark circles under his eyes from never sleeping, and he always needed a shave. He was very sexy, in his grungy way. There was some tension between my parents over his being there. Shep stayed up real late playing records, and he got drunk and passed out in his clothes on the sofa, and the guest room—his room—had an odor. I remember, at dinner, if he said something funny,

Dad would laugh, and I would laugh, and Mother would say, Please pass the carrots, with an air that turned all the food on the table cold."

Hours later, well after midnight, after Phoebe had gone to bed, Nona and Lyle were still in the library. The fire had been kept alive, and they had left their chairs for the braided hearth rug. Nona lay on her back, her arms crossed under her head. Lyle was on his side, propped on one elbow, facing her, one hand resting on Nona's stomach. Their feet were touching.

Lyle said, "What did he die of?"

"Pneumonia."

"That's unusual, isn't it? How did that happen?"

"Oh, it was totally unnecessary. If he'd gotten help in time, it wouldn't have happened. It started out as a cold, or a flu, and he didn't take care of it, so it got worse and worse. Finally one day he couldn't get out of bed. If he'd gone to a hospital then, he probably would have survived. But he was superstitious about hospitals—he was one of those people who believe that if you go into a hospital you'll never come out alive. He was living—illegally—in his studio then. It was a weekend in the middle of winter. There was no heat. The temperature went down to minus six that night. It was too much for him. His lungs filled up, and he died."

Questions. Why hadn't he called someone? Was it possible that he hadn't realized how sick he was? Had he been too weak to get to the phone? Too feverish? Delirious? Or was it pride that had kept him from calling for help. At that time his father and stepmother were still alive, and he had a brother. But he was estranged from his first family as he was from his second—and for the same reason. He would not have called any of his relations—but what about friends? Why hadn't he called one of them? He was in a huff, Benedict said. He was mad at the world. But surely there must have been *someone* to whom he would have been willing to turn?

It haunted Nona, that image of her father with only his demons there at the end, the same two demons that had tormented him all his life: fear of failure, fear of dying. Freezing, choking, alone, afraid—a torturous death, she had always imagined it. Oh, to believe what she had read somewhere, that, in the final hours, there comes a respite from the throes of dying, some physiological change takes place, a flood of endorphins bringing release from pain. Oh, to be able to believe this; how good if true, and how hard to believe because too good to be true; after all, there was so little mercy in the world.

Questions, questions. Had he known he would die? Had he, like the emperor in the fairy tale, seen Death sitting on his chest and the faces of all his good and evil deeds surrounding him? Had he spoken, had he died with a word, with a name on his lips, as people do? Had he reached out his arms, as some people do? And when it was over, when he closed his eyes, did he see darkness or light?

"Don't be sad." Lyle slipped a hand under Nona's head and lifted her face to his. He kissed her lightly once, twice, and a third time, fully. He broke the kiss, sighed, brought his mouth back down on hers. His lips moved on her lips as if he were praying. *O lovely man, what do you pray for?* She opened her legs as she slid under him, and he laid his weight upon her like a blessing. She lifted her legs and touched her toes to the backs of his knees. She was praying, too: *right here, right now—quickly.* But he broke the kiss again and moved away from her, and she did not stop him. They lay sighing, returned to their exact former positions: she on her back, he on his side with one hand flat on her stomach; feet touching. A thin whispered shriek escaped from the flames: the tiny cry of a tiny lost soul.

Lyle said, "When was the last time you saw him?"

It would take the rest of the night to tell that story. She had flown all the way across the country by herself to see him, the end of a grueling struggle with her mother. High in the clouds, her first time traveling alone, thirteen-year-old Nona had felt like a heroine. She was on her way to a reunion with the father she had not seen since leaving New York. For three long years they had been kept apart—by her mother, Nona had convinced herself, and by her mother's people. Now at last she had defied them, and she had won.

"At that point, when I went to see him, I still didn't know the truth. You see, no one ever sat me down and explained what had happened. My mother had made the whole subject taboo. It was hard enough just getting her to show me photographs. There are lines parents draw that you don't cross when you're a child. I couldn't ask certain things about their marriage. It would have been like asking my mother if she had orgasms. And there was a way in which my mother was never—I don't know quite how to put it—never entirely present, if you know what I mean. She was like someone behind a pane of glass. You could see her but you couldn't touch her. She's still like that.

"I grew up with the fear that my father had done something unspeakable. First I thought maybe he had stolen some money, and then I thought he had killed someone and that he was in jail. Later I thought maybe he had some horrible contagious disease—leprosy, I decided, after I discovered what that was. And then for a while I was convinced that he was dead and that no one would tell me. Once I knew about sex I thought: of course: another woman—what else? Just like Phoebe."

Nona's memory of the period immediately following the move to California was hopelessly confused. She could not recall when and how she understood that New York was no longer her home, that her parents were no longer together, that life had changed irrevocably. Right after they arrived in Los Angeles, Rosalind had a breakdown. At that time, Rosalind's mother had been dead for several years, and her father was living with Cady, the youngest, who had not yet married, and who kept house for him. The eldest daughter, Peg, had a fam-

ily of her own, and the two middle sisters, Mina and June, neither of whom would ever marry, had set up house together in
Riverside.

Your mother just needs to rest, Nona was told—no one
willing to call *that* by its real name, either. Your mother is in
no shape to take care of anyone but herself right now.

That her mother could have a problem part of whose solu-
tion was to send Nona away was a knife that cut deep. For the
next six months, Nona lived first with her spinster aunts, then
with Aunt Peg, then with the spinsters again.

Meanwhile, Rosalind was making peace with her father,
who had by all accounts behaved biblically, receiving back
his daughter with open arms. Nona somehow intuited that
this blessed reconciliation would have been more difficult, if
not impossible, if she, too, had been around. She saw her
mother a few times, at family gatherings, mostly. Rosalind
was thinner but always well put together, carefully dressed,
the face of grief hidden under makeup and an unvarying
smile. (Something Nona never would understand: Rosalind's
determination never to let her daughter see her suffering.)
With Nona she was tongue-tied, restless, oddly coy. Vexingly,
she used *we* for *you*: "What have we been reading?" "Have
we made any new friends?" "Do we want more cake?"
Behaving in the guarded way people behave with children who
are strangers to them. Years later, it would occur to Nona that
it might have distressed Rosalind that Nona took after Shep;
more than once she had caught Rosalind staring at her with a
strange, fixed expression, as if she were seeing someone else.
Nona had even suspected that one reason she had been sent
away might have been that Rosalind could not bear to be
reminded of Shep. She came to believe that her entire relationship with her mother had been colored by this: Nona was a
part of Shep that Rosalind could not divorce.

And when she was older and at last in possession of the
truth (and this would not be until she was grown), Nona knew

something else. Now she had a word for how she felt around her mother's people, and the word was *tainted*. Everyone kept a certain distance from her. Not at the spinsters', or at Aunt Peg's, or at her grandfather's, did anyone ever succeed in making Nona feel at home. And she saw how her curiosity terrified them all. "Aunt Peg, can I ask you a question?" "A question?" Peg would repeat faintly, eyes darting about the room as if following a fly. No one ever succeeded in banishing Nona's fear that everyone, no matter how kind—and she could not say they were not kind—would be happier if she weren't there. This was something she would carry with her into adulthood. She became used to the feeling of being tormented in the company of other people, even good friends. And this inability to relax, to be herself, and to breathe freely with others, had for long periods of time kept her a solitary.

Finally reunited with her mother, Nona discovered that Rosalind's coy, abstracted stance had become habitual. It was almost as if Nona had just been adopted and she and her mother did not share a past. In time Nona would learn that this kind of distance between generations was not so uncommon. But to Nona the child, Rosalind was a conundrum: flickering, artificially bright, there and not there, like a hologram.

"All my friends had fathers, not to mention brothers and sisters. I had one friend whose parents were divorced, but she still had a father. She said, You mean your parents didn't fight over you? It was from her that I learned about things like custody and visitation rights. No, Shep didn't fight my mother's decision to keep me away from him—not that he would have stood a chance in court anyway.

"I felt so lonely and cheated and sorry for myself. And then one day I put my foot down. I said, Okay, if he's not in jail, if he's not a murderer or a leper, if he's not really dead, why can't I see him? And then I just would not let it go. My mother kept saying things like, Oh, that's impossible, that would be very complicated—without really explaining anything, which only made me more adamant. Finally I wrote to Phoebe. I took a chance and wrote to her care of the University of Chicago. I knew that's where she'd gone to school, though by then she had graduated."

Phoebe called her parents at once. Her mother called Rosalind, Benedict spoke with Shep. It was agreed that Nona would stay with the Stones when she came to New York.

"We arranged it so I could go during Easter vacation. After three years my memories of Shep had become distorted—I was beginning to forget him, I think—and by the time I flew to New York, I had built an elaborate heroic fantasy around him: he was this handsome, dashing artist of genius—and of course what he wanted most in life was me. If it weren't for my mother, we would never be apart."

How he had missed her, how he was pining to see his little girl again. A mistress? Philandering? He needn't beg her to forgive him; she did it freely.

In New York, she was picked up at the airport by Phoebe, who had returned to the city after college and was now living with two roommates on the Upper West Side and working for a civil-liberties lawyer. Twenty-three, on her own, she seemed as old as a parent or a teacher to Nona, who blushed every time Phoebe asked a simple question. Nona was even more uncomfortable with Mr. and Mrs. Stone. By the time she saw her father, two days later, her nerves were raw.

She had wanted so much to be invited to her father's home. Of course he had a home, and Nona's imagination persisted in making it a narrow blue-shuttered house on a street like Morton Street, where they all had lived, though she knew that most New Yorkers lived in apartments.

He had arranged to meet her in a large crowded deli on Madison Avenue, not far from the Stones'. Mrs. Stone walked her there. Later, Shep would walk Nona back to the apartment building, where the doorman had been told to expect her.

It would all be over in an hour.

It would all be over, and in that hour Nona would have suffered a wound out of which her childhood bled away, drop by drop.

An adopted baby grows up, moves heaven and earth to find his birth parents, only to discover that their greatest wish was to remain unfound. It happens, Nona would hear of it happening, and she would measure her own sorrow against it.

They sat at a table in the busiest part of the dining room, hemmed in by other customers, about whom Shep seemed inexplicably curious. Even for the short time she had him to herself, she would not have his full attention. He ordered coffee only, cup after cup. Cigarette after cigarette put so much smoke between them, Nona had to squint to see him. He looked like his photographs, he looked the way she remembered him, yet, at the same time, he did not look as she had expected he would. How rough and battered-looking his hands were—yes, she remembered that. He was wearing a shirt that she knew. But mostly she was aware of his eyes—the restless eyes of someone trapped, the furtive eyes of someone hiding something.

She could not decide what she wanted to eat and was hurt to the quick when he let the waitress bully her into getting Belgian waffles, which Nona did not like.

Lyle said, "I take it he didn't tell you the truth then, either."

"Oh, no, of course not. He didn't tell me anything. He asked me questions, very stupid questions—about school, I think. I can't tell you how excruciating it was, the way he kept looking at my plate, because I wasn't eating, you see, and he was so anxious to get the hell out of there."

She would not have admitted it to anyone, but she had expected that Shep would give her something. She would not admit even to herself anymore the various wonderful things she had allowed herself to dream it would be. She had thought he would take her somewhere—his home, his studio, some special place. (She was dying to see the smoking billboard in

Times Square again.) She had thought he would take her out on the town. He would meet her at the airport with flowers and kisses. She had just known that they both would cry.

Miraculously, she managed not to cry until she was alone.

"I don't know what the plans were, whether we were supposed to see each other again, or what. I think probably everyone was playing it by ear. And who knows, had I seen him again maybe things would have improved. But in my heart I have never believed that. In my heart I knew he was trying to discourage me.

"Back at the Stones' I became really ill—I felt it physically—I could not breathe. To this day the smell of waffles can make me queasy.

"I remember I was so humiliated, because I had made such a big deal about all this, I was so triumphant when I finally got my way, and now I realized that everyone else must have known the truth all along: Shep had not wanted this reunion at all."

The decency of the Stones, which put Nona's parents' behavior to shame, their solicitude and their pity, were further humiliations not to be borne. Now it was Nona who felt trapped.

"I knew I had to get out of there as soon as possible. I said I would not see Shep again and I had to go home at once."

Unsure, Mrs. Stone made a hesitant effort to change Nona's mind, then threw up her hands and called Rosalind. "I remember feeling some satisfaction that I was causing everyone so much trouble."

On the flight home, the stewardesses had taken turns sitting with her. One of them—helpless before this grief that refused to explain itself, and perhaps divining that disappointment about a gift had played some part—removed a ring from her own hand and gave it to Nona. "In exchange," she said, "all I want is a big smile."

Back in Los Angeles, Rosalind had watched Nona anxiously. Her mother's concern was genuine and Nona knew this but sensed something else that kept her from accepting it— something that was probably closer to relief than to vindication, but that made it so that, for a long time, Nona could not stand to be in the same room with her mother.

"Where on earth did you get that ring?" Rosalind said. And when she'd heard: "Why, that's a real garnet. How odd. The girl must not have known . . ."

Shep died three months later.

When they had first moved to Los Angeles, Nona was sent to a Catholic grade school. (This was part of Rosalind's effort to make up with her father; in New York, Nona had gone to public school.)

". . . duty to inform . . . trouble getting along . . . very aggressive . . . I fear . . . Our Lady . . . no place for violence . . ." Rosalind read the letter aloud in a bewildered tone, as if she had no idea whom Mother Superior could possibly be referring to. "Hellion! Spitfire!" (Sister Agnes.) A few warnings later, Nona was placed on probation after a scuffle in which she broke the skin of another girl, with teeth and nails. At that time she was living with her grandfather, her mother, and her Aunt Cady. Her grandfather had wanted to beat her and would have beaten her if the women had not been around. (Was it just coincidence that, from the first moment, Nona had responded to this old man with an intensity of loathing to match Shep's?)

She prayed for him to die and, to her guilt-shot wonder, he died.

This happened about a year after Shep's death.

The door to her cage thus opened, Aunt Cady flew to the ready-made nest of a widower with three small children.

"We'll go mad in this big old house alone," Rosalind said. So the house was sold, and they moved to a smaller one, in Santa Monica.

Rosalind was forty-four now, and, like a certain kind of

woman in a certain kind of woman's novel, she had closed the door on public life. Dealt that near-mortal blow, she would live out her middle and old age as a semi-invalid, never taking too much on, always resting, keeping herself quiet, sedated. A funny mix, she was, of the independent and the agoraphobic. Living more frugally than she needed to on the money her father had left her, she made up her day out of cigarettes, cups of tea, glasses of gin, naps, telephone visits with her sisters, and constant reading, much of which was done in bed. Trips back and forth to the mall and the library were all the airing she seemed to need. Much of her shopping was also done in bed, through catalogues. To Nona she did not seem discontented. It was one kind of woman's life.

When Nona announced that she wanted to go to the public high school, without looking up from her book Rosalind said fine.

In high school, Nona continued to find trouble, but of a different kind. She lost—gave away?—got rid of her virginity when she was fourteen. When she was fifteen, she got pregnant and had an abortion arranged by the boy's elder sister. The operation, performed in a motel room by a man who said he was a doctor but who rumor said was a vet, hurt as in her worst fears but was mercifully brief. After that she went on the pill, which swelled her body to womanly proportions, attracting older boys, college men, who introduced her to other pills, whose altering effects were no less astonishing. This was a girl's life, coming of age in California, in the seventies.

A memory from junior year. Sitting in the bathroom one night with a glass of water in one hand and every tablet and capsule from the medicine cabinet in the other. Hours pass. From time to time, she gets up to look in the mirror and is almost surprised to see no change. Finally, exhausted, wrists aching, she puts all the pills back into the bottles, pours out the water—avoiding the mirror now—and goes to bed.

And yet, there was no doubt that Nona was happier as a

teenager. She did well in high school, she got along with people better, she had many friends. Now she discovered that there were a lot of people like herself, with problems like hers: kids with divorced parents, kids with missing parents, kids with parents who should have been in jail—girls and boys now old enough and bold enough to talk about such things.

When the time came to apply to colleges, Nona cared only about getting back to New York. By the time she graduated from New York University, she wanted only to stay in the city.

Lyle said, "So, how did you finally find out the truth?"

"It's hard to believe, but I made it all the way through high school and still no one had told me and I hadn't figured it out. Of all the things that went through my mind about him, I never guessed that. Who was gay? Did you know any gay people when you were growing up? I didn't. You heard rumors about this or that person, but no one was out. I made my first gay friends in college. And one night I was up late talking with my friend Josh, and he said, 'Did you ever think maybe your father was gay?' And, once my eyes had adjusted to the light, I saw all kinds of things falling into place. At first all I could do was laugh. I just sat there and laughed. (I should say I was pretty high at the time: we'd been smoking pot all night.) It's hard to explain what I was laughing at. My own thickness, I guess. The sheer stupidity of everyone around me. Oh, it was sad, it was pathetic, of course, but I was convinced that there was a big joke in there somewhere."

She had laughed at her mother when Rosalind said, "I was protecting you." She would hear this from a lot of people. This, and: "I didn't think I should be the one to tell you."

"What it really amounted to," Nona said now, "was that no one had the guts to tell me." A moral debacle on the part of the adults so spectacular she was devastated anew each time she remembered it.

"Don't be sad," said Lyle, catching her tear and bearing it on the tip of his tongue to her mouth.

The night had passed. From where they lay they could see, through the window, a pale bar of breaking light. It struck Nona now, as it had not the whole time she was talking, that there were people she had known for years to whom she had not revealed as much about herself as she had to this man whom she had just met. She had known her husband for months before she had told him everything she had just told Lyle.

The night had passed, and though they had not undressed and they had not slept and there had been only kisses between them, the intimacy had been accomplished and the sin committed, and Nona knew there would be no escaping that.

"Let's go for a walk," said Lyle, standing, pulling Nona to her feet.

It was the beginning of their last day, and they went out into the golden morning hand in hand, like children in a fairy tale.

At the end of that same day Lyle came to Nona's door. His knock had an urgency that made her jump, as if he had knocked on her heart. He stared at the gaping drawers and half-packed bags before throwing himself down on the bed. A coolness came over Nona at the sight of his slumped posture and bloodshot eyes. Though she damned the reflex in herself and in other women, she could not always suppress it: revulsion at signs of male helplessness.

He said, "It's impossible. Here I've gone and fallen in love with you. I knew it was happening, of course, but I didn't know how serious it was until last night. Now I don't know what I'm going to do."

Nona had managed to sleep only a little during the day. She was weary and edgy and her head ached. She wanted only to get her things packed and to go to bed as early as possible. She sat down beside Lyle and spoke measuredly, as if to a child. She said all the things that needed to be said.

"No, no, no. You don't understand—I can see that." Lyle's

tone was soft but chiding. Nona felt her cheeks becoming red. "You don't understand because you don't know me. I don't fall in love easily, not at all, not at all. You don't mean to do it, but you are patronizing me. I forgive you." But he turned away from her. There on the bed lay her blue-and-white bathrobe. He lifted the sleeve, brought the cuff to his lips, and kissed it. "I'll see you at breakfast," he said, without looking at her. He got up and left the room.

In the morning there was the letter under her door, there was the rose.

Breakfast was festive: blueberry pancakes, sausages, eggs, and everyone exchanging addresses and promises to stay in touch.

As she was hugging Nona good-bye, Phoebe said, "And don't forget: call Tim Banister."

There were several people who were driving back to the city and Nona might have gotten a ride with one of them, but she had arranged to take the train instead. She had always liked trains.

Riding home, lulled by the chugging of the train and scenes of the evanescent landscape, she was glad to be alone. Oh, the joy of the traveler who knows that tonight she will sleep in her own bed again! An extraordinary sense of relief flooded her, and one of her mother's favorite expressions kept coming into her head: "I got away with a blue eye."

chapter
seven

The young mezzo that Roy was working with this afternoon had a splendid voice but a disconcerting habit of clipping some notes, as if she had a tiny guillotine in the back of her throat. Another problem was her diction. "Kay for oh since uh your a deejay."

"Sorry, dear," said Roy. "Butter canner unnerstan awhirr Hussein." It was a mistake a lot of singers made: assuming that the words were not important because they were "foreign."

"The text and the music go together," Roy said, in a patient tone that did not betray the fact that he was saying it for the umpteenth time. "Articulate the words, and you'll see: the notes will come out purer as well. And remember, full value—full value for every note. Don't be stingy, now."

The mezzo began the aria again, and sang it just as she had before. Roy cut her off. He repeated everything he had just said, in slightly different words, in the same patient tone. The mezzo sang again, but this time he did not stop her. He let her go on, thinking of the story about Toscanini, who was said to have pointed to the great breasts of an exasperating diva and cried, "If only these were brains!"

At last the lesson was over and Roy was free. He took the subway to Union Square and stopped at the greenmarket to shop for the first real meal he would cook in a month. Cooking was one of Roy's talents and pleasures, but he never cooked for himself alone. While Nona was away, he had lived on sandwiches and pizza.

As always, the outdoor market was a feast for the eyes: pyramids of shining tomatoes and peaches—small bright yellow ones with thick fuzz and one or two leaves still attached. An acre of late-summer flowers. He bought tomatoes and peaches, he bought green beans and potatoes and fresh bread. Finally, he bought a bunch of purple dahlias. It was when he was paying for the flowers that he noticed that his hands were shaking.

Closer to the apartment, he stopped to buy lamb chops, and again, to buy wine. Loaded down though he was, as he turned onto his street, his step was light. Such a pretty street, so green and tidy. The flowers bobbed in his hand, as if they were agreeing.

Something about a woman waiting for you at a window . . . Roy's heart brimmed. She waved when she saw him. She jumped up and down like a child.

In the collision of their greeting he lost his grip on one of the bags and peaches rolled across the floor. They laughed at the rolling peaches. They laughed, rolling over and over each other on the bed. They made love frantically, as though it had been not a month but a year.

Later, she sat at the kitchen table with a glass of wine as he prepared their meal. She repeated all the Stepsisters' jokes, and he joked about his bovine mezzo.

Dinner was excellent, light and full of fresh flavor. They ate and drank and talked, their eyes and cheeks bright with pleasure. Together they cleaned up the kitchen, and as the sun was going down, they went out for a walk. As they walked, they held on to each other with crossed hands, like skaters. When they returned, they found a message on the answering machine, from Rosalind. Nona said that she would wait until the next day to call her.

That night they went to bed early and, for the first time that Roy could recall, Nona fell asleep before he did.

Something about watching a woman sleep . . . How mild and blameless she looked lying there, his beloved treacherous wife!

Roy had two sisters. Both were older than he and both loved him, but each had treated him differently when he was a boy. One was all sweet talk and indulgence, the other full of stern warnings about what would happen if he didn't watch his step. Growing up, Roy had called them Good Cop and Bad Cop. When he introduced Nona to his family for the first time, Good Cop had said, "I just know you two are going to be happy together." Bad Cop had predicted trouble.

Like other men, Roy had grown up dreaming of beautiful women, but though he had cast out his net many times, he had never managed to catch one. Good Cop thought Nona was very pretty, Bad Cop thought she looked washed-out. She was his wan, bright-haired, thin-skinned type. One of his first thoughts on seeing her that first day in class was how the veins all over her body must show through her skin. She could not have been more different from his sisters or from anyone else in their family: down-to-earth folks with the resilience and sinewy nerves of the midwestern farmers who were their forebears.

She had come into his life at a very bad time in her own. Earlier, she had been in therapy, but, for reasons that came out only later, she had stopped seeing her doctor. When Roy met her she had been eating and sleeping poorly for months. She was thin and pale and haunted-looking. She was an exaggeration of herself. An exaggeration of his type, she had enthralled him at once.

And as a voice, too, she was a type that he loved: a pure, virginal soprano with a timbre of sparkling clarity. Not a voice of great color or flexibility or range, but out of that fetching bow-shaped mouth flew tones as poignant and fateful as Cupid's darts. He had tried—unsuccessfully—to teach her to open her mouth wider. "Don't worry about how you look," he told her, and she had blushed so darkly that he felt sorry for her. The notion that singers often look grotesque when they are singing was nonsense in Roy's opinion, but, alas, women took it very seriously. (Male singers, he had observed, gave it far less thought.) Nona climbing with her voice, stretching her neck, exposing her throat, and, as she reached the climactic note, tilting her head to the side and slowly, slowly closing her eyes. What could be prettier than that? But when she tried opening her mouth wider she developed a flap. The note wobbled wildly, filling the listener with anxiety. It was like watching a juggler spinning a plate on a chopstick.

"How can you be from California and not know how to swim?" This, too, had made Nona blush. "I just never learned," she said. But, for Roy, this was a sure sign of parental neglect. The more he learned about Nona's parents the more he was indignant. He had dreaded meeting her mother, certain that he could not possibly like her, and was surprised to find how very easily he could. As for Shep, Roy was glad he would never have to meet him. To be honest—not that he ever would be honest about this with Nona—Shep gave Roy the creeps.

"I can't marry you," she said. "I can't have children." That was a blow. But it turned out Nona meant something else.

"It's not at all that I don't like children," she said. "I do—very much. I just don't have any confidence about raising them. Children have always made me nervous—I've never been able to be comfortable around them. Besides, only people who've had good parents make good parents."

Roy had objected. Surely it was possible to learn from experience, and to avoid repeating one's parents' mistakes? Nona replied by pointing to people they knew. There was their friend Lisbeth, for example, one of eight children, who had often spoken bitterly about her mother's habit of favoring each child when he or she was a baby and neglecting the rest.

Now Lisbeth had a boy of five and a baby herself. "What makes you think there's room for *you?*" she scolded as the boy tried climbing into her lap while she was nursing his brother. And they knew another woman, who'd spent a decade talking to her therapist about her hostile mother, and who confessed that every time she looked at her teenaged daughter she felt a surge of rage.

Nona said, "How will I know how to make a child feel safe and happy, when my own parents weren't able to do that for me? I'm not saying you have to be perfect. But it seems to me that being a good parent is one of the most difficult things in the world, and, as with most difficult things, only certain people are good at it, and unless you know that you're one of them, well, maybe you shouldn't have kids. You laugh, but think about it. There are so many people in the world, and so many unwanted and abandoned kids. Don't you think it's time we stopped taking it for granted that everyone must procreate? Is it really so crazy to suggest that people be more honest with themselves about whether they've really got what it takes to raise a child? Does everyone really *deserve* to have children?"

Bad Cop reminded Roy that he had always, always wanted a big family.

The period leading up to the wedding was the most tormented of Roy's life. He would have been lying if he'd said he knew what he was doing; he was sick with doubt. He who never cried, cried often during this time. At a performance of *La Traviata,* a sob escaped him—so loud people all over the theater looked his way. But, once they had settled down as husband and wife, Roy forgot everything in the happiness he found. It was true happiness—joyous, profound, and grave— and it had endured.

The five years of their marriage had been good years in other ways, too. Roy's reputation as a voice teacher was growing; he had enough students to make a decent living, and he was working mostly with professionals now. It was during this time also that Nona found her teaching job—the first job she'd ever had that she liked—and began writing her book. She quit smoking, as Roy had already done, and she never again approached the bad state she had been in just before they met. It was true that she was increasingly unhappy with her looks. "My face is getting cluttered." "Oh, no: my body is settling, like a box of crackers." Her lamentations, her anxious attention to every new sign of age, exasperated Roy in the same way as his singers' obsession with fish mouth. But he understood how the passing of a woman's looks could be reason for mourning and nostalgia, and if you loved that woman, you shared those feelings.

How well they got along was something for which Nona gave credit almost entirely to Roy. He was reasonable and tolerant and unselfish, he got along with just about everyone: it was a family trait. But Roy had never wanted to be with anyone as much as he wanted to be with Nona, and he did not believe he would have found the happiness he had found with her, or such a sense of completeness, with any other. We are different with different people, and we like who we are with some people more than who we are with others. The man Roy saw reflected in Nona's eyes was the man he himself liked best: paternal, generous, kind. Although it was true that he usually got along well with people, he had a mean streak and he knew it; it came out sometimes during lessons. He could be very sarcastic. But to his wife he never showed that mood. It came out usually when he was uncomfortable, and he was never uncomfortable with Nona.

Looking at other couples, they saw that, with themselves, there seemed to be less need for talk and analysis, for hashing and thrashing things out. They saw that, with others, not only discussion but research—reading certain books and in some cases consulting a specialist—was considered normal and good. Marriage was *work*. "There's still a lot of work to be done," their friend Lisbeth said of her own fourteen-year-old marriage. Neither of them would ever have used the word *work* to describe their relationship. As time passed they thought of themselves more and more as blessed. How little needed to be spoken for them to understand each other— surely this was a blessed thing? Could love of music have had something to do with it? A lot of their time together was spent listening to music, and, when they had had an argument, it was not unusual for one or the other of them to put on some favorite tape or CD to ease the tension, and it almost always helped. They both believed in the healing power of music and thought it a shame that more people did not know of this power and make use of it. Once, musicians had been employed by asylums to soothe the insane. Why not today?

Every marriage, even the happiest, has its secrets. Roy had two big secrets from Nona. First, during that troubled time right before the wedding, he had had an affair. Well, hardly an affair: he and a certain soprano had finished a few lessons in bed. He had no problem keeping this secret from Nona, but the other was more difficult. The first weighed on his conscience, the second on his heart: not a day passed in which he did not suffer from the thought that he would never be a father. He tried not to dwell on this, of course, but there were times when he was overwhelmed. For a while he went out of his way to avoid walking past the park in their neighborhood, which had a small playground for toddlers. He would not speak of this to Nona; he was afraid she would think he had begun to regret marrying her. (In a letter she had written him just before the wedding, she confessed that this was her biggest fear.) But Roy did not regret the choice he had made. He knew that a good life was full of such choices, and that, in the most important things—love, work—happiness always demanded sacrifice. But lately he had been seized by an idea. At some point, he thought, maybe they could adopt a child. An older child, say. Some poor kid with dismal prospects—one of those Nona had been referring to, whose parents had abandoned him or her (boy, girl, Roy didn't care which). After all, as Nona said, there were so many of them. And giving an unwanted child a home would not be the same as bringing a new one into the doomed, overcrowded world—right?

He had not yet brought up this possibility with Nona. He was waiting for the right moment. Maybe when she had finished her book, he thought. But how long that book was taking!

Phoebe's invitation had come at the perfect time. Having to be apart for a month seemed a small sacrifice. Roy hadn't realized how long, for the one left behind, a month could be.

The day after she got back Nona spoke with her mother and learned that Rosalind was coming to New York for the funeral of her old friend Muriel. They had weathered her short visit, and then they were alone again, and their life resumed its habitual pattern. Summer quickened to autumn: the days were fresh and dry. The concert season began. The greenmarket was filled with fruits of the late harvest, apples and cabbages and squashes, and the last roses.

All this time, Roy had not once brought up the name Lyle. He had promised himself that he would not mention him unless Nona did first. He did not want to seem to be accusing her. Oh, many times he was tempted. It would have been so delicious to fly into a fine, righteous rage. But whenever this feeling rose in him, that soprano rolled over, like a naked sleeper, on his conscience. And after all, he reminded himself, fairness was his middle name—right? A sterling quality. A family trait.

Lyle. Something sinister and repellent, something *reptilian* about the name. *Lyle, Lyle, rhymes with vile*, he repeated to himself shamelessly—as if it didn't rhyme with a hundred other words as well.

AGAIN: WE ARE DIFFERENT with different people, and we like who we are with some people less than who we are with others.

The woman Nona saw reflected in the eyes of the man sitting across from her now was the woman she wanted to kill.

She lit a cigarette. He reached into one of his desk drawers, took out a small glass saucer, and slid it toward her. "When did you start smoking again?"

"On my way over here."

He said, in the very mild voice that was his professional voice, "You used up that last prescription awfully fast. You have to be careful with this drug."

Nona shrugged.

"It's not impossible that some of the problems you had while you were away—the anxiety, the confusion, and so on—were caused by the pills. This is a funny drug, you know. A lot of doctors won't even prescribe it anymore."

Nona ground out the unfinished cigarette with so much force and such an air of menace, he had no trouble imagining she wished the ashtray were his flesh. She had been furious even before she walked in—furious with him for insisting that she come into the office instead of doing as she asked and calling in the prescription to her pharmacist.

"This is a controlled substance," he'd told her on the phone. "You know I can't do that. Besides, it would be pretty irresponsible of me."

Her laugh had hurt his ear.

"Just give me the fucking prescription."

Had there been a witness to this scene, he or she might have guessed that here were not just doctor and patient, but former lovers. A brief, wanton affair that had ended bitterly, of course. They were anything but friends. She had turned to him only after both her internist and her gynecologist had refused to write her the prescription.

She said, "Look: if you don't give me those pills, I'll try to get them on the street."

As soon as she had the prescription, Nona got up to leave. He got up, too, and came around his desk, moving more quickly than she, so that they arrived at the door together. This was how it had begun. After every session, he would get up and go to open the door for her, and every time, as she went out she had noticed, out of the corner of her eye, how his gaze traveled down her spine. Every single time. It had amused her and irritated her—not so much because he did it as because he let her see him doing it. And one day, instead of passing through the door, she had spun around and pressed herself into his arms.

His hand went out, but instead of reaching for the door-knob he touched her arm and he said, "Nona," and again "Nona," in a voice softer even than his professional voice. She shook off his hand, yanked open the door herself and stepped out into the waiting room, where a young woman half rose out of her seat and looked at them with such an awkward, innocent, and pathetic air, Nona could have slapped her.

We are different with different people, and the woman who stalked out of that office was someone Roy might have had trouble recognizing. Not at all like the woman who stood before him in tears that night and announced that she had to go to Tucson.

chapter
eight

Nona arranged to leave for Tucson on a Friday morning and to return the following Monday. That was all the time she could take off from work. Because she was traveling at the last minute, she could not get a cheap fare. "Don't worry about that," Lyle said. "I'll write you a check when you get here." She had been moved by his generosity, because she knew that he was anything but openhanded. There had been grumbling from the others (and how she had blushed for him to hear it!) about the small contribution he had made to the collection taken up to buy thank-you gifts for the cleaning women and the cook.

There were not many people whom Nona would have told. She and Roy were friends with another couple, Anthony and Tess. Anthony, the least judgmental person she knew, advised her not to go. "You will regret it if you do."

"She will regret it if she *doesn't*," his wife disagreed. "Her whole life she'll always be wondering."

"I hope I'm not the one being tested here," Roy had said—using the same tone, it struck Nona, that Lyle had used when he said, You are patronizing me. "I hope I'm not expected to—to—lock you up or something?" And, without waiting for a reply, he left the room, stepping strangely and cautiously, as if across a wet floor. Nona saw his back bristling with arrows, and by the odd angle at which he held his head could measure the degree of his hurt.

This has nothing to do with you, she would have screamed after him had she dared. But she didn't have to tell him this; he was busy telling himself: nothing to do with me . . . not about her and me . . . between her and her demons . . . Throughout the whole bitter ordeal, this would be a kind of consolation to him. To Anthony and Tess he confessed, "I've always been afraid something like this would happen." And what did he think would happen next? "He'll disappoint her," he said. "She'll come back." Said it with such solemn conviction they half expected him to add: "It is written." But they, too, saw the arrows sticking out of him, and even Tess, who had egged Nona on, now found herself wondering how her friend could do such a thing.

Had Roy demanded an explanation (which he would never do), Nona would have been helpless without showing him the letters (which she would never do). Timber Lake had receded and seemed now far away and not quite real, as happens with most trips and vacations after one has returned from them. She had not been unhappy to leave Lyle then. There had been much about him that put her off: the moroseness that made him seem at times so cold and spiritless, the suspicion that he did not really like women, his hesitation to possess her in the library— she disliked hesitation in a man. But this Lyle of the letters was different. *Now* he declared it his biggest regret, what had happened, or, rather, failed to happen, in the library. Now he sang of the agony of love he was going through, and, yes, Nona wanted a closer look at that: the suffering she had caused. Whenever she thought about what she was doing, she found herself struggling to make it so that curiosity did not weigh too much in the balance. She had always been too curious for her own good. (That, and her anxiety about traveling, were two of several traits that made Roy tease her about having once been a cat—which, though she loved cats, annoyed her no end.) She knew perfectly well that there was something reckless and backsliding about her behavior—something of the same order as drinking too much or taking too many pills or spending money she didn't have on things she didn't need—the sort of behavior to which she'd been prone when she was younger. She saw now that she had not outgrown what had once seemed a frightening capacity for mischief. She saw that she was still prey to that unruly amorousness (another catlike trait, known also by some less pretty names) that had complicated her youth. A weakness that did not age well, she warned and warned herself.

It was on the telephone that Nona first told Lyle that she was coming to Arizona, and his response had perplexed her. To Nona, the meeting was inevitable; he had begged for it, in letter after letter. Say the word (he had written), and I will be on the next plane. Name the place, and I'll fly there and meet you. Why then should it surprise him that she had bought a plane ticket? But he had been more than surprised, Nona thought, hanging up: he had been dumbfounded.

Immediately she gathered up all the letters—there were over a hundred pages of them now: a little book—and reread them, to see if she had misunderstood. She had not. He had said the word, many, many times.

She was reassured the following day by the arrival of an express-mail letter in which Lyle described his joy at her coming in delirious terms.

For the moment he was living with a graduate student who had found himself in a similar fix. Only in this case it was the wife who had moved out. Lyle described the house, which was near the university, as "a bit shabby and needing repairs but comfortable." Nona, who had spent the summer of her freshman year on a commune in Vermont, imagined a house like that one: a funky place with tight windows and loose floorboards, each room painted a different color, and a pungent smell that might be incense or scented candles or pot. Indian-print cloths thrown over furniture, bamboo blinds, plant holders made of macramé. In the kitchen with bright yellow walls, or yellow curtains, or in the bright yellow sun of a porch, she pictured the two of them drinking wine or tea and talking for hours. Earnest, hushed—a silver river of talk: lovers baring souls.

She was jolted out of this fantasy when she learned that Lyle had made a reservation at a bed-and-breakfast a few miles outside town.

Though she could not say why, Nona knew that this was all wrong. Pleasant and easy it was for her to picture them in that shabby, comfortable house. But when she tried moving them to the bed-and-breakfast, a scrim dropped; stagehands in black whisked the furniture away. . . . Besides, an inn meant extra expense—but again Lyle insisted that she not worry about money. "It's just that I don't know how much privacy we'll have in the house," he said. But how much privacy did they need? He had his own room, didn't he? Oh, setting was so important.

On the flight out, Nona might have been ill: pulse irregular, temperature fluctuant, smothering sensation in the chest. She could not read any of the magazines she had brought with her, or correct the autobiographical essays she had asked her new students to write. She had to change planes in Dallas. With an hour to kill, she strayed into a coffee shop—one of those paradoxically unwelcoming places with harsh lights to hurt your eyes and singsong music to hurt your ears—the same awful music that was piped everywhere in the airport and that you could not escape, not even in the restroom. Nona recognized the tunes, old rock-and-roll songs of her youth—or, rather, slow, flabby versions of them, as if the songs themselves had grown middle-aged. It was like a punishment, having to hear this done to the music you had once danced and made love to.

When Nona had bought a cup of coffee and sat down, she took a sip and involuntarily made a face. A rusty nail boiled in

water would have produced such a taste. There were few people in the coffee shop, but Nona was aware of one man sitting
near the entrance who had been watching her since she came
in. A sickly-looking man, unnaturally thin, with a caved-in
chest, rough skin, and long stringy hair hanging like a soiled
fringe from under his cowboy hat. He kept playing with his
fork, prodding his thumb with the tines, as if testing their
sharpness. He had seen Nona make that face and now, as she
lowered her cup, she happened to look up and meet his eye,
and she caught her breath at the malevolent expression she
saw there. He looked as if he hated her. She was sure that he
hated her, and for what? For being used to better coffee, better
music, better places than this. He looked as if he would have
happily driven those tines into her heart.

Nona was staring miserably into the black hole of her cup
when she heard a sharp crack—like the report of a small
gun—that made her jump. A woman who'd just sat down at
the next table was lighting a cigarette, though there was no
smoking allowed. It was the striking of the match, the head of
which had popped, as sometimes happens, that had startled
Nona. The woman chuckled as she shook out the flame.
"Here, honey," she said, holding her pack of Marlboros out to
Nona. "Looks like you need one more than I do." She laughed
again, louder this time, a laugh that was followed at once by a
whispery echo, a faint ghost-laugh from deep in her chest: the
afterlaugh of the heavy smoker. The hand offering the cigarettes was dimpled and pudgy with a crease at the wrist, like a
baby's. "I get nervous when I travel, too," she said soothingly,
and Nona smiled at her and exhaled smoke, grateful, soothed.
No ashtrays, no smoking allowed, but no one seemed to care.
The sinister man was gone, though Nona had not seen him
leave, and she couldn't help connecting his disappearance with
this woman who'd taken an interest in her. An unlikely fairy
godmother in a beige pantsuit, one of those expansive types,
large of heart and hip, that you meet everywhere when travel-

ing out in Real America. Nona watched her empty three pack-
ets of Sweet 'n Low into her coffee. Beige was her color: her
skin and her teeth were beige, and so was her stiff bubble of
dry hair, which was also so thin that Nona could see where it
had been teased. Her eyes—beige, too, where they should have
been white—were magnified by her glasses and had been made
up to repeat the sweeping upward curve of the frames. She
was the kind of woman who would be nostalgic about Elvis,
though Elvis was before her time; who would be thunder-
struck to learn that she and Nona were the same age. A kind
woman, Nona judged her, simple, honest; a generous type,
dying to talk but no less eager to listen.

She was on her way to Phoenix, to stand by a sister with
what she called husband trouble.

"She's got a restraining order, but that won't do her a heck
of a lot of good if he decides he wants to see her. Well, she's a
big girl, I guess, she made her own bed, but what about the
kids? Them's the ones you got to feel sorry for. Then I got a
brother who's just been fired—not for the first time, either—
for drinking. He drives a bus—just what you want behind a
big ol' bus wheel, right?" And she laughed her double laugh.
"And listen to this: he's got a daughter, my twenty-year-old
niece, right? Well, do you know, the very same week he gets
fired she gets *her*self hauled into court for knocking down
some poor old man crossing the road. DWI. Can you beat
that? Honestly, sometimes I think the whole family's heart-set
on becoming white trash. Still, family's family, and when family calls for help you got to come running. Even if they killed
someone, right?"

It was awkward for Nona when the woman stopped speaking. Having laid so much out on the table, she would be
expecting a confidence or two in return. When Nona said that
she was on her way to Tucson to visit a friend, the woman
looked at her shrewdly, knowing that she was being lied to,
and probably making a close guess at the truth.

* * *

LYLE WAS THERE TO MEET Nona when the plane landed. Their embrace was clumsy, as he tried to take her bag at the same time. He pulled away from her—why so gruffly? she wondered. Perhaps because there were so many people around. It struck Nona that this was the first time they had ever seen each other in a public place. But, once they were in the car, she discovered what the real problem was.

"When I was growing up," he said, rolling down his window, "the whole house reeked of stale smoke and stale beer."

Nona apologized. "At least I don't drink beer." She was trying to speak lightly, but she was stung. She had not dropped everything and flown all the way across the country to have him wrinkle his nose at her.

It had been in the fifties and drizzling when Nona left New York. Here it was sunny and hot. The bright parched air took her all the way back, to Los Angeles, but the sky was a clear delft blue that had not been seen in Los Angeles in years, and there was a delicious fresh clean smell that seemed to come from it.

The bed-and-breakfast was an old ranch house in the desert foothills. A man in a wheelchair greeted them. "I'm Walt, and this here's Bathsheba." An enormous brown-and-white rabbit sat on his lap. He wheeled ahead of them to their room. "It's nice and private—you have your own separate entrance—but I hope you don't mind if it's a bit small." A reasonably-sized room dwarfed by a king-sized bed. Canopied. "Let me know what time you'd like breakfast tomorrow, so's I can tell the girl Rosita."

It was only five o'clock, but Nona, who had been too nervous to eat on the plane, was starving. They agreed to eat dinner early, after she'd taken a shower.

Nona believed that you could tell a lot about a person from what he or she ate, and in this regard she didn't know much about Lyle. At Phoebe's she remembered only that he had not been one of the fussy ones. She was surprised when he said that they were going to a health food restaurant.

"I've gone on a pretty strict diet," he said. "And I've been trying to run two extra miles every day." He, too, had put on weight at Phoebe's. Nona, who hated health food restaurants, said nothing. But she could not suppress a twinge, thinking how, if Roy had been there, he would have pored over the guidebook, seeking out the best restaurants in town.

The restaurant was a somber little place near the university. Plainchant on the stereo, votive candles, mission furniture— had they come to dine or to worship? The menu began with a little essay on food, disease, and longevity. *Growing old is not inevitable.* Nona laughed out loud when she read this. "Something I have never understood is why people who are supposed to be so concerned with the spiritual side of life have so much trouble with mortality."

"What do you mean?"

"Well, all this New Age emphasis on staying young and living forever. Doesn't that strike you as pretty worldly?" She was reminded of Phoebe's daughter-in-law assuring them that yoga reversed the aging process. When Ralph pointed out that, alas, the only alternative to growing old was dying young, she had given him a smug, having-it-both-ways smile and said, "No one ever really dies. It's just a migration of energy."

Lyle closed his menu and said, "You want to go somewhere else."

"Oh, no, no, please," Nona said, instantly ashamed. "I'm sorry. I don't know why I'm being so— Let's order. I'm sure it's good."

And as it turned out, the food, though not what Nona wanted, was better than good, and beautifully served. Wine would have been nice, but wine was apparently one of those fermented foods associated with disease and with negative emotions like anger and lust. *Tamasic*, warned the menu: to be avoided.

Halfway through the meal, things still had not warmed up

between them. Conversation was the small talk of people who did not really know each other. Nona tried telling a funny story. One of her students, desperate for work, had put up signs in his neighborhood, offering to walk dogs and board them in his apartment while the owners were away. At the bottom of the sign he had added: "And your pussy is always welcome!"

Lyle smiled. "That *is* funny," he said. "But I have to tell you, in general, I don't like toilet humor."

Nona's face burned as if she'd been slapped. She *had* been slapped. *Toilet humor?* She thought of the poems Lyle had left on her bed that day, and she wondered.

They talked about Nona's trip out, about Timber Lake, and the other people they had met there. Lyle had had a letter from Ralph, Nona had heard from Josie.

Nona said, "Rita and I promised to stay in touch, but I haven't called her and she hasn't called me. Have you heard from her?"

Lyle did a funny twisting thing with his head and right shoulder: he had no interest whatsoever in hearing from Rita, that gesture said. "By the way, there's something I wanted to ask you. I'd appreciate it if you didn't mention any of this to Phoebe. She takes a pretty dim view of this sort of thing."

Nona knew that. Nona knew that her friend had a puritanical streak; it was the one thing she didn't like about Phoebe. Though Nona hadn't planned to say anything, Lyle's request mortified her. Any of *this*? This sort of *thing*? Without the help of a fermented bite, her stomach was churning. She wondered whether sometime in the past, back in college, say, Lyle and Phoebe had been more than friends. Nona laid down her fork. She was aware of a trembling and tottering inside her: something on the verge of collapse. What was wrong? Why wouldn't he look at her? Was it the cigarette, still? She had taken a shower. She had washed her hair and brushed her teeth. . . . He would not meet her gaze, and whenever she sought his, she was daunted by the hardness and immobility of that face, more like a wood carving than ever. He seemed full of dark emotions, like one who had gorged on tamasic foods. Twice, the waitress had to be told to bring them water. "All that fat makes her brain sluggish," Lyle said. She was a girl, the waitress, not even twenty, and she was not fat at all. She had full round cheeks, and she was not thin; but she was not fat. I outweigh that girl by at least ten pounds, Nona thought. What must he think of me? And wasn't it strange: at Phoebe's, when Lyle would make cracks like that—about the cook, for example—Nona had found him wicked but funny; but here, now, when he said that about the waitress, she thought: how stupid, how mean.

"I don't think I'll have any dessert," said Lyle.

"Me, either," said Nona, carelessly, and was brusquely corrected.

She looked at her watch, which she had not yet set to Pacific time. If she were home now, she would be getting ready for bed. She wished she *were* going to bed. She felt as if she had been up for days. She had a headache coming on. Her right eye kept watering, and she could feel the pain boring its way through her temple. Good hot strong coffee was what she needed, but, remembering where she was, she told herself, Don't be ridiculous.

The waitress had just taken their order for herbal tea when Nona noticed that Lyle was frowning, staring at the lower part of her face. "What's that?" His tone was sharp, accusing.

Nona spread her hands—?

"It's a piece of spinach."

Nona touched her napkin to her lips.

"Now it's on your chin." Still staring, frowning, merciless. Nona wiped her chin, checking the napkin to make sure she had got the green speck this time, and saw that her hand was shaking.

Later, in bed, waiting for her pill to take effect, Nona went back over everything that had happened since her arrival.

If he loved her, she asked herself, would he have jerked away from her in the airport like that, even though he did hate cigarettes? If he loved her madly, as he said he did, wouldn't he have taken her in his arms the moment he got her alone? He would have asked her where *she* wanted to eat, wouldn't he, if he loved her? And then, in the restaurant, how different he would have been, a man in love, unable to resist, his eyes and his hands constantly seeking her own.

How did Nona know these things? She knew because she had been loved. And it wasn't true, what was often said, about the unpredictability of love. What love would do was the easiest thing to foretell in the world. He would have reached across the table with his napkin and tenderly wiped that piece of spinach from her mouth.

When the check came, Nona had had to pay; the restaurant did not take credit cards (tamasic, possibly), and Lyle had forgotten to bring cash.

In the ridiculous king-sized canopied bed, Nona lay as far from her lover as she could. His snoring was light but enough to disturb her. (Who thinks to bring earplugs to a tryst?) Again, she thought of the poems Lyle had left on her bed that day. What he wanted to do to her. What he would do to her if he could. What he had done to her tonight she could have done to herself. She opened her eyes in the dark and saw clearly. In a canoe in the middle of a mountain lake on a radiant summer's day, he had been bewitched (his word) by a woman's back, by her song, and by the color of her hair. *Daylilies*? "Penny Red" on the rinse she had been using for over a year now, ever since her hair had begun to turn gray. A red-haired Siren. A blue-and-white kimono. A letter slipped with a rose under a bedroom door at dawn. *Farewell, my love, my dearest dear.* Letters: that little book into which he had poured out his heart, carried away not by love but by the vocabulary of love, the adjectives and verbs of love, one smooth golden word following another, like honey dripping

from a spoon. She had accomplished nothing by coming to
Tucson except to destroy his fantasy, and for this he could not
forgive her. It had been a lot of work, that fantasy. They had
been together only a few hours and he had succeeded in making her feel wholly undesirable: fat, smelly, food stuck to her
mouth. It was her punishment.

Nona lay on her stomach, her head buried in her arms,
homesick and miserable and defeated and ashamed. She had
been in Tucson only a few hours, but already she knew everything she had come to find out. Alas, there remained Saturday
and Sunday to get through.

Nona awoke the next morning with a curious sense of lightness. It was as if a burden had rolled from her while she slept.

She was alone—Lyle was not in bed with her—and someone
was knocking at the door. Nona sat up. Lyle, dressed in his
running clothes, came out of the bathroom and went to
answer the door. It was the girl Rosita, with their breakfast.
Nona eyed the tray greedily as Lyle set it down on a table near
the bed. There was a basket filled with different kinds of
bread, tiny pots of butter and marmalade and prickly-pear
jelly, a milk jug, a sugar bowl, and a carafe of coffee. There
were two bananas, an orange, and an apple. Lyle said he
wanted only some fruit, which he would have after he came
back from running. He ran first thing every morning, and usually once again, later in the day.

Nona, who had already eaten some banana bread and was
now buttering a scone (still warm!), said, "Are you sure you
don't want any of this? It's delicious."

"No, thanks," said Lyle, on his way out the door. "I'm not
interested in clogging my veins."

"What are you keeping them open for?"

"I can't understand if you talk with your mouth full."

Nona shook her head never mind and waved good-bye.

With Lyle gone the room seemed at once cozier and more

spacious. Nona, still eating happily, could not help thinking just how cozy and how much fun it would have been if Roy had been there; they always had such a good time when they went away together. And then it struck her that this was the source of that strange sense of lightness. A burden had indeed been lifted. She did not love Lyle and he did not love her. She had no business being in Tucson. She wanted to go home. She wanted her husband! Of course!

But this elation gave way swiftly to fear and remorse. Tears filled her eyes and she said aloud, "Oh, what is wrong with me? Am I a child? Am I mad?"

There was no telephone in the room. If there had been one, Nona wondered whether she would have been able to resist calling Roy. She jumped up, hurried to the door, and threw it open, as if someone had knocked again. Outside, it was dazzling: the same bright cloudless blue as yesterday, and already hot. There was that smell—Nona did not know what it was, but she had caught whiffs of it several times already: strong but delicate, at the same time sweet and sharp, floral and peppery.

Though she was in awe of the beauties of the desert, Nona did not think she could ever live here. The lack of trees induced true anxiety—further proof, Roy would have said, of a former life as a cat. Something moved at the outer corner of her vision. Nona saw the coyote, just a few yards off, sniffing at the roots of a cactus. She whistled and he raised his head. He measured her over his shoulder with something of the same cold narrow gaze with which Lyle had looked at her. Nona closed the door and went to take a shower. By the time she was finished, Lyle had returned.

When Lyle himself had showered and eaten his fruit, they went out. Had they been real lovers, Nona thought, they would have made love first; they would have taken a shower together.

They spent the morning at the desert museum, observing hummingbirds and bighorn sheep and prairie dogs in their natural settings, and German and Japanese tourists out of theirs. Nona had forgotten to bring a hat or sunglasses, and the heat and the glare affected her like an antihistamine: she was thirsty, drowsy, and her ears kept ringing. Later, Lyle took Nona on a tour of the city, driving through the historical district and around the university. They stopped at Lyle's office and at the house where he was staying, so that he could get his messages and his mail. The house was not as Nona had imagined it, not funky, not like student digs at all, but orderly and carefully decorated with pale carpeting and matching upholstered furniture. *Shabby*: why had Lyle described it so? (This would not be the only time that weekend that it would occur to Nona that Lyle might be an habitual liar.) The only shabby thing about the place was his room. The smallest room in the house, it seemed cluttered even though it was almost empty. A bureau, a bookcase, a desk chair but no desk, a mattress on the floor. Nona could see now why Lyle had not wanted to have her stay here. She thought he might have been ashamed, a man his age, without a home of his own, sleeping on the floor in a room in some student's house. *She* would have been ashamed. She would have felt pathetic.

The student was not home. Had he been, Nona thought, she would have flirted with him. Had Lyle left them alone for an instant, she would have been all over him. Lyle would have walked in to find her on her knees before him. . . .

"It's me. Please call."

"It's me again, Lyle, please call."

"Lyle, are you there? I guess not. It's me."

Long-suffering, humble—the voice of one anticipating pain. *It's me, it's only me.* Who else but his wife.

Lyle filled two tumblers with lemonade from a jug in the refrigerator and handed one to Nona. "Come see the backyard."

The student's wife was a talented gardener and had created a small patch of Eden, with an astonishing variety of cactus plants and a collection of antique garden statuary. How sad she must have been to have to leave this, Nona thought. The spicy smell was especially strong here. Nona was about to ask Lyle what it was when he said, "Charlotte knows about you."

"What?"

"Charlotte knows about you. I mean, not that you're here, she doesn't know that."

"Well, then, what does she know?"

"She found one of my letters to you on the computer. Or part of a letter that I'd forgotten to delete."

"That was very careless of you."

"It doesn't matter now."

"Of course it matters."

If it were me, Nona thought, I would feel worse if I caught Roy writing like that to another woman than if I caught him in bed with her. "What is she like, anyway?" (Why did she ask, when she didn't really want to know?)

"She's—like a lot of women. Like most women, I'd say. She has a way of deciding that she's right about something, she knows exactly what the story is, she's got it all figured out, and that's that. She's never gotten along well with men. Her first marriage was a disaster. She has an explanation, of course. Men are stupid, men are unkind, men are insensitive, men are unjust. Men don't understand the first thing about anything, a woman doesn't owe them the time of day. Be that as it may, all she's ever really wanted was a man. Like most women, she wouldn't know how to define herself without a husband and children. She has very few interests, Charlotte. She's had various jobs but no real career. She never had any ambition. She . . ."

Had Charlotte recognized Lyle in that letter, or part of a letter, that she found? Or was this a side of her husband she had never seen?

"This sun is too much for me," said Nona, shielding her face with her hand. Very foolish, to have forgotten a hat.

"Oh, I can't get enough of it," said Lyle, tilting his own face up worshipfully. "I've always loved the feeling of basking and baking in the hot, hot sun."

Like certain other cold-blooded creatures, Nona wanted to say.

"Speaking of weather," Lyle said, "it's very unusual for this time of year, but we're expecting a lot of rain tomorrow. So I was thinking, why don't we drive up into the mountains today, maybe go for a hike? That's one thing you shouldn't miss while you're here."

Grateful for this crumb, Nona said that she would like that very much.

They climbed the steep winding road slowly, stopping the car several times along the way to take in the view. An unearthly landscape, more strange than beautiful, with its mammoth, artificial-looking rock formations and forbidding brown chasms. If you were filming Dante, Nona thought, you might shoot scenes here. Soon they had left the desert behind; chaparral and saguaro gave way to conifers. Every thousand feet up was said to be like going three hundred miles north. In less than an hour they had arrived not only in a different landscape but in a different season. Ten degrees cooler, yellow and brown leaves among the green, and a stiff breeze to shake them. No more the spicy smell of below but the fresh tang of pine.

"We could be back in the Adirondacks," said Nona.

Lyle nodded. "Out here they say that the Adirondacks are the only part of the East that Western folk respect."

They put on the jackets they had brought along and entered the woods, following a trail that Lyle knew well but that he warned Nona might be difficult for her. The path was strewn with pine needles. As always when hiking, Nona felt an urge to sing, but she suppressed it. Besides, the path was steep and full of loose rocks and treacherous hollows, and her breath was soon short.

"I don't want to go much further," she called out to Lyle,

who was well ahead of her now, "unless we take a rest."

"Hang in there," he called over his shoulder. "Spectacular view just around the corner."

But it was not just around the corner. It was another half mile, at least. Uphill. When they finally arrived, Nona's shuddering legs crumpled under her and she sank to the damp ground, heaving, her blood pounding, her lungs like pincushions. Lyle, whose breathing was almost normal, grinned down at her. "All those cigarettes. Do they seem worth it now?"

Once, she had found him charming. Once—mere weeks ago—she had desired him.

"I did quit, you know," she panted, as much with indignation now as with strain. "Years ago—and it wasn't easy—and I did make it here—without resting—out of shape though I am."

It was like the fairy tale in which the wicked trolls build a mirror that makes handsome men look hideous and the most beautiful landscapes like boiled spinach—and Nona was one of the unlucky people who get a shard blown into their eye when the mirror breaks. That view, which had cost Nona so much effort to reach, was utterly spoiled for her now. As for Lyle, he might have been one of the trolls himself bending over her, all big hairy nostrils and sneer. A large fly hovered between them, and she imagined him darting his tongue forth to catch it.

Something came back to her—something Rita had said—a kind of warning, it seemed, but Nona couldn't remember the exact words.

A gust of wind raced in circles around them, like a dog chasing its tail. From the forest rose that restless, troubled, sighs-of-a-thousand-burning-lovers sound, and Nona's heart ached.

On the slow spiraling drive back down, unable to bear the silence between them, Nona asked Lyle about his job. She knew that he was not happy teaching, but they had never talked about it.

Lyle said, "'By the time the author wrote this book he wrote many others.'" Nona stared at him blankly. "'When they got married they knew each other for five years.'"

"Ah." In fact, she had heard about this from other academics she knew: the disappearance of the past perfect tense.

"Only some of my foreign students use it," said Lyle, "because they've studied English. The American students of course haven't. Hard to believe, isn't it. Every new class knows less than the last. Soon we'll be teaching Shakespeare to illiterates. These kids don't read, they don't come to class, they don't study—a lot of them don't even seem to know what studying is. They think of spelling and grammar as some kind of specialized knowledge that the average person shouldn't be expected to bother with—like tax laws."

"I have to admit, I didn't work very hard in college, either," Nona said. "At least not the first two years." Understatement! Her freshman and sophomore years had been a history of missed classes, late papers, dropped courses, and make-up exams. One semester she had taken a course in which she did not lay eyes on the instructor until the midterm. As Nona explained to her adviser, "There's just so much other stuff going on."

Nona still remembered the first college paper she wrote. "*Romeo and Juliet* is certainly a tragedy." She remembered the time she confused Graham Greene and Kenneth Grahame, attributing the creation of Toad to the former. The professor was a gentleman from Cheever country, dapperly suited in browns and grays, lecturing in his much-mimicked boarding-school drawl. He always wore a hat. He loved his cigarettes, and he loved his gin and, when he'd had too much, he loved acting out scenes from certain books that he read. They had laughed about Toad as he bound her wrists to her ankles with his necktie. She was somewhat surprised but secretly pleased that her final grade for that course was no higher than she deserved. The old satyr—Nona had not thought of him in years. Already in his sixties then—was he still alive? She had let him shave her pubic hair and lived in dread of her room-mate's finding out. And then came appendicitis. Quite a buzz at the infirmary. Later, the nurse's aide who came to prep her for surgery raised an eyebrow and said, "Well, little lady, I see you done already prepped yourself."

They had reached level ground again. A kit fox dashed into the road right in front of them and narrowly missed being struck.

Nona said, "My friend Tess was teaching at a Baptist college in Oklahoma, and she was appalled when her students told her that they thought Anna Karenina deserved to be punished—deserved to die—because she had 'destroyed the nuclear family.' I was appalled, too, but then it occurred to me that Tolstoy wouldn't have been; he would have agreed with them."

As if she hadn't spoken, Lyle said, "I was so different at that age. I loved school, I loved to study. I had the feeling that I was saving my life with every book I read. I wasn't just a good student, I was an excited student, you know? I thought that what my teachers had to give me was the sweetest thing in the world, not some bitter medicine. If I had known that this was the kind of student I'd have to teach, I would have done something else with my life."

A hopeless marriage, no family, memories of childhood so grim you wanted only to forget, a job that you despised—Nona had a glimpse then of the depths of Lyle's isolation and unhappiness: it was like peering down one of those endless rocky chasms they had just left behind. And yet, she could not feel sorry for him. He wrote everyone off: his family as white trash, his students as cretins, his wife as being like most women—or was it most women as being like his wife? Nona wondered when he ever intended to return his wife's calls. Poor Charlotte! And the shameful thought rushed to its shameless conclusion: Charlotte could have him.

They drove to the Indian reservation, to see the mission. The church was the color of good strong teeth, smiling against the bluest sky, color of peace or virtue or healing or truth, depending on your religion. Outside the church, Indians sold their handmade wares and cold soda and rounds of bread fried in hot oil. As she approached the entrance, Nona had the sense that she had seen all this before, in a movie, a Western—yes, she remembered that tall skinny black dog walking into the frame. Other dogs lay listlessly about the parched courtyard, their gaunt ribs and weepy eyes stirring concern among the German tourists. Inside, though it was cool, there was a feeling of heat and closeness unto suffocation because of the crowds and the smell of candles and incense and the clutter— no space anywhere that was not filled with some painting or ornament—and the colors were so throbbingly garish Nona found herself reaching back for a word she hadn't used in years: *psychedelic*. A taped voice came through the speakers, repeating the story of the mission over and over. Indian worshipers moved among the tourists, lighting candles, genuflecting, kissing the frayed hem of the shiny blue skirt that had been hung on a statue of Mary. Nona had joined a group of people in the chapel where a figure of the patron saint lay under a gold-sequined blanket. The figure was about three feet long with a head carved from dark wood. Various items had been pinned to the sequins: Polaroid photographs, a sonogram, bits of cloth, a pair of worn pantyhose, a set of car keys, folded pieces of paper—thus were the needs, dreams, and fears of the believers communicated to the saint. The blanket, like the several small pillows that had been placed under the wooden head, was badly soiled. Worshipers approached, cradled the head in their hands and kissed it, then carefully rearranged the bedding.

Down the main aisle of the church came a young woman whose hair was so long Nona guessed it had never been cut, leading a hunchbacked child on legs so crooked and thin it was miracle enough that they could support him. He cast a shadow like Humpty-Dumpty. As they drew nearer, Nona saw that the woman was much younger than she had seemed and her companion was much older. Not woman and child but girl and man. What could their relationship be, the hunchbacked dwarf and the girl who picked him up by the waist so that he could kiss the wooden cheek, the hem of Mary?

String ties with crucifix tie clasps, belts with the face of Jesus on the buckles, biblical knickknacks, and plastic bottles of holy water were on sale in the gift shop. Nona had to resist the temptation to pick out something for Roy's sisters' children, for whom she always bought souvenirs when she traveled.

"Shall we go now?" said Lyle.

"Sure: mission accomplished," Nona said, and Lyle winced.

Outside, sunlight momentarily blinded them, exhaust from a tour bus befouled the air, and a German couple who had bought some fry bread was feeding it to the dogs.

Back at the bed-and-breakfast, Nona was left alone while Lyle went for another run. A complimentary decanter of sherry had been brought to their room. Nona poured herself a glass as she sat on the bed with her folder of student homework. *Write ten sentences telling me about yourself.* "When I was a child I lived in a privy house." "I got married in 1982nd, and every year I had a daughter and every other year I had a son." "Right now my country is out of order." "I forsook the Damascus and came flying to New York." "Boys are more interesting than girls, which is why I have two sons." "I received my education and my breeding at Gdansk." "In my country I worked as a bard." "I have a grandson half past two." "Every year my family was resting on the sea." "My mother is animate still." "In school I did not snatch stars from heaven, but I learnt well." "My father and mother were at war before my birth." "As teacher I had intercourse with many childrens." "My wife is a prattler like all women." "My daughters are good wenches."

Nona plucked a tissue from a box on the night table and wiped her eyes. Had there been a phone in the room she would have called her mother that instant and read the best lines to her. But when she heard the key in the lock, Nona put the folder away in the night-table drawer. She would not share one word with Lyle. He didn't deserve it.

It was Lyle who suggested that they go to a movie that night. The movie they chose was one neither of them knew much about, except that it was a big hit. As it turned out, there was some resemblance between the plot and their own story. A woman married to an exemplary husband pursues another man, a perfect stranger, all the way across the country on a hunch that he is the one with whom she really belongs. In the end she marries this man, with the first husband's blessing. (Certainly a comedy.) Both Nona and Lyle hated it. Afterward, they went to a taco restaurant in the same mall as the theater.

"Why did this movie get such great reviews? Why did all my friends tell me to go see it?" Nona was genuinely puzzled.

"It's a love story," said Lyle, "with a happy ending. Of course people are going to like it."

But this was just what Nona could not fathom. "Let's say that everyone who sees this movie has been in love—I mean, most people have been in love, at least once. And if they have, then they know what a rich, mysterious, complicated experience love is. So why would they want to see it portrayed in this shallow way? Why would they find it entertaining to see their deepest emotions cheapened and falsified like that?" Why don't they feel betrayed, she wanted to know, as I do?

With horror Nona realized that she was not far from tears. She knew, somehow, that to break down in front of Lyle would be a calamity, that he was the kind of man in whom the sight of a weeping woman aroused not tenderness but rage.

But Lyle was not looking at her. Across the booth he sat smiling, staring into space. Half grieved, half disdainful, that little smile—a smile Nona had seen on his face before—an almost habitual expression. She sat quietly and waited. At last he shook his head gently and said, "You wanted to know what Charlotte was like."

"Charlotte?"

"She's been trying to get me to see this movie for weeks."

"So she liked it," said Nona, with a sickly little smile of her own.

"She's seen it three times."

The next morning they fought. The rain had come—was coming down now—steady and hard, the room was so dark it might have been dusk. They had been talking about what they should do that day. There were a few museums they could visit, but it was Sunday: nothing open till noon. Lyle was sullen because he couldn't go running. He was slumped in an armchair near the door. Across the room, Nona sat propped up against the pillows in the unmade bed. She had slept poorly, in spite of the pill she'd taken, starting awake every hour or so. Ravenous dogs and a ventriloquist's dummy had been in her dreams.

"What's wrong?" said Lyle. "You look—*upset*." Same disgusted tone he had used to point out the spinach on her chin.

Would Nona speak? Would she tell the truth? That she wished it were not raining so that Lyle would go out and run—as far away as possible? That she had no desire to visit any museum or to do anything else in horrid Tucson? That she wanted only to get away, that she was homesick, that she wanted her own bed—that she wanted her husband?

Yesterday, she had gotten a light sunburn; now the tears stung as they wet her cheeks.

Lyle got up and went into the bathroom, returning a moment later with a washcloth he had dampened with cold water. He stood over Nona and rubbed the washcloth over her face. He did this with incredible roughness. For Nona was right: he was the kind of man who, when he saw a woman crying, wanted to hit her.

Nona stopped crying. Lyle dropped the washcloth on the bed and went back to his chair. They sat in silence for a few moments. Outside: rain, laughter, and voices (his, hers), car doors slamming, the car pulling away. Other guests: some normal couple, Nona saw them, enjoying a nice weekend in scenic Tucson. Her skin felt raw.

"Look," said Lyle. "I know you're upset. I know you've been unhappy with me this weekend and I'm sorry about that. But I'm not going to let you push me into the role of the bad guy. I haven't done anything to you. I haven't done anything to make you cry."

He looked suddenly old, slumped in his chair. Fifty is old, Nona thought. She exhaled a shaky breath and said, "But you must be aware how hostile you've been, Lyle. How you've made me feel as if you didn't want me here."

"You are married, you know."

"As I was when you asked me to—"

"Ah!" he cried, holding up one palm like a traffic-stopper. "I never asked you to come. I was very careful about that. I simply wrote to tell you how I felt. *You* decided to come."

Oh, the petty, legalistic male mind. Nona never ceased to be amazed. She said, "Oh, Lyle," but she meant *for shame*, and so he understood her.

"Why did you come?" He had raised his voice. "Can you even answer that?"

Could she? "I came—I came to see you. I came—"

"And tomorrow you'll go!" Shouting now. "Back home, back to your husband."

Nona covered her ears with her hands. "I never said I was leaving Roy!"

"But then why did you come?"

"I came because I wanted to see you—"

"You said that already," said Lyle. "You're just repeating yourself." And the look he turned on her now was so full of loathing Nona had to fight the impulse to crawl under the covers.

When he spoke again it was softly. "Look. There's no mystery here. I met you when I was feeling particularly hopeless and weak. I went a little crazy, that's all. If you hadn't come, the whole thing would have died a quiet, pretty death. But you had to go and turn it into a farce." After a pause he added, in a tone that gave Nona goose flesh, "Did I hurt your feelings? I know how sensitive women's feelings are. What about my feelings? Ever consider those?"

A Frenchwoman Nona had met in one of her voice classes once told her that she had given up trying to have affairs with American men. "The American men are not grown-up enough for thees."

His feelings. "You do make it remarkably easy to forget that you have any."

Bitter laugh. "You sound like my wife."

"Fuck you."

"Say that again." It was a warning and Nona heeded it. Just because she wasn't crying anymore didn't mean he would not hit her. It occurred to her, then, that no one back home knew exactly where she was.

Nona reached for the sherry.

"You're not going to drink that?"

"Oh, yes." Nona filled a glass. "Take me out to the back and shoot me."

Each had a few more sour lines to deliver before Lyle made his exit. He was going home, he said. Nona could call him later if she wished; there was a telephone in the office.

Rosita arrived as soon as Lyle was gone. She tidied the room around a constantly moving Nona, who felt foolish and underfoot. Nona told her to leave the bread and fruit that she and Lyle had hardly touched that morning. "You like more wine?" asked Rosita, holding up the empty decanter. Nona nodded eagerly.

When she was alone again, Nona pulled down the just-made bed and lay down. She closed her eyes and fell asleep at once. When she awoke, about an hour later, it was still raining, but quietly. Nona ate a banana, and as she leafed through a copy of *Arizona Today*, the rain grew fainter and the room brighter. When the rain had slackened so that it was too soft to be heard, she went out. It was like stepping into a mirage. Everything shimmered. There were a few drops still coming down, but the sun was out, shining through them, and every raindrop held a tiny rainbow.

Nona took a walk around the house. She passed by the office, which was really part of the owner's living quarters. In the room next to the office the window blinds were open, and Walt was there, parked in his wheelchair before the television. The screen was very large, the picture vivid: a young man wearing a bandanna, in a wheelchair, his face distorted by emotion. Nona had seen this movie, too: another cheap, sentimental, falsifying story—not about love this time, but about war. Walt had Bathsheba—he was hugging Bathsheba to his chest—and Nona could tell from the movement of his shoulders that he was sobbing. Tiptoeing by, Nona wondered how many times Walt and Bathsheba had seen this movie.

Nona kept going, taking the dirt road that led away from the house. By the time she reached the asphalt, the rain had stopped; from horizon to horizon the sky was clear. A road-runner appeared, head down, tail up, out for a jog—probably just what Lyle was doing at that moment.

On her way back to her room Nona glimpsed the couple heard leaving before, returned from wherever they'd been, and they looked just as she had imagined them: young, normal, carefree.

Walt had provided Nona's room with a few books, mostly about the region—landscapes of the Southwest, natives and wildlife of the Southwest; Southwestern houses, furniture, food. They were beautiful books, picture books, the kind Nona never looked at now but that had enthralled her when she was a child. She felt like a child, sitting cross-legged on the floor with a large book open on her knees. Hours passed. She turned the pages slowly, trying to ignore how hungry she was. At last she put the books away. She ate an apple and some cornbread. She read a chapter of the novel she had brought with her. Then she took a long bath, and after she had dried herself she got into bed and she lay on her stomach and gave herself an orgasm. Just before she would have fallen asleep again, she got up, put on some clothes, and went out. She took a longer walk this time, admiring the big sky turning deep, vibrant colors—turquoise and violet and mauve—just like the picture books. The air was still moist. It was pleasantly cool. Nona saw, for the first time since she'd arrived, why so many people loved this part of the country, why people came here to be cured. That rainstorm had been like a consecration. There was that hallowed hush upon the land. No bird sang. The first star caught her eye and the stillness was broken by that unmistakable yipping cry. Did coyotes mate for life, like other wolves? Nona remembered hearing a story about a timber wolf that had mated with a golden retriever and was later left bewildered and heartbroken, troubling that Canadian village with his howls. *O bitch, I thought you loved me, but now you go with every mutt in town!*

That evening Nona finished reading her novel. She finished the little food that was left, she finished all the sherry. She was in bed by ten. But one more time she got up and put on her blue-and-white robe, and her jacket over her robe, and her shoes, and went out. It was so cold now she could not stop shivering. One last look at the blueberry-colored sky throbbing with stars, a few more deep breaths of that healing air. Once more a high plaintive cry came out of the darkness, and an answering cry rose in Nona's breast. *Oh, Roy, how could you let this happen to me?*

The next morning Nona packed her things and went to call a taxi and to settle the bill. Except for the deposit on the room, Nona had paid for everything that weekend. She knew that Lyle was never going to write the check he had promised, and that was all right, she accepted this; it was part of her punishment.

It was not until the plane was landing in Dallas that she remembered that she had left the folder of homework in the night-table drawer. She called Lyle from the airport, at home (knowing that he would be teaching then), and left a message asking him to get the folder and mail it to her as soon as possible. After she hung up she wanted to kick herself: I could have called Walt and asked him—why didn't I?

One of the worst feelings in the world: this shuddering distaste that set in when you had been intimate with someone and later regretted it. A feeling men experienced only rarely, it was said, and women, over and over again. It plagued Nona sorely on that flight to New York. Two drinks—one on the flight to Dallas, another in the airport—had not washed it away. Suddenly Nona remembered something that had happened a few years ago. She had been at a party where she and three other women had agreed to drive home together. They had gone about a block when one of the women cried *stop*. This woman then confessed that, at the party, the host had followed her into the bedroom where she was getting her coat, had taken her in his arms and begged her to stay with him. Alarmed, she had fled. But now she didn't know. She was torn. Had she made a mistake? Should she go back? Nona would never forget the helpless look in her eyes. Advice was given all round, including this, from the oldest among them: "Go home. Trust me, you'll have such a better time in bed tonight by yourself."

The cocktail cart arrived, and Nona ordered a screwdriver.

Of course she would have nothing to do with Lyle ever again. Vile Lyle—why should she waste any more time even thinking about him? He was history. She had a life. And she was damn eager to get back to it, after this—farce. Much to do when she got home. One of the first things she would do was take Phoebe's advice and try calling Tim Banister again.

Maybe this time he would be willing to talk with her.

Nona shuddered—so hard the ice rattled in her drink, and the woman sitting beside her turned to her curiously.

Oh, the way he had looked at her. The contempt with which he had treated her. The searing contempt of men for women. And another shaft of memory came flying at her. Just out of school, she and a boyfriend had gone to a wedding where they met one of his uncles. When uncle asked nephew what was up, and her boyfriend just shrugged, Nona burst out: "Oh, but he just won this fabulous fellowship!" And without looking at her the uncle said, "Why don't you just shut up and let the man speak for himself."

She had been mistreated, misunderstood. She had been seduced and rejected. She had been humiliated. She had suffered enough. Already it seemed too absurd to have actually happened. She could not get Bathsheba or the hunchbacked dwarf out of her head.

That foolish woman: she had lasted one more block before crying *stop* again and jumping out of the car.

Nona was drunk. She kept seeing Lyle, bending over her, all hairy nostrils and sneer. A fly hovered between them and he darted his tongue out to catch it—oh!

It was not the first time she had kissed a prince and got a frog.

By the time the plane landed, she had told the curious and sympathetic woman beside her the whole sad story.

chapter
nine

It was four months before Nona got around to telling her mother that she and Roy had separated.

"Oh, Nona," Rosalind said when she heard. Not in the sense of "Oh, my dear, how terrible, what happened?" but, rather, "Oh, Nona, how *could* you." A mother disappointed and exasperated with her child. Nona was reminded of a time back in grade school when she and another girl had been assigned to work together on a science project. They each had started plants at home, then brought them to school and arranged them together in a terrarium. The project was a success, the seedlings were thriving, but one day the girls had a fight and Nona's classmate insisted she wanted her plants out of there. When she could not change the girl's mind, Nona dug them up. "Oh, Nona, how could you," said the teacher. "Now you've gone and destroyed something beautiful. And why? Just out of spite, out of wicked, wicked spite." The other girl had stood there, clean-handed, beaming. It had frightened Nona then, how that nun, without knowing what happened, had decided that Nona must be guilty, and it frightened her now, too, how Rosalind automatically assumed that if Roy and Nona were breaking up, Nona must be to blame.

In spite of herself, though, Nona was touched by her

mother's response. So Rosalind cared about Roy after all.

"I don't know why on earth you'd want to leave him," Rosalind said. "He was a good man."

"He's not dead, Rosalind," Nona said, though she knew perfectly well that Rosalind had used the past tense because by "man" she had really meant "husband." "You never said that about him before."

"I didn't have to say it, did I? It was obvious. I hate it when people state the obvious."

Nona knew she had better get off the phone. "I'm sorry, but I can't explain everything now. It's too difficult, especially on the phone. All I can say is, some—some things happened, and I—we—started thinking maybe we got married before we were ready."

"For God's sake, Nona, you talk as if you were twenty years old! You talk as if you were married a week ago!" The second arrow drove the first one in deeper. Nona agonized in silence. When, before hanging up, Rosalind asked whether there was any hope, Nona said yes, but she lied; she was sure she and Roy would get a divorce. But she couldn't talk about this with Rosalind. If only she could. If only she could tell her mother everything. How many times in her life had Nona wished for a family to turn to. When she was growing up she had indulged such dreams all the time, sighing and pining like a character in a romance: *Oh, for a sister to confide in! Oh, for a brother to protect me!*

When she finally got off the phone, Nona took her new dog out for a walk. She had got the dog after Roy moved out, choosing him from a group of strays brought to the greenmarket by ASPCA volunteers. But she had not been acting on an impulse that day. The only useful thing she could remember her psychiatrist ever saying was that getting a dog would spare many a person a breakdown, not so much because of the love the dog provided as because of the responsibilities that came with it. Nona named the dog Pip. He was fawn with black markings, small but robust, still young. Definitely part beagle, Nona had been told; and, she thought, looking at his short legs and large head, maybe also part corgi. At night he lay on the floor while she read, and, as soon as she closed her book, would jump on the bed and curl up at her feet, where he stayed till morning. She bought him a bright red leather leash and walked him several times a day, no matter the weather, and the sight of him marching briskly ahead of her, chubby legs goose-stepping, head high and an expression of grave self-importance on his face, cheered Nona unfailingly.

It was winter. Nona wore a heavy coat with a hood, thick woolen gloves, and fleece-lined boots. The season had been rather mild so far, but where Nona walked, in the direction of the river, there was often a sharp wind blowing. She and Pip kept up a good pace, past the antique dealers and boutiques and restaurants, and the handsome town houses, and the play-ground, where Nona had to be careful, because Pip was apt to snap when charged by toddlers. Once, he bit a little boy on the cheek, and though he had not broken the skin, the boy, his mother, and Nona were all quite shaken. On the way back Nona would stop at her café for hot chocolate and a cheese roll. Here Pip was welcome in spite of health codes, and the regular customers greeted him. Nona had noticed, before she got Pip, how pleased people often were when you paid attention to their dogs, how they would stand there smiling, patient, and now she was one of those smiling people, patiently answering those silly questions: "Does he like people?" "Does the cold hurt his paws?"

The sky was dull. Snow was forecast by nightfall. Here and there on the pavement: a skin of brittle ice. Up from the river the sharp wind blew. A loose Labrador came bounding over and slobbered on Pip, who bristled with pique.

Nona remembered that she had not told Rosalind about Pip. Of course she had not told her earlier, because it would have been odd to mention getting a dog without mentioning Roy's moving out—the two things were so connected. Now she had finally told Rosalind about Roy but forgotten all about Pip. She knew just what Rosalind would say, though: "Why didn't you get a cat? Cats are so much easier." True. But that self-possessed species was surely not what the psychiatrist would have ordered. It was Roy who happened to be living with three cats at the moment. They had come with the apartment he was sitting, the home of a friend, a pianist who was away on tour. The apartment was on the Upper West Side. The day she got Pip, Nona had taken him up in a cab to meet Roy, and the three of them had played Frisbee in Riverside Park for hours. Since Roy had moved, he and Nona had been seeing each other now and then. But these were wrenching times, increasingly difficult for both of them. So many important things they had to discuss, so many hard practical questions to decide, such as how Nona could afford to keep their apartment herself, and where Roy was going to live after the pianist returned. But whenever they tried to talk seriously and make plans, it seemed these questions led only to bigger and even more daunting questions, which overwhelmed them. Much easier to talk about the animals. "It's so strange," said Roy. "Suddenly we've acquired all these pets." He had never lived with cats before and was finding them full of surprises. "I never knew they could have so much personality. I always thought of them more as beautiful objects. And what is this problem they have with closed doors?"

Nona thought Roy was probably taking better care of those cats these days than he was of himself. He had started smoking again. Nona felt especially sorry for him, because he had been so good for ten long years, never cheating, as she had, incorrigibly.

That night four months ago when Nona returned from Tucson, Roy was at home waiting for her. Smoking. They had sat together for a while, not speaking, until Roy announced that he sure as hell did not feel like cooking, and they agreed to go out to dinner. They went to the same restaurant where they always took Rosalind. It was not as good as many other restaurants they knew, it was overpriced, but it was around the corner, it was their place, where they were known and where they were always comfortable. There was a dilemma in Roy's life at that moment involving a student who owed him money, who kept taking lessons and putting off paying for them, and though they had talked about this before, they talked about it now, again, for some time. Then came an endless silence. It was Roy who broke it, gruffly. "You look exhausted. Busy weekend?"

Nona was still a little drunk. Though to her it seemed she was speaking slowly, her words came out in a rush. "There might come a time, I think there will come a time, when we can talk about all this, Roy, but not now. All I can tell you now is that I've made a terrible mistake, and I'm sorry. I have been selfish and stupid and crazy and I've suffered for that, but I don't want to talk about how I've suffered, you just have to believe me."

Roy peered more closely at her. "Nona, are you all right?"

Here their waiter approached, hovered, sensed something, and withdrew.

Nona sighed. I have everything in him, she thought. I have what every woman wants. She slumped in her chair, suddenly weak. She reached across the table for his hand. "Oh, Roy, Roy. Why are you being so good about this?" And it was then that he flinched and turned his eyes away. Fatally. For that was when she knew.

"WHY DON'T YOU TWO JUST call yourselves even and stay together?" Advice from Tess. It seemed that she and Anthony had saved their own marriage this way, letting one betrayal cancel out the other, giving themselves a clean slate. "Couples do it all the time."

Naturally Nona had wanted to know more about Roy and that soprano—and was told there was nothing more to know. Well, could Roy at least say whether he had cared about the woman? He had not, he said; not really. So Nona asked him whether he thought the woman had cared about him, and that, said Roy, he really didn't know. Well, maybe. He supposed, yes. So then Nona wanted to know whether he thought that the woman had ended up being hurt, at which *Jesus Christ,* said Roy, his voice rather high, it was over five fucking years ago and he didn't remember, but if she had been hurt, that was her lookout, after all he hadn't raped her, for God's sake, and she was an adult. And Nona had shouted, "You're as bad as *he* is, damn you!"

But, for the most part, they had managed to talk without shouting. They talked a lot, trying to stay calm, and to be honest and fair, and to see their situation truthfully. It was hard: the body of their love laid out on the table like this. They talked and they listened to each other, and they examined the bruised, battered body of their love, and it was in the course of all this earnest discussion that Roy's other big secret came out: his pain over their childlessness, his wish to adopt. And, unlike the first secret, this was something Nona had always suspected.

To the end Roy insisted he did not want a divorce. Poor Roy. He was suffering—with astonishment Nona realized that she had never seen him suffer before—and it shook her heart but not her conviction. She had been happy with Roy—that was no lie; but it was possible to be happy with someone in a relationship and unhappy with yourself in that relationship at the same time. This was what Nona had discovered. She was not suited to marriage. It seemed to her now that she had always known this. She had just proved it, hadn't she? Roy was suffering now but in time he would be grateful. He would marry again, it was not too late, he would have those children he so wanted—and so deserved, thought Nona, for a more wonderful father she could not imagine. And they, he and

Nona, would remain friends. She would be like an aunt to those children, as she was to his sisters' children (three nieces and two nephews whom she loved, and whose love for her was one of the great surprises and delights of her being). And wouldn't that be better for everybody all around? But Nona knew that her remaining close to Roy would depend largely— no, entirely—on the new wife; and when she peered too closely at this, her part-of-the-ex's-big-happy-family fantasy, she saw the worms on the rose, and was forced to acknowledge how unlikely such an arrangement was. And then her courage failed her. To have to face a future in which her Roy not only belonged to another but was completely estranged from herself? No, no, no, no, no.

Turning the corner of Perry Street, ducking her head at a blast of wind, she was simultaneously blasted by the thought that to lose Roy would be to lose all his family, too, her in-laws, the five nieces and nephews that she loved. She tightened Pip's leash—they were at a red light—and, gazing down the wintry avenue, she seemed to see herself ahead, old, solitary, bent, a bare tree in a bare landscape, and the gabble of a homeless man wrapped in a tarp sounded to her like: You will die all alone.

She did not stop at the café where she usually had her hot chocolate: not today. Back home, she checked the mailbox as she had checked it on leaving: empty then, empty now. She closed it gently. In weeks past she had slammed it so many times she had loosened the lock, and now, though she closed it gently, the lock rattled.

A week after she had returned from Tucson, the folder Nona had left behind and asked Lyle to send her had not arrived. She had told her students that she was merely late in getting their essays corrected and would be returning them soon. She left another message on Lyle's machine, and when after a few days he had not called back, she called the bed-and-breakfast and got Walt. "Your husband came by and picked up that folder, oh, I'd say ten days ago." Her *husband?* Nona shuddered. Another week passed. Nona tried calling Lyle again, at his home, at his office, at different hours, always getting a machine, always leaving a message. She remembered Charlotte's strained little voice on the tape. Hating herself, appalled at whatever this force was that kept her calling, Nona kept calling. Had he moved again? Was he out of town? One day his roommate picked up. "Oh, sure, he's around. I'll tell him you called." Oh, sure. Didn't say he'd call back.

And so Nona sat down and wrote a brief letter, coolly asking for the return of the folder. She understood that Lyle might be upset with her, but this was her job after all, and why take it out on her students?

Silence.

At last, blushing with the lie, Nona informed her class that she had lost their homework. And she wrote another letter to Lyle, this one also brief but crackling with dudgeon. Not only the folder did she want back this instant, but also her letters, and the photographs she had sent him. As soon as these were safely in her hands, she would be only *too happy* to return *his* letters and *his* photograph to *him*.

You are ridiculous, she told herself. You are sinking lower and lower. What do you really want?

Closure. A word—was that asking too much? One last letter: he owed her that. And she knew exactly what that letter should say; she had written it herself many times.

It was now that Nona received a notice from the company with which she and Roy had taken out a health-insurance policy when they got married. Their quarterly premium had just been doubled. Nona called the company at once. "Last year this premium went from five hundred to eight hundred dollars. Now it has gone up to sixteen hundred. What I want to know is, if we keep this policy, is it possible that the premium could double again next year? Or triple? Or quadruple?" The woman at the other end of the line replied that this was indeed possible. "I see. And I understand also that the company has the right to terminate this policy at any time?" "Yes, ma'am, that is also correct." "Well, then, why do you call yourselves an insurance company?" "Ma'am?" "I mean, what good is our paying you all this money if you can raise the premium to whatever you want, whether we can afford it or not, or cancel the policy entirely, at any time? In practical terms, then, we have no insurance." The woman hesitated. "I don't know what you mean, ma'am. If you're covered and you make a claim, the company will pay it. Of course you're insured." "Yes, but say I pay you this—what is it?—sixty-four hundred dollars a year. And then one day I have a bad accident—" "God forbid," the woman interjected, automatically and without irony. "—and I wake up in the hospital and my first thought is: Thank God I have health insurance! Now I know why I've been paying all that money! But what I *don't* know is that at that very moment sitting in my mailbox back home is a letter from you informing me that you have terminated my policy—" "That is an extreme scenario, ma'am." "Impossible?" "Well, no, I cannot say it's impossible. Anything is possible." "Just listen to what you're saying," Nona said, her voice cracking. "'Anything is possible.' Sixty-four hundred dollars a year for that." The woman said, "I don't know what to tell you, ma'am." She sounded truly at a loss, a tired woman doing an unpleasant job. Nona imagined her divorced, with a deadbeat husband and two children to support. I'm losing it, she thought. Tormenting helpless clerks on the phone.

Roy said, "Look, we have too much to deal with right now. Let's just pay the damn premium for this quarter and we'll try to find a cheaper policy later." But Nona was truly worried. Rent on their apartment had also just gone up. And could they find decent health insurance for less? And if they got a divorce they would need two separate policies. Oh, money! And it was now that Nona sank to her lowest point. She wrote to Lyle again. Where was the check he had promised her? Writing her letter, Nona felt calm, reasonable, perfectly justified. She wasn't asking for everything, just his share of the plane fare and the bed-and-breakfast bill. But the instant she mailed the letter she regretted it. She would have given anything to have it back. Oh, how much trouble might the world be saved, how many tragedies might be averted, were mailboxes made with slots large enough to reach in a hand.

Trudging back home that day, her heart in her boots, Nona had opened the door to hear the phone ringing. Rita, of all people. Finally calling . . . hadn't forgotten . . . so much catching up . . . fabulous news . . .

Walking downtown to the bar where Rita had suggested they meet, Nona thought that Lyle's name was sure to come up, and she resolved to be discreet.

Background is important. Upstate, Rita had been out of her element: unsure of herself, vulnerable. Here, in this elegant new Tribeca bar, she was at home. Nona, who had arrived first and was sitting at a table facing the door, smiled as Rita entered. She had forgotten what an impression that woman made. Today, clothes had a lot to do with it. Such unusual pants, cut wide in the hips and skintight in the leg, like modified jodhpurs—only a perfect figure could carry them off. The pants fit snugly into tall black leather boots. Under a thin black leather jacket she wore a pink angora sweater that clung to her bosom but flared out a little an inch or so above her waist. Her skin glowed, her makeup was immaculate, and her long blond hair was pulled back into a French braid that looked so glamorous Nona thought, if enough people saw her, that style might well become ubiquitous again. Certainly enough people in the crowded bar had noticed Rita. The waitress, a very attractive young woman herself, appraised her shamelessly, tapping her pen against her pad. Nona was drinking white wine. Rita ordered a Pernod. A rose-tinted alabaster sconce was mounted on the wall of their booth, and Nona could only hope that it was illuminating her face as magically as it was Rita's.

As soon as she had her Pernod, Rita gave her news: she had sold her screenplay. Nona looked blank for a moment; she had completely forgotten that Rita had been writing a screenplay when they met. Now she listened as Rita filled in details, mentioning an agent of whom Nona had never heard but whose name was evidently household, and the astonishing—to Nona, at least, but what did she know?—figure of two hundred thousand dollars. No wonder Rita was radiant. "Don't look so shocked," Rita said, her face darkening, and Nona remembered: always quick to take offense, Rita was. "So what happened with that book *you* were writing?"

Nona smiled wryly. Had she been writing a book? "I've had to put it aside for the moment. But I'll get back to it."

They reminisced about Timber Lake. "That awful place," Rita said. "Those awful women!" And she twisted the corners of her mouth down and flared her nostrils in such a true imitation of Pearl Verga Nona had to laugh. And what about Ralph, Nona wanted to know. Had they stayed in touch? "We didn't leave on good terms," Rita said, with a sly look that suggested there was more to tell. Nona waited, but Rita appeared to have fallen into thought.

Nona had not eaten lunch that day and the glass of wine had gone right to her head. She blamed that glass for allowing her to order another, and she blamed the second glass for allowing her to forget her resolution and blurt: "I saw Lyle."

"You mean, he's back in New York?"

Nona lowered the glass she'd been about to bring to her lips. Lyle in New York. And when would that have been?

"Right after he left Phoebe's. He came down for a few days before he flew home."

"And why did he come to New York?" Stunning a blow

though it had just received, Nona's mind was moving nimbly, rushing to abominable conclusions.

Rita's expression had turned sly again. "To see me, of course." And for the second time she told Nona, "Don't look so shocked."

"I'm just—confused, that's all. As I recall, you didn't like Lyle, or so you said the last time we spoke, and I certainly don't remember you ever saying anything about planning to see him in New York." Nona was amazed at how steady she was managing to keep her voice. Meanwhile, under the table, she had curled her shaking hands into fists.

"Ah, yes," Rita said. "You don't know the whole story, do you. How could you? It was my last night up there—you and I went for a walk after dinner, remember? And after that, I went to my room, to pack. I told Ralph that I'd come to his room after I was finished—it was our last night together. But first I took a shower, and then I decided to go downstairs and get something to eat. I was always hungry at night up there, because we ate dinner so early—too early for me—and I hated Eva's cooking so I never ate that much at dinner anyway. I thought I'd go get a piece of fruit or something. The house was quiet, I guess everyone was in their rooms, but there was Lyle down in the kitchen. It was odd, because he wasn't doing anything, not eating or making a cup of tea or anything like that, just sitting at the table, alone, as if he was waiting for someone. I wasn't wearing anything but my bathrobe. I don't know if you ever saw it"—a scrap of flowered silk unfurled in Nona's mind—"but it was pretty skimpy. Well, Lyle just sat there staring, just looking me up and down, you know, in the most incorrect way imaginable. I said something to him, I think, something jokey and inane—I was actually kind of nervous, the way he was looking at me—and I went and got a plum out of the pantry. Then I went to the sink to wash it, and the whole time he just kept staring at me, not saying a word. I was leaning against the sink, I had just taken a bite of the plum, and he leaped across the room and pounced—I hardly saw him. And I don't know quite how he did it—he's had a lot of experience at this sort of thing, I gather—but he got the robe off. Whoosh—it was gone. And I still had the plum in my hand and hadn't swallowed what was in my mouth, and he started kissing me very hard, mashing the plum in my mouth. Let me tell you it was just about the sexiest thing that ever happened to me. Picture it: there I was, naked in his arms, and all the kitchen lights ablaze—anyone could have walked in on us, but I didn't care. The window over the sink was open, and I could hear the crickets and smell the trees out there, and then I felt my throat tighten up. I don't know what happened to me, but I thought I was going to cry. Then Lyle said, Someone's coming—he must have heard something—and we slipped up the back stairs to my room. We had quite a night there."

"I heard you."

"What?"

"That night. In my room. I heard you."

"Oh. Sorry about that." Not sounding sorry at all. "Anyway, you can imagine Ralph wasn't too pleased with me."

"And that's when you and Lyle arranged to meet in New York?" Fuck Ralph.

Rita shook her head. "We spoke a few times on the phone after I left. It was his idea to come to New York, but I wasn't so sure, so he had to do some sweet-talking. He came down just for three days. Just long enough to get me hooked. Then he went home, and that was the last I heard from him. Typical. He hasn't called me and needless to say I'm not going to call him." Her braid had slipped forward over her shoulder while she was speaking, and now she took hold of it and tossed it behind her as if it were the cad himself. Then she remembered. "Wait a minute. What were you saying? You saw him? How could that be?"

"I flew out to Tucson a couple of months ago and spent a weekend with him." In the midst of her own devastation, Nona drew a sliver of satisfaction from Rita's chagrin.

"*You?* What on earth did you do that for?"

"To sleep with him. Don't look so shocked."

"I don't believe this." Rita appeared to need air. "What about your husband? What about his wife?" But before Nona could respond she said, "Never mind. I don't want to know. It doesn't matter. I'll never see him again anyway. I don't want to talk about it." Oh, Rita was miffed.

She did not want to hear Nona's story. She did not want to know what had happened in Tucson, or what Nona's feelings for Lyle might be. World of contempt in that *you*. What did Rita want? Men. Their worship and devotion, their hearts en brochette. But it was not enough. Other women must be rejected. Already she had hurried on to another topic, and Nona had to resist the impulse to drag her back by that pretty French braid.

They parted soon after—though on the phone Rita had said something about maybe following drinks with dinner—and Nona knew that they would not see each other again. But she had decided that this would probably have been the case even if Lyle had never come up. She had decided that Rita had arranged this meeting not because she wanted to see Nona, but so that she could announce her fabulous news—hoping, no doubt, that Nona would repeat it; say, to those awful women who had been so mean to her at that awful place.

And now, when Nona thought of Lyle, she found that no memory of hers—not of that first kiss by the lake, or of their night in the library, or of their time together in Tucson—was as vivid as the scene that had been described to her: the two of them, Lyle and Rita, that night in Phoebe's kitchen. This scene stayed with Nona, and was a torment to her.

Picture it, Rita had said, and Nona did so even now, as she entered the apartment and looped Pip's leash around the door-knob. Rita naked in Lyle's arms, the robe a silk puddle at their feet, the crickets, the plum-filled kiss—in wonder and in pain she pictured it, her own throat tightening as Rita had described her throat tightening.

Going into the kitchen, Nona glanced out the window and stopped, amazed: in the few minutes since she'd come indoors the snow had begun and was coming down now as swiftly as rain.

Nona filled Pip's water bowl and set about making herself some coffee.

She had lived through hours in the past four months that she would rather have died than live through again. But at last she seemed to be regaining a measure of calm. Nothing so appealed to Nona as an image of herself calm. Taking proper care of herself, eating right, getting enough rest, working. Not scribbling unseemly letters, shrilling into telephones, spilling her guts to strangers on airplanes—please! To do the work before her, letting nothing distract her, looking only to the work and never to the fruits of work, expecting nothing, fearing nothing—the way of the Stoics—this was the ideal. Could she ever learn it? Why, the most beautiful and most satisfying image of herself she could conceive was this: a calm, dignified woman, writing a book. And though countless matters remained to be settled, there were at least moments now when she could believe that her life might return to normal. She made it to her job every day, she was doing without cigarettes, and she had gone almost a month without sleeping pills. As for her book—didn't she have a meeting set up with Tim Banister that very Friday?

Having drunk all his water, Pip lay down in the middle of the floor, resting his head on his paws. Nona watched him, and for a moment all thought faded, her mind was peacefully blank, numb—as the tips of her toes were still numb from her walk. He was in excellent health, she had been assured by the vet, who had given her some cream for Pip's only problem: a small patch of eczema between his shoulder blades. It was too early for his dinner, but Nona thought he might want a snack. She was careful not to overfeed him—she did not want to be one of those owners who turn their poor beasts into hassocks. She took one biscuit from a box on the counter and tossed it to Pip, who caught it without getting up.

In a car, his rescuers had found him. Locked in the trunk of an abandoned car.

The phone rang and Nona answered it: a wrong number. As she hung up she remembered her conversation with her mother, and she winced. Her coffee was ready. She poured herself a mug and carried it to the kitchen table, and suddenly she thought of Mr. Vaughan. The high school choral teacher. He had looked hulking and out of place beside her mother on the living-room sofa. He had come to the house to speak to Rosalind, about Nona. He had already spoken ("ad nauseam, I fear") to Nona. (Nona had rolled her eyes.) Just doing his duty, he said. A fine voice, a good ear—these were things to be taken seriously while a person was still young. He had some advice, about training, what should be done at this stage and what should be avoided. A talent was a sacred thing, a gift of God, a thing to be respected and nurtured wisely. Yes, he had indeed spoken to Nona about all this before, and now she was not listening. She was watching her mother, who was listening raptly and giving the distinct impression that she really would have liked to please this nice Mr. Vaughan. And now Nona had to wonder: just how much had her own resistance had to do with a desire to disappoint her mother? She and Rosalind were not getting along at all in those days. Later, Rosalind had tried to reason with her: couple of lessons, work with a pro—what could that hurt? Summer music camp, sing all day, make new friends, sounded like fun—why not? And when Nona would not budge: "Oh, Nona. Don't be like this. You never know. You could be somebody." Which had sent Nona slamming out of the house. "I'm somebody *now!*" Twelve hours later, dawn breaking over the rooftops, she arrived home in a squad car. The police had found her loitering on the pier. "Anyone might have thought she was soliciting," one of the cops said. "Anyone with a dirty mind," retorted her mother. But Rosalind gave up after that. Mr. Vaughan did, too. Nona, who belonged to the high school chorus, had threatened to quit but changed her mind; so long as everyone left her alone, she enjoyed singing. For the graduation ceremony the chorus was going to perform a medley of traditional American songs, and Nona would be the soloist, singing "Beautiful Dreamer," with Mr. Vaughan as accompanist. A certain tension between them during rehearsals, but Nona didn't care. Everything was set now, she was going far away to college in the fall, she felt safe from Mr. Vaughan and all his plans for her. Besides, he was something of a heartthrob, with his athletic physique (Mr. V, the girls called him), his dark, sleepy-looking eyes, and daring habit of lighting up now and then in class. After graduation she had sought him out to say good-bye, and found him alone in the basement of the building, in the music room.

"Have you really come to say good-bye? But don't you know, dear, wherever you go, you'll always be on my conscience."

She was aware that something awesome was taking place: her good ear heard it in the pitch of his voice, and his eyes were shining. Smell of tobacco, and the sweet citrusy scent of his aftershave. He was trembling all over, and the heat of his hard chest melted her. He stroked her head as he was kissing her, as if to console her. When he let go of her, he sat down heavily in a chair and stared at the floor. His face: dazed, bloodless, as if some vital fluid had been drawn out of him. And wasn't Nona soaring, keen, more alive than she had ever been, as if she had taken some vital fluid in?

He had made her promise not to tell anyone.

Mr. V.

Nona sighed. She remembered. She drank her coffee, brooding.

And suppose it was true, and she really had thrown it all away. Her gift from Apollo. Her chance to be somebody. Her good man. *Oh, Nona. Look what you've done.* Suppose it really was all her fault, and she had destroyed something— something beautiful—many beautiful things. *Out of spite, out of spite, out of wicked, wicked spite.*

The sound of snoring disrupted her thoughts. Pip, tired from his long walk, had rolled onto his back and lay with his front paws crooked in the air. Nona watched him and listened to him and was filled with a quiet astonishment. I have saved this dog's life, I take good care of him, and he is grateful to me.

chapter
ten

Tim Banister lived in one of those handsome town houses that Nona often passed on her walks with Pip. His apartment was a one-bedroom on the first floor, and he lived there alone. The man with whom he had moved into the apartment eighteen years ago was dead. Two other men with whom Tim had shared that apartment were dead. Shep Shelton was the first lover who had died on Tim, and that had been twenty-seven years ago. Tim often thought that if he had been told back then how many other lovers he would be burying in the years to come, he would have buried himself first. He had been just twenty-three when Shep died, and death was still strange; now it was his daily bread. Tim had been keeping a journal since he was twelve. In the back of his journal he kept a list. Intimates, acquaintances, neighbors (the man upstairs: even now, dying). Friends and the friends of friends, the man who had cut his hair for years, the manager of the neighborhood movie house, the manager of the health food store, six colleagues at the library where he worked, his doctor, his cleaning person, his high school math teacher, two of his college professors, both owners of his favorite restaurant—the endless list at the back of his journal. Every day when he read the newspaper he checked the obituaries first, just as he turned first to the In

Memoriam column of his alumni bulletin when it came in the mail. Those he had known and loved—and those he had not known, but loved: his favorite writer; his favorite dancer. In his journal Tim had written:

"It cannot go on like this, of course. Something must, something *will* be done." (July 7, 1984)

What Tim had done: stood vigil at sickbeds and deathbeds, comforted, prayed, carried out last wishes, arranged funerals, volunteered, given time, given money, hounded his government representatives, spoken out, acted up, voted with his feet, attended memorial services for people he had not even known because others who had known them needed the support. *It cannot go on.* Fifteen years, thirty-two funerals. Tim's mother, Grace, whom her sons called Amazing Grace, kept reminding him: God sends a man only as much suffering as he can bear. But men had died in his arms suffering more than they could bear. An immense fatigue sank into Tim, he felt it bone deep. He did not want to read another book or article about AIDS, or see another play or movie about it, or attend any memorial service he didn't absolutely have to attend. He did not want to smell that smell again, or hear that breathing, or hear it—stop.

"A whole way of being and seeing, of enjoying and interpreting life and making love—a whole world is dying." (December 31, 1987)

His world.

The last name on Tim's list was that of his oldest friend—he who had been Tim's rock, the one helping him get through it all. A man of peerless goodness. A death of spectacular brutality. And now Tim came nearest to snapping.

Mother, he cried. *Help me, Mother. I cannot, I cannot—*

But you are negative, she said. *Think of poor Billy.* (First cousin: dying.)

He went on.

* * *

Years ago, during the time he knew Shep Shelton, Tim had worked as an assistant at an art gallery on Madison Avenue. But he had left that job, gone back to school, become a librarian, gone back to school again, and was now a specialist in manuscript conservation. He worked for a private historical society. Good work, good pay, he was happy with his job—especially happy not to be like so many he knew: actors and artists working at jobs they despised while waiting for the big break or a grant. Other ways in which Tim was happy: in his apartment, its beautifully renovated rooms, its excellent light, and in his part of the Village (Boys' Town, Amazing Grace called it), the only neighborhood where he would have wanted to live, death-haunted though it might be. And he was happy in the house he owned on Long Island, where he spent most weekends, spring, summer, and fall. The house had a garden, and Tim was convinced that working there, on his knees, hands in the good earth watered by his tears, had helped save his sanity more than once. And he was in love.

Love. How many times in the past fifteen years had Tim warned himself to keep a distance from people. But he had never been able to do this. (Overheard in a bar: "Safe sex, okay, if I have to. But I will not wear a condom on my heart.")

Tim was in love with Andrew. Andrew was getting his doctorate, in history, at Columbia. He was not really Tim's type: too stocky, too dark, and of course too young, but—Cupid. Tim was at Stage One: up and down, this way and that—rapture, melancholy, hope, despair—the whole bumpy ride. This cold clear winter evening, with the light turning blue, and blue frost bordering the windowpanes, all he wanted to do was think about Andrew and how they were going to see each other later.

But first he had to deal with this woman.

Oh, why had he agreed to talk to her? *Why* had he invited her to the *apartment*? Once before, she had called, and Tim had been rude to her—he had shocked himself, how nasty he'd been—and that had gotten rid of her, at least for a time. And that, of course, was precisely why he'd been so nice to her when she called again, that nastiness having troubled his conscience ever since. Still, as he'd told her on the phone, he didn't know how much help he could be. After all, it had been a long time, and he and Shep had known each other not much more than a year. Theirs had not turned out to be one of the more important relationships in Tim's life. He had ended up playing a much larger role than he should have in Shep's last, grim year because there was no one else. Shep had broken with just about everyone by then. And after Shep's death, which had happened, to Tim's abiding guilt, while Tim was in Arkansas, the business of dealing with Shep's estate had been thrust on Tim.

"We want nothing, my daughter and I. Do as you think best," Rosalind had instructed him. "Just send me whatever papers I need to sign." And what about the work? "Ben Stone is the one who can help you with all that." And Benedict had helped. But it was Tim who had cleaned out Shep's studio—no small task: Shep was incorrigibly messy. It was Tim who had arranged to have all the paintings photographed and, later, wrapped and stored. And so it was Tim who discovered that Shep had destroyed or painted over not only almost all the abstractions he'd done toward the end of his life, but many earlier canvases, from the forties, as well. Tim could tell you exactly where, in what museum or collection, the fourteen paintings Shep had sold in his lifetime were to be found. Some thirty paintings and several boxes of drawings were now stored in the basement of Tim's house on Long Island. Other paintings Tim had given away to friends over the years, and because so many of these friends had died, these paintings had been moved around a lot, with Tim fastidiously keeping track. Fastidiously, too, he had begun by keeping Rosalind informed, sending her documentation of everything he did, until she moved and did not send him her new address. Tim had judged

Rosalind harshly back then, for having, in Benedict's words, buried Shep long before he was dead. Tim could still call up the resentment he had felt toward her and her family, and which he thought might be even now coloring his feelings toward her daughter, though of course Nona had been too young at the time to have had any say in things. And it was young Nona, after all, who had put up such a fight to see Shep again, Tim recalled—mostly because of the unspeakable anxiety this had caused Shep, so broken in health and spirit at the time. ("What the hell do I say if she starts asking questions?" Tim didn't know; not then, not now.)

The only person from those days with whom Tim was still in touch was Pearl Verga. She had already closed her famous gallery when they met; but when she was invited to curate a show for a gallery at a college upstate, she had hired Tim to help her. They had hit it off hugely. Tim had a weakness for dragons—as, often, they had for him. (Just a sand of Pearl's grit might have saved his mother a heap of suffering, Tim always thought.) It was Pearl who had warned, in a letter she wrote him that summer:

> Be prepared to hear from Ms. Shelton again—and you can blame Ms. Stone for encouraging her. Last night after dinner she read to us from that book she is writing. Afterward, she spent the rest of the night in the library with a man she's been hanky-pankying with here. My room is right next door, so I *know*. She's married, of course. Must be in the genes. As far as looks go, she definitely takes after the spear side. I don't *dis*like her, but she's not exactly my kind of person. One of those types for whom *everything*, no matter how small, is enormously complicated. I've seen her sit at dinner for a full five minutes, trying to decide whether to have the casserole with the meat in it or the vegetarian one. And by the way, what is it with all these girls?

Scribble, scribble, scribble, every one you meet. There's another one here writing a screenplay. If anything ever happens with either book or screenplay, I'll eat my Picasso.

Shep had not been Pearl's kind of person, either. "I *do* not see the fascination." Nor had she seen why Tim should be the one taking care of everything at the end. "How did this become your job? Why take it on?" Questions best answered with a question: if Tim didn't do it, who would? He had always had a very strong sense of responsibility, Tim. In high school the girls had voted him Best Future Husband, and though he'd taken a lot of razzing for that, secretly he was pleased. Pearl warned him that if Shep's paintings ever turned out to be worth any money, he'd find himself swarmed by relations "who won't give a damn anymore *how* queer Shep was." But immediately she hastened to assure him: except for the *Shoeshine Triptych* and perhaps one or two of the portraits, the work was second-rate. That had been another occasion on which Pearl had vowed if proved wrong to eat the Picasso still life she and her husband had acquired on their honeymoon in Paris—"not exactly for a song, but for a whole lot less than an opera."

"And do you think it's the paintings his daughter is after now?" Tim asked Pearl.

"I don't think she knows what she's after, to tell you the truth. Strikes me as a bit of a case, just like *him*."

Tim glanced at his watch, saw that Nona was five minutes late, and sighed. She would be like everyone else who embarks on this kind of search, he thought: desperate for confirmation that, in spite of all evidence to the contrary, Mom and Dad really were good people and that they had really loved each other and their kids. Tim had had too many long talks with the dying not to know all about this. His own father had walked out two days before Tim's twelfth birthday. Before that he had done so much damage that when he reappeared—just once, four years later—Tim and his brother had hidden Amazing Grace in a closet and driven him away with baseball bats.

It would be different if he had something to tell this woman that he knew she would want to hear. "A family is like a noose around an artist's neck," Shep once told him. And: "Let's face it: artists make rotten parents." (A conclusion any reader of *Children of Artists* would also be forced to draw.) What he had felt more than anything when his wife and child were gone, Shep confessed, was a tremendous sense of relief. "It gets to you after a while, you know, two pairs of eyes following you around the house, ready to fill with tears if you reach for your jacket. I would rather have spent twenty hours in the studio alone than twenty minutes in the park with them. What can I tell you? That's how it was." And, of course, he hadn't always been alone in that studio when he wasn't with them. And there were others he was spending twenty minutes with in the park.

Tim looked at his watch again. She was now fifteen minutes late. He had just time to hope that perhaps she was not coming when the downstairs bell rang.

Now remember, he told himself, as he buzzed her in: Keep it short. You have a date. No alcohol—you don't want things to get too cozy, or, God forbid, maudlin. Let her do the talking, don't volunteer too much, just answer the questions, you're not a priest or a therapist, you don't have to—

Oh, my. The mouth. The chin. But of course: he should have been prepared. And she was around the same age, too.

What a lovely apartment, she said, echoing just about every other person who saw it for the first time. And always when he heard this, Tim bowed his head for Russell, who had designed it eighteen years ago, when they both moved in.

She did not want anything. Maybe just a glass of water. She had sat down at the table in the dining alcove and was looking out the window, or it might have been at her reflection (it was quite dark out now). Tim was relieved to see that she had not brought a tape recorder. He set a bottle of Evian water and a glass before her. As for himself, he was having nothing, and dying for a drink.

She did not speak. She seemed tense, or rather more than tense, she seemed in a trance. He wondered if she was on medication. He wondered if she'd inherited her father's proclivity to substance abuse. Which reminded him. "Feel free to smoke, if you wish." She looked at him then and smiled (a sad, private little smile that jolted him again, it was so like Shep's) and shook her head.

The silence was getting to Tim. It was like one of those excruciating moments in the therapist's office. He wondered what she did for a living. He wondered about the husband.

"I'm sorry," she said at last. "I seem to be a little out of it today. I didn't sleep last night." So she got that gene, thought Tim, as a pair of sexy, dark-ringed eyes regarded him from out of the past.

What was happening? Now it was Tim who felt suspended in a trance. Incredible enough had it seemed when he discovered that the daughter of his old lover was living a few blocks away. But that she should be sitting here across from him, bringing Shep back with every remark, every gesture. And it occurred to Tim that Nona herself might be unaware of the resemblances that were striking him. Yet she would want to know about them, and Tim saw that it would be his duty to tell her. But not now, of course. Now: "How is the book coming along?" he said.

She did not reply at once. Tim thought she looked truly worn out, more so than from just one night without sleep.

"Oh—" Weary flip of the hand. Was she left-handed like Shep? (No.) "I'm having a lot of trouble with it. It's become something of an embarrassment to me. How it doesn't get written."

Of all things, may she not have inherited that: his supersensitivity to humiliation, his morbid fear of failure.

"I've talked to other people," she went on. "My mother, of course. My aunts. Benedict Stone right before he died. There was one brother, who's still alive. I tracked him down and we've talked on the phone a few times, but he didn't have much to say. He and Shep were practically strangers. That's the thing: so many people seem to have been strangers to him—I mean, people who shouldn't have been strangers. Myself, for example. But you. You were close to him. I want to know about you and his relationship with you." She was looking directly at him now, and as distracted as she had seemed minutes ago so she now seemed intent. "You can tell me everything, really."

Well—no. Tim smiled to himself. He took a deep breath. He spoke slowly, choosing his words with care. They had met at an opening at the gallery where Tim was working. It was Tim's first year in New York, and just about everyone he met then seemed glamorous and exciting and superior—no one more so than the artists. That was a time when Tim was prone to crushes on men twice his age. But Shep did not seem much like a man in his forties. *Youthful, intense, romantic, troubled, dedicated, solitary*—these were some of the words that came to Tim to describe Shep. *Arrogant, irresponsible, paranoid, bullying, selfish,* and *drunk* came also but remained unspoken.

Nona said, "I was wondering, since you were so much younger than he, did you ever have the feeling that you were like a son to him? I mean, was he ever—paternal?"

Yikes. "Well, it's funny that you should say that, because I remember that I often felt as if *I* were the father to *his* child—one of those wild, hyperactive kids who run their parents ragged," said Tim. "A real enfant terrible," he added, laughing, whereupon a pain he had no idea he'd been carrying around with him all these years made itself felt. It propelled

Tim right up out of his chair. "Um—I was thinking of making myself a drink. Are you sure you won't join me?" he asked, and was relieved when Nona said that, after all, she would.

He mixed them each a vodka martini, and as he was setting the glasses down Nona said, "There is a French proverb that goes, In love there is always one who kisses and the other who offers the cheek."

Tim laughed again. "Oh, yes, I suppose you could say we were that kind of couple—if you could call us a couple. The last thing in the world Shep wanted was another marriage. He insisted on his freedom, and he didn't like it if you crowded him. He hated it when I tried to take care of him, or even if I tried to get him to take better care of himself. Don't get wifey on me, he'd say." It was disconcerting to be watched so closely as you spoke. Outside, a truck horn blew, sirens keened in the downtown distance, and his upstairs neighbor, who was dying, put on Billie Holiday. More horn-blowing from below, a voice cried "Asshole!" very loud, and then came, louder, "Asshole your fucking *self!*"

Nona said, "When I set out to write this book, I don't think I had any doubt that Shep was going to come out as some kind of hero. To hear someone like Benedict Stone talk, you'd think he *was* a hero. And maybe, in the way he was devoted to his work and kept on working even when he was having no success at all—I suppose there was something heroic about that. But I keep coming up against all kinds of things I'm having trouble getting down on the page. I've only just begun to realize how much must have been concealed from me when I was growing up. I knew our family was not perfectly happy, of course, but I thought we were normal enough. Mother always home, father always out—that wasn't so unusual. Mother wanting more attention, father too busy—you saw that everywhere you looked. But I know I had no idea back then how miserable my parents must have been. My guess is Shep wanted out of that marriage from the time he arrived in New

York and discovered the possibility of a whole other kind of life—the kind of life he was living when he met you. I've been told that he was not very discreet about his affairs, and if my mother had been a little sharper, she'd have caught on a lot sooner, and maybe that's precisely what he wanted to happen. I think my mother must have figured all this out for herself, and maybe that's why she wanted nothing to do with him after they broke up. I used to be outraged when she claimed that she was only trying to protect me by keeping me away from him, but maybe she really was trying to do that—protect me, I mean, not just from the knowledge that he was gay, but from the knowledge that he didn't care about me. She, of course, knew better than anyone how devastating the truth could be."

This is unbearable, Tim thought. "But had he lived, everything might have been different," he said. "Times change, people change. I've seen it happen a lot—estranged kids and their parents getting back together." For two long years he and his mother had not spoken, during which time she consulted her clergyman and her heart and, thank God, chose to heed the latter.

"Yes. Had he lived. But it seems he was as careless with his life as he was with everyone else's feelings."

If he'd been worried that alcohol might turn things soppy, he needn't have been. Nona had drunk her drink rather quickly, but it seemed to have affected only her pallor, suffused now with pink. What Tim saw of her father in her now was his utter lack of sentimentality. Tim was grateful for this. It helped him to be honest.

"I suppose what I am looking for," she said, "is some evidence that he cared about someone else besides himself."

Tim shook his head. "No, I can't say that I'm that person or even that I know that such a person existed. I have loved and been loved, and I know what love is, and what love does and doesn't do. The truth is, I had left him. Life had become intolerable. He was very unhappy at that point and he took everything out on me—I was his whipping boy. He was always making fun of me."

"For—?"

"Oh, let's see. For having a degree in art history and for taking my job at the gallery so seriously. For having any interest in art at all."

"Why?"

"Because I wasn't an artist myself, you see, so what could I possibly know about it. And he hated dealers and curators and critics—anyone connected to the art world who wasn't an artist—and most artists, too, for that matter, at least among the living. They were all parasites, they were the enemy, and I worked for a gallery, so I was one of them. I sometimes think one of the reasons I changed careers was because Shep had spoiled that whole world for me. What else did he make fun of me for. . . . He made fun of me for using emery boards, I remember, and hand lotion. For being concerned about paying the rent on time and for talking too much to my mother on the phone. He said I was servile, said I was a namby-pamby, he made me cry, made fun of me for crying, told me to run home to Mama, which is what I did. I mean I went home to Arkansas for a couple of weeks—just to get away from him. I told him I was going, but I didn't give him my mother's number. He died while I was gone. I'll never know whether he would have tried to reach me and whether I could have made it back in time. You know, I was too young then to understand what was happening. Those last months he was so far gone. He was drunk most of the time, he'd stopped washing, he reeked, when he talked he didn't always make sense, and sometimes he'd break off in midsentence and stare into space. If I saw anyone I cared about behaving that way now, I'd get him to the doctor—at gunpoint, if necessary. Obviously he was having some kind of breakdown."

As if to herself Nona said, "Runs in the family."

Tim cringed. Had he said too much too soon? Nona had

turned to the window again, and now he could see: she did appear to be studying her own reflection. Upstairs, his neighbor, who was sometimes light-headed these days, dropped or knocked something over. "I'm sorry—" Tim began.

"Oh, no, no," she said. "I was just thinking how lucky it is that I don't have children." She was looking at him intently again. "I understand you still have a lot of Shep's paintings."

"Yes," he said, only too happy to turn from the man to the work. "I've taken good care of everything. I'm not sure how familiar you are with his work, but some of it is very fine." He shook his head to clear it of an image of Pearl Verga sneering. "Every couple of years I make the rounds to see if I can interest some gallery in doing a show. So far all I've gotten is offers to take certain paintings on consignment, though, and that's not what I want."

"Why do you do it? I mean, you don't owe him anything."

"Oh, I want to do it. I like the work, first of all—always have. And think of all the art that would have been lost to the world if someone hadn't stepped in to take care of things after the artist died. Over the years, I've turned a lot of friends on to Shep's work and it's been very satisfying. Now you come along—and how would you feel if you discovered that most of the work hadn't survived? How would I feel being the one to have to tell you that? Besides, it's not a lot of trouble, really. I don't do that much. And you know what Shep would say, don't you?" Nona shook her head. "'You're not doing *enough*.'" Which reminded Tim of a funny story. "You remember about ten years ago when the van Gogh *Irises* was sold, and it was front-page news? That day when I went to the newsstand the man there said to me, 'Look at that, forty-nine million bucks, and the guy died broke. You know, his brother used to be his dealer. Can you imagine if van Gogh knew what was going on today? Kicking his brother in the pants: And *you* couldn't sell my goddamn paintings!'"

They both laughed. Tim explained to Nona how most of

Shep's paintings had ended up on Long Island. "You're welcome to come out sometime. I'd be delighted to show them to you. I'll be opening the house up again in April."

There was one painting he could have shown her right now, but he hesitated. Then he noticed the time.

"Oh, dear. It's seven-thirty already and I'm afraid I made plans for tonight and I have to go meet someone." He also had to bring dinner to his neighbor upstairs before going out, but this he did not mention. "Of course, we can get together again. And I was thinking. There's so much I don't remember. I don't know if it will help, but I could go back over my journals from that time and see what might be in there about Shep." Had anyone suggested an hour ago that he even consider doing such a thing—how Tim would have balked! But, like the invitation to his country house, this offer had come to him quite naturally.

Now Nona was gone and Tim was alone again. As he was changing his clothes in the bedroom, he studied the painting he had been unready to show her: an unframed oil, four feet by three feet, hanging on the wall above the bed. It had not always hung there. Tim had rediscovered it and taken it out of storage only about two years ago. A male nude, very flat and angular, and very pale against a maroon background. When it was done, Shep, who belittled the results, had given it to Tim, who was at first too self-conscious (it was not a shrinking pose) and later too bereft to want to display it. Now it reminded him of his youth and of his early, happy days with Shep. Brief but incandescent that time had been, when love meant being worshiped head to foot.

In the kitchen Tim piled a plate with food he'd picked up on his way home from work: an herbed chicken breast, risotto with truffles, lima beans with spinach and artichokes. Less than half would get eaten, he knew—all the more reason that it must be delicious. He heated the plate in the microwave and placed it on a tray along with a bowl of chilled fresh fruit salad.

Music swirled through the hallway as he climbed the stairs. "Oh, what a little moonlight can do—" Tim was one of about half a dozen people who'd been given keys to that apartment. He sang out cheerily as he opened the door: "Hel—lo—oh!"

A wraith in pajamas gestured feebly from the place where he had fallen on the floor. His name was Lloyd, he was thirty-one, and he would not live through the spring.

chapter
eleven

With an hour free between lessons today, Roy went to a coffee bar. He ordered a cappuccino and sat down at the counter with his book, but he could not read because there was loud music playing. The number of places you could go where music was not playing was getting smaller all the time; he supposed public libraries would be next. He was amazed at how willing most people were to give up quiet. Once, in a restaurant, when he asked to have the stereo turned down, he got dirty looks from everybody and someone said, "That's the saddest thing, man, when people hate music." But how could people who loved music stand hearing it as background for every banal human activity? Why was it assumed that because he wanted a cappuccino he wanted also to hear this schlocky recording of *The Four Seasons*?

Two young women sat down next to Roy and, because of the music, they almost had to shout at each other. Roy slammed his book shut and thumped it down on the counter—if you can't beat 'em, join 'em—and turned his attention to the scene outside the window. Now this, at least, was entertaining: Broadway—the most diverse promenade in the world—stepping to the strains of Vivaldi. Faces of fascinating beauty and no-less-fascinating ugliness. A bevy of young dancers in pink tights and Psyche knots followed by a heavy-muscled, tattooed gnome who might have been the eunuch escorting them back to the harem. And—was it possible?—every tenth person on wheels? Roy started counting—until something brilliant caught his eye: the red hair of a woman stepping from a cab into the sun—a flame that singed his heart.

"I can't believe she's going to marry him."

"What do you mean? You said he was real nice and real smart."

"Yeah, but he's also real short and real bald."

"Oh, god."

"And he's got these, like, funny lips."

"Funny lips?"

"Yeah. I don't know how to describe them. They kind of, like, stick out?"

As the women laughed, Roy indulged his mean streak by imagining the shoe pinching the other foot. "I can't believe he's going to marry her. She's real nice and real smart, but she's got no tits, and she's got these funny hips." "Funny hips?" "Yeah, they kind of, like, stick out?"

Just last night, over drinks with his friend Anthony, the conversation had drifted into these waters.

"It's okay for a woman to put down a man's body," Anthony said. "Tess says to me, Anyone who believes in penis envy has never seen one up close. She would never understand if I were offended by that."

"Were you offended?"

"No. I thought it was funny. Are you offended?"

"No."

"Well, there you go."

("Are you offended," a woman once asked Roy, "because I didn't swallow? My ex-boyfriend—it really bothered him that I didn't swallow. I said to him, Are you crazy? That shit is *alive*.")

Anthony said, "I remember, years ago, when AIDS first

appeared, and this lesbian comic said, It just confirms what I've always known: semen is poison."

They both thought that was funny, too.

These days, Roy had on his mind certain things he'd more or less not had to think about for the past five years. He had entered what was the second of only two periods in his life when he'd been promiscuous. The other time was during his last year of school, and the difference between then and now astonished him. Unless he'd been kidding himself, the women he'd had sex with in school had enjoyed it as much as he had. He was unprepared for the gamut of pleasure-diminishing anxieties that now went with the territory. (Because times had changed? Because he was older? Both, of course, but hard to say which weighed more.)

Channel-surfing late one wakeful night, Roy tuned in to a female talking head: "Any time a man sleeps with a woman without any emotional feeling for her, without having at least some idea that he might want to have more than just a sexual relationship—that man is abusing that woman, and he should admit that that's what he's doing."

Not exactly "All intercourse is rape," but dishearteningly close.

Maybe he *was* fooling himself about those women back in school.

The new etiquette said it was always better to wait for the woman to bring up the issue of safety first. "It's okay for her to imply that she's afraid you might have a sexually transmissible disease, but for you to do the same—that would be like calling her a whore" (Anthony).

The bars of the Upper West Side were filled with women looking for a good time: a man could make this mistake. What they were really looking for was the other thing. Each and every one Roy met. It was a shame, because— (Here he scrupulously squelched a thought that was just a hair's breadth away from Why can't a woman be more like a man.) In fact,

Roy believed he was seeing something for the first time: there was nothing more vulnerable than a woman who'd been drinking going home with a strange man. And what did that say about him? What was all this screwing around about, anyway? *Do not let my penis make a slave of my neck.* Back in school, Roy had split his sides when he came across this, in an anthropology book. Do not let my penis make a slave of my neck! So prayed the Ashanti. Now it kept coming back to him. He would often repeat it, almost unthinkingly, to himself. O Lord, do not let my penis make a slave of my neck. Not laughing now.

He had made one friend, at least. This was Francesca—Fran—who lived in New Jersey and worked in Manhattan (she was a proofreader), while dreaming of making movies in Hollywood (she had gone to the NYU Film School). She knew a couple who lived on the same floor as the apartment where Roy was staying. Fran and Roy met at the elevator one evening—she'd been visiting her friends, he was going out to a bar. Sixteen floors later they had reached the lobby and a decision: straight back up they went. ("Oh, wow, a Steinway. Oh, wow, I *love* cats.") She was one of those people who often point to their ethnicity to explain things about themselves. ("You have such beautiful skin." "All those generations eating olive oil." "Do you like opera?" "It's in my blood, isn't it?")

Hint of panic on both sides when it came out that Roy was not the concert pianist whose playing Fran had once admired from the hall. . . .

She left before he was up the next morning, and he was still asleep when she called him an hour later, from work.

"Listen, about last night? I have to tell you something: that was one big terrible mistake."

"I was that bad?"

She laughed. "No, no. What I'm saying is, I broke my own rule. Never get involved with a man who hasn't been single for at least one year."

"I see. Well, sure, that makes sense."

"I mean, I could tell you some sob stories."

"Oh, no, that's okay. I understand."

He paid no attention when she said she wanted them to be friends and was surprised to discover that she meant it. Things were awkward at first, but then Fran met another man, also once married but unattached for the required twelvemonth, and the new romance was thriving. She was warm and gregarious by nature, Fran; love made her only more so. Roy enjoyed the time he spent with her. She was a good friend and a comfort to him. She was easy to talk to, and they talked a lot. She knew his whole story and she said that she was worried about him, and when she said this to Roy, that she was worried, it was a great comfort to him.

Later that day, after Roy had given his second lesson and Fran had finished work, they met at a bar in a midtown hotel. Hotel bars and restaurants were Fran's favorite places. Being surrounded by tourists gave her the illusion that she was traveling abroad, she said.

Whenever they met, they talked about Nona. Fran liked to be kept up-to-date. Not that there was much to tell. Things stood pretty much the same between Roy and Nona. In the beginning, he had been certain that they would be back together even before word of their separation got widely around. So certain that, when his mother happened to call on the very day Roy was moving, he said nothing—why worry your mom unnecessarily? But as the winter dragged on, he had been forced to break the bad news, and to see the future differently. He could tell that Nona missed him, but he could tell also that she wanted to be alone. Fran said she did not believe that anyone ever really wanted to be alone. The few times Roy and Nona saw each other, they managed not to quarrel but seemed to be under some kind of spell that made talking difficult. An eerie calm had settled between them. At times Nona seemed to Roy almost dangerously withdrawn. He tried not to perceive this as coldness toward him, but there were moments when he was shaken by the unthinkable: she was slipping away from him. And something else was tormenting Roy. From time to time he caught himself accepting that she was gone, almost resigned, as she seemed to be resigned, to the inevitability of divorce—and in the wake of these feelings came convulsions of guilt. Giving up—accepting that Nona was gone—wasn't that in some way saying that he did not want her back?

To Fran, it was all a conundrum.

"She goes to Arizona to spend a weekend with some guy, she realizes her mistake and that all she really wants is you, she comes home, you forgive her, she leaves you, you want her back. What's right with this picture?"

It was happy hour. The bar was packed. Again, everyone had to scream to be heard. Roy and Fran were sitting at a chessboard-sized table squeezed between four Japanese men on one side and a family from Montreal on the other.

"See what I mean?" said Fran. "We could be in Rome, right?" Roy laughed. She was funny, Fran. She leaned forward over her Mai Tai (Fran liked tropical drinks no matter the season) and said, "Don't you wish you really were in Italy right now?"

The next ten seconds belonged to another world. The room before Roy dimmed and blurred, a whirring sound filled his ears, and something grazed his cheek. It was as if an invisible bird had circled his head.

"Are you cold, Roy?"

"What? Oh, sorry, no. I was just thinking about Venice."

"Oh, no wonder. I take it you've been there, too?"

"Yes, but it was long ago and only for a few days." His first trip abroad, just out of school: two dozen cities in one scalding, penniless, exhausting summer. He had a story about Venice he thought Fran might appreciate, but she jerked him back to the here and now.

"Why on earth did you let her go to Arizona in the first place?"

How Roy had come to hate this question, which nobody seemed willing to spare him. "Because I didn't think it was for me to stop her, okay? Because I didn't think you could tell other people what to do with their bodies. I knew the guy was a jerk. I knew she making a mistake. I'd already tried to warn her. What was I supposed to do—tie her up and sit on her? I thought women didn't want to be treated like property anymore." He stopped, aware that he had raised his voice even louder than necessary.

Fran said, "It sounds like you're still pretty angry."

Roy shook his head. "Right now I'm more desolate than angry. I think she's behaved badly, of course—destructively, stupidly. I'm disappointed in her for that. I'm disappointed in both of us, to be honest. For not taking better care of each other, for letting the marriage fall apart—because I refuse to believe any of this had to happen. And I feel—humiliated by the whole business. I feel there's something, I don't know—regressive about it. Do you know what I mean? I look at myself and I say, This is not where I should be at this point in my life. That goes for her, too. It seems to me we should be past this sort of thing. I'm beginning to think maybe it's true what they say: people who never have children never really grow up."

Although Roy was usually comfortable talking with Fran, today for some reason he could not bear to go on and he turned the subject to Fran's new boyfriend, to whom she had introduced Roy just recently. He listened with melancholy envy as she talked about this actor/bartender—not at all the handsome charismatic genius Roy had been told to prepare himself to meet, but nice, very nice. And lucky, thought Roy. She was salt of the earth, Fran. He saw them married, of course—Hollywood dreams hung back among the stars; he saw children with beautiful skin and strong white teeth, one big beaming healthy family, everyone thriving on love and olive oil.

"Hey, hey, hey now." Fran reached for his hand.

"I'm sorry. It's the alcohol, I guess."

The clatter had died down on either side of them. The Canadians stared. The Japanese looked away.

"It's going to be okay, Roy, you'll see. The world will turn right side up again. Everyone has to go through times like this. You'll get over it, I promise."

The tender clichés poured from her lips. Her hand on his hand, her knees against his knees under the table were a comfort to him.

"I'm sorry," he said again. "It's just—everything—my whole life—is different. Not really knowing what's going on—being here with you—not sure how I feel—" He hiccupped. "Oh, dear. I think I'd better be going, Fran."

Outside, she held him a long time before saying good-bye. "Call me," she said as he put her in a cab for Penn Station. "I'm worried about you."

The temperature was below freezing and he was thirty blocks from home, but Roy decided to walk. He was faintly woozy from the Scotch he had drunk, and the thought of getting into any kind of moving vehicle sickened him. He had no scarf. He had no gloves. These were among several items, like his umbrella and his Mont Blanc pen, that Roy had managed to lose recently—a measure of his distraction.

It was good to walk, good to breathe the frosty air. His head grew clearer with every step—or, rather, stride, for he was covering ground at an athletic pace. The best ideas come while walking—didn't Nietzsche say that? So maybe Roy would have a brainstorm. But the only idea that came to him was that he should eat something. He stopped at a pizzeria and had two thick hot oily slices: dinner. Since moving uptown, Roy had yet to cook a meal.

Those dinners he used to prepare every night—the pleasure

he took in cooking for Nona—her requests for certain dishes—his chicken with couscous, his avocado mousse, his lemon pound cake. That was him? That was his life? That was just a couple of months ago?

He was shivering by the time he got home; small creatures were hanging by sharp teeth from his ears and his nose. Without taking off his coat he went straight to the phone and dialed his old number. Oh, what a bitter moment that had been, when Nona changed the message on their answering machine, letting the whole world know: "If you're calling for Roy . . ." He winced each time he was forced to hear it.

Getting the machine did not mean that she wasn't there; Nona often screened her calls. Nevertheless, Roy hung up. He could not have said why, other than that he was feeling too raw. If he spoke and she didn't pick up he'd spend the rest of the night plucking petals off poison daisies: She was there. (She just didn't want to hear from him.) She was not there. (So where the hell was she?)

He thought of calling Fran, but it was too soon; she would be on the train still. He wanted to apologize for spoiling their evening—or did he really just want to hear her voice again?

Still wearing his coat, Roy went and sat down at the piano. He played for about an hour—pianissimo, so as not to disturb the neighbors. Some Chopin, some Satie. No, Roy was not a concert pianist, but he could play. He played very well. Smetana waltzes—pieces he used to play way, way back in Minnesota, when he had an after-school job at the local ballet studio. All those pretty dancing girls, one of whom, he had no doubt, he would grow up to marry. Finally, he played "In My Life," softly singing the words.

Thank you, thank you—bowing to the three cats who sat in a row on the carpet.

There—that was better. At last Roy took off his coat.

He tried calling Nona again, and again he got the machine and hung up. He thought of calling Fran, who'd be home by now, but decided she'd probably had enough of him for one night. He shook his head, remembering his peculiar baffling response at the mention of Italy. Venice. In the pensione where he was staying, an American woman whose room was on the same floor passed him one day on her way to the shower, wearing nothing but a towel. Ten minutes later she knocked at his door, her hair slicked back, in her towel. "I'm all squeaky clean now. Would you like to make me dirty?"

Better he had not told that story to Fran, now that he thought about it. Probably she would not have believed it. Women often had trouble believing that women like that existed outside male fantasy. But she had been flesh, all right, that Ohioan: stripping her towel away, narrow-eyed, gently gloating at his excitement.

The cats followed Roy into the bedroom, watched him take off his shoes, and then everyone got onto the bed. I will miss them when I move, he thought, rubbing the head of the nearest one. He turned on the television and stared at the news without listening, fighting the desire to get up and put on his shoes and coat again and go out to a bar. The weatherman filled the screen with maps and smiling sun-faces and frowning cloud-faces. Roy was thinking about something that had happened about a year ago. He'd been walking in the street, a few steps ahead of a man and a boy. They passed the windows of a lingerie shop. "Look," said the man. "Brassieres. Do you know what a brassiere is?" "Stop it," said the boy. "Just stop." "Tits. Do you know what titties are?" "*Stop!*" Not— oh, surely not father and son? Roy had prayed as he turned to look at them. He would never forget the taunting leer on that man's face; and that boy, no more than eight or nine, slinking near the curb with his fingers in his ears.

The incident had haunted Roy for weeks. When he told Nona about it: "Poor Roy," she said. "You've lived such a sheltered life." But she said it coldly, with a touch of exasperation and perhaps even contempt, as if she thought he had no right not knowing that this was the sort of world it was. "Of course they were father and son."

He was not in the habit of looking at himself critically, Roy; the sheltered rarely are. Only now, for the first time, did he expose himself to this merciless light in which he appeared neither bad nor good but small, feckless, superfluous, with no special purpose or reason for his being. His work still brought him rewards, and he thought that it always would, but there were others who could do his job just as well as he, and he knew this. And none knew better than he the difference between his own calling and that of, say, the musician on whose bed he now lay, or the baritone he'd been coaching that afternoon and whose Iago that season would bring down the house. As he had said to Fran, he did not think he was where he should have been at this point in his life. Just where he thought he should have been he wasn't altogether sure. But if true success was what he believed it to be, that is, making at least one other person happy, well, certainly he had not done that. Worse: he had not even tried to do that. It had been part of his perfect stupidity to assume that all he had to do was to be himself, and the rest would follow. After all, no one had ever demanded more of him than this: that Roy be Roy.

He didn't need people to keep asking him why he had not stopped Nona from going to Tucson. He knew the way he answered that question was dishonest and irrelevant and unworthy of him. He had been weak when she needed him to be strong. He knew that this was what his real mistake had been.

He wanted to say all this to Nona—all this that he was just beginning to understand and that, while it filled him with pain filled him also with awe, for he was aware that something immense was taking place, working changes in him that would mark him forever. But whenever he tried to express these things, the words would not come—as if, for having been silent when he should have spoken, he were now struck dumb.

Here was a lesson Roy was learning about life: innocence is punished more swiftly than evil.

Tits. Do you know what titties are?

"You think that's bad," Nona had said. "This guy in the Bronx has just been arrested for sewing up his daughter's vagina."

Stop!

For some weeks now Roy had been living with the sense that he was being tested. Everyone had to go through times like this, as Fran had reminded him. On every human map: the cloud-faces and the sun-faces. But what troubled Roy—what kept him constantly on edge—was the belief that a much graver ordeal was in store for him—an ordeal he feared he would not have the strength to meet and so he would be destroyed by it. He had lost the gift he'd always had—and that makes the happy happy—of abiding in the present, and acquired the curse that keeps the anxious anxious: the imagination for disaster. A sense of failure and futility, of the inevitability of loss and the end of love—this was always with Roy, now that Nona was not. Let no one say he had not loved her. But it was not enough. It was not enough.

chapter
twelve

Tim had invited Nona to spend the weekend at his country house, but that Wednesday his neighbor Lloyd died, and the funeral was on Saturday; and so it was another week before they all drove out to Long Island: Tim, Nona, and Andrew, in Tim's car. Tim apologized for not being able to extend his invitation to Pip: Andrew was allergic. Nona asked another dog owner in her building to walk Pip while she was gone.

"You'll like it," Tim told her. "It's my favorite time of year out there, even though we can't swim." The daffodils and the cherry blossoms were in bloom. The house was old and roomy and smelled of earth. It had white shingles and blue shutters. The perfect spring weekend: equal parts sun and rain. Of course they could not swim: just to walk near the water they had to wear coats. In the evening Andrew built a fire while Tim cooked. Andrew would eat no meat or fish or dairy products, and Tim rose to this challenge with platters of vegetables and grains and beans—all delicious, though still Andrew complained: too much garlic. When he said that, about the garlic, Nona avoided looking at Tim. She didn't like Andrew—and not just because he was allergic to Pip. She had the impression he had stayed in school not so much because he wanted to further his education as that he was afraid to let go of his youth.

He had had the kind of beauty that can inspire fear in the beholder. Now he was merely good-looking. Lately he was despondent about his hair. "I keep telling him to get a crew cut," Tim said. "It would minimize the receding hairline and accentuate his great bone structure." But to sacrifice what remained of that thick, blue-black glory—the hair of an Indian brave, Nona thought—Andrew could not bring himself to do that. He was also despondent about his waistline: "If it gets any worse, I'm going to start using a body double for sex." All this kept his lover on tenterhooks. Tim had once described Andrew as the kind of person who could breathe all the air in a room, whose funks and peeves were impossible to ignore. Tim fussed ceaselessly over him. Was Andrew tired? Was Andrew bored? Tire*some*, bor*ing*, amended Nona, who felt sorry for Tim. Long before he lost his figure or his hair, Andrew would be gone. And Tim would suffer—but then, very soon, he would fall in love again. He was like Chekhov's Darling: always devoted to someone, unable to exist without loving. He was like the one in the French proverb who is always doing the kissing.

"You know, Shep wasn't a bad cook," Tim said. "I'd forgotten all about it, but now I recall he had a way with omelettes."

Nona was learning more and more about her father like this. Little things, like Shep's way with omelettes, kept occurring to Tim, who would share them with her. And no matter how small the detail, Nona seized it. She was seriously back to work on the book now, and it was because of Tim that she felt much encouraged. She had grown very fond of Tim over the winter. Like most people, she had found that making friends came less and less easily as she grew older; she had not bonded with anyone like this in a long time.

And so, to be fair, wasn't her dislike of Andrew partly jealousy? She wanted Tim all to herself, didn't she. Yes—but it didn't help that Andrew reminded her of someone she hated.

"Well," said Tim, when he had heard about Lyle, "I hope he

was worth it." A remark that made Nona cringe. There was something that had been preying on her since Tucson. When Tim heard, he said, "Why don't you go get tested—set your mind at rest?"

Saturday afternoon was spent hauling canvases up from the basement into the brighter light of the living room. It was the first time Nona had seen so much of her father's work at once. The paintings with which she was most familiar were the three from the *Gladiator* series that had belonged to Benedict. Years ago, when Nona moved back to New York for school, Benedict had wanted to give her one, and she had refused. Now they belonged to Phoebe. Not long after Nona had started writing her book, she and Roy traveled to the Cleveland Museum of Art, where she saw the *Shoeshine Triptych* for the first time. And by now, of course, she had also had a chance to study the nude hanging in Tim's bedroom. It had always troubled Nona that not a single work of Shep's had ended up in Rosalind's possession. This had everything to do with the circumstances of their divorce, but Nona thought things might have been different had Rosalind appreciated the paintings more. "Boxers! Why boxers? And why did everyone he painted look like they'd been stretched on the rack?" It was an agony to sit for him, Rosalind said, knowing how you were going to turn out. And it wasn't that she didn't have any faith in his talent or his vision, but of course she would have been happier if he'd done something more to her taste. In that respect, she said, "I wouldn't have minded being Mrs. Bonnard."

Shep's own idols had been Goya and Manet, early Manet, especially: this was a detail Tim had culled from his journals.

Nona had never seen her father paint, but she had a clear memory of his studio. The Chock Full o'Nuts cans chock full of brushes, the stained floor and the stiff, impossibly filthy rags—she would not have believed any adult capable of such a mess and was amazed that her mess-hating mother did not seem to care. Rubbery blobs of color sat on the metal tabletop he used as a palette. Some of these looked hard and dry, but if you squeezed one, out plopped a smaller, brighter clot, which delighted Nona—she could have done that all day. Windows, windows everywhere—even in the ceiling: Nona thought it must be the sunniest room in the world. And that smell, which her mother claimed always gave her a headache but which Nona (to this day) loved to inhale. Turpentine: *her* madeleine.

Arriving at the studio one day. All the windows open to the fine spring air and the jazzy sound of traffic rising from Broadway. Her parents kiss, and Nona is seized by a giddy joy that sets her spinning in circles around the room, faster and faster, as they kiss and kiss, until she is stopped by a wall. Shattering pain on the right side of her face. She slides to the floor, leaving a stroke of cadmium red on the white wall. When she comes to she is aloft, embraced in strong arms against heaving chest, looking up at the most beautiful face she has ever seen. And even then—even as a child—she knew: love does not go deeper than this.

He struck her once, on that same side of her head. Forgotten for long periods of her life but never forgiven. Punished for speaking her wish: "Why can't Mommy just die and leave us alone?"

"As far as I'm concerned," Tim said, "these paintings are yours. You can take whatever you want."

Nona would have liked to take them all, but where would she put them? With an impulse that was half mischievous, half sentimental, she set aside two: a self-portrait and a portrait of Rosalind. Both had been painted around the same time, the mid-fifties. "It's wicked of me, but I can't resist." She meant to bring them together on her living-room wall.

"Was he really that weird-looking?" Andrew asked.

Tim laughed and said no. "Even so, that's a pretty good likeness."

"He looks like he's had his nose broken a couple of times."

"And I can assure you my mother's skin never looked like that, either," said Nona, also laughing.

"Really," said Andrew, examining the impastoed surface up close. "She looks—*flayed*."

Sunday night they drove back to Manhattan with the two paintings strapped to the roof of Tim's Volvo.

THAT SPRING, PHOEBE'S aunt Josie died. Phoebe, who had spent the coldest part of the winter elsewhere, as usual, was now back in Timber Lake.

"She knew she was dying last summer when she was here," she wrote to Nona, "though she didn't tell us then. She was seventy." Nona grimaced. Her mother's age exactly. "Toward the end she refused all food and medication, and she suffered a lot." Phoebe's letter was full of bad news. The house had been broken into while she was gone. "They shat on the carpets, gutted the sofas and chairs, carved obscenities into the dining table, and smashed most of the dishes. Every room in the house—it must have taken them all day. They poured water into the piano, tore pages out of books in the library, and slashed Josie's portrait of you." But here Nona's heart lifted: she was not at all sorry to hear that that painting had been destroyed.

It had happened once before, when Nona's hairdresser died: for months afterward, she kept seeing him. Now, at the supermarket, in the subway, at the Museum of Modern Art, Josie appeared. In the museum Nona forgot herself and uttered an astonished *hello!*, startling that poor old unsuspecting woman.

BY NOW THE FRIEND IN whose apartment Roy had been staying had returned and Roy had moved. Another friend, a composer who lived in Chelsea, had gone off to an artists' colony for two months and was only too glad to have someone stay at his place, which had been burglarized twice already.

Meanwhile, Nona had taken on a second job, teaching private lessons at a language school near Rockefeller Center. Most of the students were businessmen whose companies paid the high fees that the school charged. All except one of Nona's students were Japanese. The exception was a thirteen-year-old Korean boy who had been sent to live in New York for several years to learn "American." His father wanted him to go to an American college. A great round jolly boy built like a young sumo wrestler. For homework one day Nona had asked him to write a letter to someone—anyone he wished—back in Seoul. She read the letter after their lesson, when she had a few minutes before her next student. He had written to his father— although, as he explained, his father could not read English.

> Dear Father, who are you? My English teacher asks I write you. She is nice but she teaches at other school and private lesson is for her only subsidiary business. Father, I am homesick! Many times! And many times I think of you! Why I have to be go so far away from you? Father, I know I am not always good. Sometime I don't study. Sometime I think to the girls and I want to go to the girls but from girls I know I could go to drugs, and I am afraid! Father, I know sometime I am thinking bad thoughts and how you can become angry with me. But I am not the bad son! Father, you know I only helpless teenager! Father, father, why you never hold me to you! Why you never speak the loving words!

Mr. Toshida arrived right on time, as usual, and as usual he was beaming (Mr. Toshida loved his English classes), but as he sat down at the desk across from Nona, his face changed. "Something wrong?"

Nona shook her head and reached into her book bag for *Idioms in American Life*. "How are you today, Mr. Toshida?"

"Yes," he said. "Something wrong. Please." He held his palms out to her. "Spit out. Spit out."

Nona smiled and shook her head again. "I'm all right, really, but thank you. Thank you." And as she opened her book she thought how kind Mr. Toshida was, and how we are saved by this, again and again: the unlooked-for kindness of other people.

She still had the garnet ring that stewardess had given her.

ONE OF NONA'S NEW YEAR'S resolutions had been to join a health club. She was there one day when, passing by one of the studios on her way to the weight room, she glanced in and saw that the entire class was standing on their hands. She watched the class for a few minutes and, later, happening to see the teacher as they both were leaving the club, Nona asked, "Was that a gymnastics class?" The teacher smiled. "Yes. Indian gymnastics. Otherwise known as yoga." Yoga? But Nona had taken yoga; it was nothing like what she'd just seen. "There are many kinds of yoga," the teacher explained. "There is hard yoga and soft yoga. You find the style that's right for you. Now, if you're feeling adventurous and want something challenging, you might try my class."

And so it began. No one could have been more surprised than Nona herself. She had never done much strenuous exercise—she had never done any sports at all. To balance on her hands, or on her head, or on her forearms (most difficult of all)—this was asking a great deal of Nona. The yoga she had done before—for example, with Phoebe's daughter-in-law, last summer—might have been soft, but for Nona it was hard enough. She was not double-jointed: how would she ever be able to do those contortions? By doing them every day, was the simple answer. And if she did them every day, with courage and integrity and a full heart, she would be transfigured, inside and out. So promised the teacher, whose name was Nika.

Impossible to say what age this woman was: her hair was completely gray—almost white—but she had huge eyes as limpid as a baby's, and no wrinkles at all. Her bones were birdlike, her muscles as small as a child's, but she was stronger than most men. She had an accent Nona could not place, either. In the dressing room once, she overheard someone say that Nika was multilingual and had lived all over the world. Nona would not have been surprised to hear that she had lived on other worlds as well. *Otherworldly* was a word Nika brought to mind. Also: *incandescent*. To burn with a hard, gemlike flame—Nika was the first person Nona had ever met who appeared capable of Pater's famous strange ideal.

Yoga was work: sweaty, arduous, often frustrating work. According to Nika, it was meant to be frustrating. "And you must be grateful for that. Give thanks for any resistance or discomfort that you feel, because this gives you something to overcome, and that is how you become strong."

The next step, as Nona understood it, was to bring what you had learned through yoga to the rest of your frustrating life.

None of this would have made much sense to Nona, except that, after yoga class, she did not feel frustrated or fatigued or uncomfortable in any way. Vibrant, light, purged—her mind calm but alert—Nona left the health club feeling like singing. And, in fact, the chanting and the breathing exercises that were part of class brought Nona back to her singing days. Vibration was intrinsic to yoga. Tension and release—the basis of all music—was at the heart of yoga as well.

Not everything Nona heard in class was she able to swallow. She knew that aging no more than time can be reversed and that daily practice of the Forward Bend, the asana said to eliminate all diseases from the body, could not have saved Josie from hers. She doubted whether turning upside down for five minutes a day could strengthen the heart as effectively as jogging. She almost laughed out loud when she heard women compared to vacuum cleaners, forever sucking up negative energy and needing a way to get rid of it—hence, menstruation. She had the same problem with the explanation for tightness in the hips: most childhood trauma is stored there. As ye sow so shall ye reap? Yes, Nona believed in some kind of karma. But transmigration? "Remember, it is only in this life that you have your physical body to work with. After this life your energy goes elsewhere." (Why should Nona care where her energy went, if she didn't get to go with it?)

Generosity: this word came up a lot in yoga. The class was often reminded of the need to be generous when attempting certain postures—the Backward Bend Cycle, for example—and urged to *lift* or *open* or *offer* the heart. If you were getting tired, and the posture seemed impossible to hold even for another second: "Try doing it for someone else. Do it for the person next to you." Sometimes, at the beginning of class, Nika suggested that everyone dedicate that day's practice to another person, and Nona had dedicated classes to different people, like Roy and Tim—she had even dedicated a class to Pip, though she wasn't sure dogs could be included and she would have died before asking. A meditation exercise they were often asked to do was to send a ray of bright caressing light to someone that they loved, and again Nona sometimes sent her ray to Pip. Once, Nika gave them what she called a much more difficult exercise: sending that ray of light to someone they hated. "I cannot tell you how many years it took me to be able to do this exercise," she said. Nona, squeezing her eyes shut and struggling grimly, knew that, for her, a lifetime would not be enough.

Be generous. Open your heart. Like any good exercise, yoga could make you stronger—but could it also make you kinder? Could it make you braver, as believers said it would? How many Hero and Warrior asanas would you have to do, say, before rape held no more terror for you? Or before you could face with serenity the kind of suffering Josie had endured? Could the yogi really learn to lose all fear of death? Certainly, from the very first class, Nona was happy to have discovered yoga. And, once she had practiced enough to be able to hold the postures reasonably well, if not perfectly, she was happier still. She understood that the goal was to become so adept that you needed no teacher, but for now Nona enjoyed being part of a class. To be one in a large crowded room, everyone standing tall, heads arched back, arms up, hands in prayer pose and extended toward the ceiling—all this was very grave and beautiful. Stronger, more confident, better able to cope with stress—Nona had no doubt that yoga could make you all of these. But she did not believe it could make you a better person.

"Oh, all that stuff just gives me a headache," said Rosalind. Nona had called her mother to wish her a happy birthday. "That's one thing I don't like about the West Coast—all these goofy gurus and goddess worshipers. *Please!* What's wrong with people? Isn't life mysterious enough? Isn't there enough magic right here in this world—haven't they ever seen the ocean or listened to Mozart? If that isn't manifestation of the spirit enough, to hell with them."

Nona amused herself imagining Rosalind's response to the suggestion that the consequences of her early maternal failings were now stored in Nona's hips.

"Speaking of gurus," Rosalind said, laughing, "the other day I saw this scrawled above the cash machine: Jesus Saves, Why Can't You?" As always, Nona was touched by how easily her mother succumbed to mirth. "Now, tell me about those funny students of yours."

Nona told her mother about her young private student, who'd gone with a group of Koreans on a trip to Washington where, he said, they visited the house of the great Korean general Lee. "I tried to explain that Lee wasn't Korean, but he insisted. He said Lee was a Korean name and that the tour guide told them he was Korean. I said he must have misunderstood the guide's English, but it turns out the tour was in Korean. I guess the guide was making a joke, and the poor kid believed him. I taught him the idiom 'to pull someone's leg.'"

"Oh, that's priceless!" Rosalind cried. "That great Korean Civil War hero—Robert E. Lee!" And she laughed and she laughed.

When he heard that Nona was taking yoga, Tim remembered that Shep had once turned briefly to Buddhism. "He didn't go too far with it—he just read a few books and tried to teach himself meditation. A lot of artists he knew were getting into it. He thought it could help him stop drinking."

"And?"

"He decided he didn't really want to stop drinking."

You have to want to change—you will not change unless you really want to. Every time the yoga teacher said this—and she said it a lot—Nona thought of psychotherapy, which began, of course, with the very same premise. And there were different kinds of therapy, too, there was hard therapy and soft therapy, and there was a time when Nona had hoped to find the kind that was right for her. Now she often found herself comparing how she felt after yoga with how she had felt after therapy sessions: never like singing, then; never light or calm, but small and crumpled and dark, like something stuffed deep into someone's pocket and forgotten. The ugly therapeutic jargon—*help-rejecting, ego-alien*—had always put her off. The ineluctable banality of the clinical. *Padmasana*—Lotus, *Anjaneyasana*—Crescent Moon, *Akarna Dhanurasana*—Shooting Bow. The language of yoga: beautiful alike in Sanskrit and in English. *As a child I was not loved enough, not loved enough, not loved enough*—this was psychotherapy's mantra, and Nona had dutifully repeated it. But nothing like enlightenment came. "You cannot change," she was told, "unless you stop observing and talking about yourself as if you were observing and talking about someone else." But detachment—anathema to psychotherapy—turned out to be the yogic ideal. "If you really want to change," said Nika, "you must learn to separate yourself from your emotions. Step back from your anger and your discontent and watch yourself, *as if you were some-one else.*"

Was Nona changing? Was she being transfigured with every asana and every om?

When it came right down to it, Nona thought, she shared her mother's way of thinking. Yoga didn't have to work mira-cles. It didn't have to make her young or fearless or one with the Divine. It was enough that it gave her pleasure.

Kapalabhati was a powerful breathing and purification exercise whose name meant "shining skull," and the heads of yogis who practiced it devotedly had been known to radiate light. Nika demonstrated for the class, pumping her stomach hard and blowing the air out forcefully through her nostrils— and everyone with eyes could see: her white hair blazing like an aureole. At that very moment the sun had moved into the narrow gap between two buildings across the street, and a fin-ger of light reaching through the window had found her, sit-ting in lotus posture at the front of the room. Nothing miracu-lous, nothing supernatural about it. But a coincidence like that? It was close enough.

"WELCOME TO YOUR FORTIES. From now on you ought to be coming in once a year. Do you eat any beef? Better not—or if you must, no more than once every six months or so. Other meat is okay, but beef—it's not the beef itself that's the prob-lem, it's the hormones. And, by the way, you should have a mammogram."

Nona could hear the gynecologist, but she could not see him. She supposed it was his way of saving time: talking to her while the examination was in progress. She lay staring at the ceiling, wondering, as she always did when she was on that table, how she and other women managed to survive this exam. And how about that first woman, whoever she was, who'd allowed herself to be talked into it? There were plenty of women, like Nona's mother, who had never been able to do it.

"Do you like mushrooms? Eat them. For the iron." The doctor recommended also a daily multivitamin pill. "Later, we'll add some calcium. Okay." He stood up and patted her knee. "You're shipshape." He was a burly, bearded, kindly old man not many years away from retirement. Nona had always trusted him. Before the exam he had taken a blood sample. He would have the results of the AIDS test in about a week, he said. He gave her the name and number of a radiologist, but when Nona called the next day, she was told that the earliest available appointment was three months off. "Unless you can come in half an hour from now; we've just had a cancellation." Why not: it was a fine afternoon and Nona did not have to teach that day.

She had heard that mammograms could be unpleasant, but she was not prepared for the X-ray technician who kept tsking as she fitted Nona's breasts between the compression plates. "Small breasts are the *worst*," she grumbled. Her skin was rough, her breath medicinal-smelling. After she had taken X rays of both breasts, she left Nona alone for a few minutes, returning grim-faced: "Have to do the left one *again*." When she had squeezed Nona's sore breast between the plates, she snapped, "Now don't *move*," leaving Nona with the impression that it had been her own fault that the first X ray had not come out right.

The technician was gone much longer the second time—for good, as it turned out. Another woman appeared in her place: older, gentler: the radiologist. "That left breast," she said. "Something's showing up—that's why I asked to have it taken again. It's probably nothing, but I have to recommend that you see a breast surgeon and that you do it immediately."

Surgeon. Immediately. Two blows of a hammer shattering *probably nothing*.

Nona knew as many breast surgeons as she did tree surgeons. "Your gynecologist will refer you," the radiologist said.

"Why don't you call him right now?" Such urgency. And yet, except for that cancellation, Nona would not have been here for another three months.

And that is how, X rays in hand, Nona ended up at the breast surgeon's office first thing the next morning. She had looked at the X rays when she got home the day before and seen the dark mass for herself. Roy happened to call that evening, but Nona had made up her mind earlier not to tell him. She was far from being mistress of herself on the phone, but the good thing about being a nervous type was that no one ever got too suspicious if you sounded weird. They agreed to have dinner that weekend, and for the rest of the evening Nona kept seeing herself then, bursting into tears: "Roy, I have the most terrible news."

The doctor's office was in the wing of a large hospital and medical center, and when she stepped into the elevator Nona saw a plaque warning personnel that this was not the place to discuss patients. She shuddered to think of the incident that had led to the hanging of that plaque.

She was right on time, but after she had given her name and her X rays to a receptionist, she had to wait forty-five minutes. She tried reading the paper and could not. She tried reading the faces of the other people in the waiting area: who was a patient and who was just someone accompanying a patient. Everyone looked to her harried and gray. This was the department of thoracic surgery.

How young he is, Nona thought when she finally saw him. Sign of middle age, someone once said: when the doctor is younger than you are. They were in the doctor's tiny office. Nona's X rays were displayed on one wall. The dark mass looked bigger to her now, as if it had grown overnight. The doctor asked her the usual things: age, pregnancies, family diseases. "Do you smoke?" Nona swallowed—with difficulty, her throat was so dry. "I have—smoked." "Do you drink?" "I have—drunk." As if this were a drill in the present perfect. He did not ask anything else about her habits—not whether she ate lots of fruits and vegetables, not whether she exercised regularly—no, all he cared about was whether she smoked or drank. Nona kept up with things and she didn't have to ask why. She knew the connection, and her heart sank.

"Everything will be a lot easier," said the doctor, dropping his pen, "if I can actually feel this thing." He led Nona down the hall to an examination room where he left her alone to undress. Five, ten, fifteen minutes. How long did it take to unhook a bra. When he returned, he had a nurse with him. Throughout the exam she would stand aside with her arms crossed, her face expressionless. A witness. Nona was mildly astonished. It was pretty ludicrous, when you thought about it: copping a feel during a breast exam. Then Nona remembered a conversation she'd had with her psychiatrist, after they had become lovers: about anesthesiologists. "And when they get caught they often get away with it," he said, "because doctors are so reluctant to blow the whistle on one another." And when Nona had asked why: "Every doctor knows how much effort it takes to get that degree and that license. To want to ruin a colleague's career—well, he would have had to do something really bad." Worse, Nona was left to believe, than molesting a woman while she was unconscious.

The exam was painful. The doctor dug and dug his fingers into her flesh, turned her this way and that, placed her arms here and there. Lie down, sit up, lie down again. Nona followed instructions, now stiff now limp, like two different types of doll. She was sure the doctor could feel her heart pounding. She wondered what this must be like for him, how he ever got used to it. The entire time he avoided eye contact—as did the nurse, another one of those granite creatures: the X-ray technician's sister. But of course, thought Nona, she is not here looking out for my interests. She is here to protect *him*.

In the end, the doctor said he could feel nothing.

When she had dressed and joined him back in his office, she

found him at his desk, looking up at her X rays on the wall. Nona looked, too: the mass had grown again. He drew a little picture on her chart—it looked just like a frying pan with a fried egg in it: her breast. He marked an X above the yolk. He said, "Okay. Here's the story. When something like this shows up on a mammogram, you don't mess around. We have to go in after it, get it out, see what the hell it is. In this case our only option is surgery, and it would not be a very smart thing to put it off. So, with your permission, I'd like to get going immediately." *Surgery. Immediately.* Oh, why wouldn't he look her in the eye? So far Nona had not spoken more than about a dozen words. Now she simply nodded her head. The doctor picked up the phone and dialed an extension. "Hello, Fred! It's me— how're you doing? Great. Hey, listen: can you do a localization for me tomorrow morning, say around eight? No? No? What do you mean, no? What've you got, a golf tournament or something? Hah-hah. Oh, okay. What good are you, Fred? What? Janine? *Janine?* Uh-uh, Fred. No way. Janine's going to have to practice on a few more service patients before I let her have a private patient of mine. How about the next morning— Friday? Okay? Great. Thanks, Fred."

That settled, the doctor pulled out a form and began rapidly filling it out while explaining the procedure to Nona. Always looking to save time, these doctors. Friday morning, Nona was to report first to the radiology department for the preoperative spot localization. An X ray would be taken from various angles to determine the exact location of the mass. Then, a long needle would be inserted into her breast to mark the spot, more films would be taken to check the placement of the needle, and Nona's breast would be injected with a blue dye. All this would take about an hour. Next came the biopsy, which would take somewhat less time. The dye would be the surgeon's guide, showing him what to remove. As soon as the tissue was out, it would be sent to pathology. "Twenty minutes after that and we won't know everything, but we'll know the worst."

"Will I have to have anesthesia?" Nona managed to ask, envisioning a frothing man in a surgical gown bearing down on her.

"Just local. You'll be awake the whole time, though of course there won't be any pain. Later, after the anesthetic wears off, there might be some pain, but I can give you something for that. We do the surgery right here—we have our own little operating room right on this floor. Come on, I'll show it to you." He seemed to have perked up quite a bit, as if he were actually looking forward to the operation, which puzzled Nona. But as he led her through the halls again, stepping lively and even whistling (though still not looking her in the eye), she decided that his chipperness was for her benefit, an attempt to hearten her—and though she was not heartened, she was grateful.

In the operating room, a nurse (not the witness) was eating her lunch. She was sitting near the door, dressed in scrubs, her feet propped up on a desk.

"This is my beautiful young assistant, Lynn. She'll be there Friday morning, too. Mm—smells good. What is it?"

"Turkey and mustard," said Lynn. "Hello." To Nona the sandwich did not smell good at all. In fact, it smelled inexplicably strong, like something that had turned. Her eyes barely took in the room, which did not look very different from the examination room, except that it was larger and had windows.

So far not a word had been said about money. Thank God I have health insurance, Nona thought wryly, remembering "Janine." What Nona and Roy had finally decided was to keep the policy they already had, agreeing to pay a higher deductible so as to reduce their quarterly premiums by about two hundred dollars. Now they would have to have spent four thousand before the insurance company began paying any part of their bills. Impossible to say how much it would all amount to until they knew "the worst," as the doctor put it. Nona could only pray that he was less clumsy with his hands. The famous tactlessness of doctors. A couple of months ago, she had watched a documentary on television. The cameras were in Japan, where a surgeon had just operated on a young woman. When he went to meet with her family, he brought along the breast he'd just removed, in a pan. Nona had admired the stoicism of the woman's husband and her other relations, who sat listening to the surgeon explain why there was no hope, with the ragged breast thrust under their noses and the movie cameras rolling.

"Be sure to eat breakfast that morning," the doctor told Nona. "God knows, it's going to be uncomfortable enough, I don't advise doing it on an empty stomach. And bring someone with you, you know, your husband, a sister—someone to keep you company. And try not to worry too much. By Friday noon it'll all be over—and who knows? It may turn out to be nothing."

As Nona stepped through the office door, some demon in her forced her head around so that she caught the doctor's expression—the pursed lips, the lowered gaze, the frown—and that was when she knew she was going to die.

Outside, the day seemed unnaturally bright and had grown much warmer. Nona blinked and set her feet down gingerly, like someone emerging from a cave. The rancid smell of that sandwich was still with her. She would never be able to eat turkey again. She hailed a cab and got a maniac who veered so wildly from lane to lane Nona was afraid she might be sick. Reaching out for something to hold on to, she thought of the phrase "for dear life" and a heave of sorrow rose in her, so strong it made her back arch.

Oh, that her energy should have to migrate so soon.

From the moment she learned the results of the mammogram, Nona had had these intermittent symptoms: ringing in her ears, shortness of breath, leaden-leggedness—going from the cab to her front door was like walking underwater—and a bad, metallic taste in her mouth, as if she'd been sucking on a coin. Now added to these was that smell—she moved in a cloud of it, as if it had been dabbed on her pulse points. All these symptoms would persist over the next two days, but to her surprise Nona had no trouble sleeping at night. She went to bed early, fell asleep at once, and did not wake until six or seven. She did not remember her dreams.

The time went by faster than Nona would have expected. She taught her class on Thursday and arranged for a substitute (what some of her students called a "stepteacher") for Friday. She went to yoga, walked Pip, corrected homework, listened to music—this was business as usual. Reading was difficult, though, and writing, impossible. She let the machine answer the phone when it rang. She did not return calls.

Many times in those two days the thought came to her: and there I was, worried about AIDS. And if she hadn't been worried about AIDS, she would not have gone to the doctor.

When in her life it had ever occurred to Nona to wonder how she might face the prospect of death, she had known it would not be the way of the Stoics. Not with courage or serenity or understanding, no no. She had always seen herself just as she was now: terrified, outraged, heartbroken. To die now, with so much left undone, so little resolved, and all the big questions still unanswered? She could not bear to think that all she had managed to make of her life up till now would be all that it would ever amount to. For in that case, she did not understand: what had been the purpose of this incarnation?

Late Thursday, Nona went out to the florist's and returned with one enormous white peony. She put the flower in a vase of warm water on the kitchen table and spent the next hour or so leaning on her elbows, watching it unfurl. At first she simply drank its beauty in. After a while she tried concentrating absolutely, her face only inches from the swelling blossom. One-point meditation, it was called. It was very difficult, but for the moments in which she succeeded she was lifted out of herself and found a breath of peace. She kept trying. It was as close to praying as she had come since she was a child.

At last she got up and moved into the living room where her eyes went at once to the portrait of Shep that she had taken from Tim's basement along with Shep's portrait of Rosalind. She had hung them not side by side, as she'd originally planned, but on opposite walls, facing each other. She had studied both portraits minutely when she first put them up, but, as happens with one's constant surroundings, she was beginning to forget them. But now she stood arrested in the living-room doorway, her gaze fixed. *Dear Father, can you see me? Have you been watching me all these years, and do you understand me? Rosalind has never forgiven you—you must know that. Have you forgiven her? Did you know that you took all her love and there was nothing left for me? Dear Father, who was so poor a father to me, do you know what trouble I am in? Have you any power to help me? If I am wrong and need not be afraid, is there some way you can let me know this? Here I am, almost the same age as you when you died. Are we as alike as I sometimes believe we are, and is that why my life has to be cut short like yours? Will I, too, have to die alone?*

Wiping her eyes, Nona passed through the living room and into the bedroom, and though it was only ten o'clock she went straight to bed. Just before she fell asleep, she remembered her father's superstition, that if he ever went into a hospital he would not come out alive.

The next morning Nona arrived at the hospital a few minutes before eight. The radiology department was in the basement. A receptionist had Nona fill out a form. "That'll be six hundred and fifty dollars." Nona had not thought of this. "Can't you bill me?" The woman chuckled. "I can see you've never been here before. Those days are over. We won't do the procedure without the money up front. Doctor should have told you that." "But I didn't bring a check." "But you have a credit card, don't you?"

And if she hadn't had a credit card? Nona wondered as she sat down to wait. Someone called her name, and Nona looked up to see a tall woman in a white coat and jeans, beckoning her. Nona rose from her chair and almost sat down again when the woman said, "Hi, I'm Janine. Follow me." Nona did, as if to her own hanging. But the confusion was soon cleared up. "Fred" (the radiologist) "is on his way." Janine was just the tech. "I'm sorry, I know this is no picnic," she said, as she prepared to take the first set of X rays. Struggling to get the correct angle, adjusting and readjusting the plates, she tsked several times—just like the other tech. "Damn machine is *impossible*. Don't see *how* it can be accurate." Well, Nona thought: at least she didn't blame my size. "There. Now, try not to move, honey." She might be incompetent, Janine, but she was kind. Nona asked her about the anesthesia. "Anesthesia? For this? You don't need anesthesia for a localization." Nona said, "You're going to stick a needle into my breast, and I don't need anesthesia?" Janine shook her head. "The breast is just one big piece of fat. You won't feel a thing." We are talking about one of the most sensitive parts of my body, Nona cried—silently, but Janine heard and said, "Do you really think we'd lie to you and then go and hurt you?" Just then Fred appeared. A clownish-looking man with tufts of white hair growing on either side of a freckled bald crown, and a large red nose. He went about his business with nimble fingers and scarcely a word. Janine was right: the needle did not hurt. "It is imperative that you hold still while we take the next films," said Fred, and Nona sighed. All these X rays over a period of four days. Nona kept up with things. The breast: known to be highly vulnerable to radiation. Radiation: known to cause cancer.

Nona found the surgeon waiting for her, not immediately recognizable in his scrubs. Lynn was there, too, as promised; and there was another person, whom no one thought to introduce: small, dark, foreign, and too young, Nona would have said, to be a part of this. But it was in fact this girl who would stand at the surgeon's elbow throughout the procedure. Lynn—once she had arranged Nona on the table and started the IV—stayed pretty much out of the picture, looming into view every now and then to ask Nona how she was doing.

"Now, listen to me," said the surgeon. "If you feel any pain at all, let me know right away and we'll give you more juice, okay? No reason to be a martyr, do you hear me?" (He had already expressed disapproval that Nona had not brought anyone to the hospital with her.) Nona told him there was no chance of that. "Good. Now, the other thing I have to tell you is that this is going to leave a scar. I'm sorry about that." "I don't care," Nona said. "Oh, yeah, sure, you say that now, but you'll see: you'll be cursing me next summer when you put on that bikini." "I don't wear a bikini," Nona said. She hoped he would be quiet now.

No, she didn't feel any *pain*. But the *cutting*, the *probing*, and the *snipping*—Nona felt all that. The tissue requiring removal was stubborn. Once, he drove his instrument so deeply into the wound that he moved her slightly on the table. Blood leaked into her armpit and seeped under her back. His hands were only inches from her chin. She turned her head to the right, toward the windows: all the blinds were down. She tried conjuring up the white peony of the night before, to make that image stretch from one end of her mind to the other.

"Don't you want to see?" the surgeon interrupted.

"I don't think so."

"It's not so bad, really. It looks just like—blue chicken fat." The girl laughed. She was holding a dish on which were deposited the pieces of tissue. After a pause, he said, "Did you eat anything this morning?" Nona rolled her head from side to side. "Why not? I told you to eat breakfast, didn't I? You must be starving." He was different. His voice was different. It was his intimate voice, Nona thought. She was sure he used it with every woman he operated on, but still, it was his intimate voice, and she responded to it. "I can eat later," she said. A much longer pause, and then came: "You know what I think?" She had been wrong: *this* was his intimate voice. She turned to look up at him and for the first time his eyes met hers. "I think you've been just terrific." Uh-oh. Didn't he know about brave fronts—how they crumbled the moment someone acknowledged them? The next few seconds were the hardest for Nona. At one point she thought her throat might explode. When she had gotten control of herself, she dared to look at him again. Rather sexy in his face mask. Fine gray eyes set in thick black eyelashes. Handsome young doctor. If those two other women had not been in the room, she would have flirted with him, Nona thought—not without shame—and then, self-mockingly, Oh, but I must look a fright! It wasn't the bared breast with the bloody gash that she was worried about. It was the hideous shower cap. In the last few minutes it had puffed up over her brow, but, with her arms pinned under the sheet, Nona was helpless. When Lynn next appeared to see how the patient was doing, Nona asked her to please push the damn thing back.

The thread broke while the wound was being stitched. "Shit." The surgeon turned to his assistant. "This patient has good insurance. We can use the expensive thread."

A joke, Nona thought. But then, remembering Janine and the service patients, she thought: perhaps not.

It was over. The wound had been bandaged, the dish of blue chicken fat whisked away, surgeon and girl were gone. Lynn removed the IV, helped Nona up, wiped the blood, and left her alone to get dressed.

Back in the waiting area, Nona sat down to count the minutes until "the worst."

It was less than twenty. It was less than fifteen. Dressed now in a baggy brown suit, the surgeon strode up to her chair, stuck out his hand, and pulled her to her feet. There were other people sitting all around them, but instead of taking her back to his office he announced right there: "It's nothing. No malignancy. You're fine." The expression on his face was both joyful and sheepish. "What a relief, huh?" He squeezed her hand. "I know I had you scared. Let me tell you, I had myself scared. I was pretty sure this time." "I know," said Nona. "I know you were." The famous pessimism of doctors. She should have remembered that. And how embarrassing this was—with everyone listening and looking on. Ah, but who cared. Nona forgave him everything. His hand was so warm. He kissed her good-bye. "Now go get some lunch."

A few hours later, Roy burst into the bedroom where Nona was lying on the bed. He had been beside himself since he heard the news. "Oh my God, oh my God," was all he could say. He had insisted on coming over at once. He had taken a cab, and now here he was, his hair uncombed, his glasses askew, the pullover he was wearing inside out. "You should have told me, you should have told me." His agitation infected Pip, who kept barking and leaping at him.

"It's okay, Roy. It's okay, Pip. Calm down, everyone." Nona was in a mellow state, which was partly relief and partly codeine.

Roy wanted to see. Nona took off her shirt. Her left breast was hugely swollen and had begun to turn a deep purple—the first of many hues that would appear over the next few weeks. She said, "I'm afraid to see what it looks like under the bandage. The doctor says it's going to leave a scar."

"Oh, your poor breast, your poor breast."

"Be careful," Nona whispered. And he was—very—never putting any pressure on her there.

"Wow. I didn't know you could do that, Nona."

Yoga, she explained.

A long time passed. They were on a raft. . . . Lying side by side, on their backs, hands entwined, they were crossing the wide blue sea. . . . Nona started awake to hear Roy saying, ". . . away."

"Away?"

"Yes, I mean, on a trip—like a vacation. I really could use one, Nona. I've been so unhappy. We've been through so much, and now—you—this. And we always have such fun when we go away together."

"Oh, I don't know, Roy. Where do you want to go?"

"Anywhere. Somewhere special. Europe. Italy. Venice! Let's go to Venice."

"Venice?"

"Yes—why not—the most beautiful city in the world."

"Oh, Roy, this is all very romantic, but—"

"Please."

"But I don't know, Roy. Think about the money. The surgeon's bill alone is going to come to something like two thousand dollars. And—well, is it reasonable—?"

"Please, please, Nona. This is really important to me." Sounding as if his life depended on it. "Do it for me."

"A second honeymoon!" Rosalind shrieked into the phone—forgetting, of course, that there had been no first. It was Nona's opinion that, for couples who'd been living together before they got married, honeymoons, like big church weddings, were rather absurd. "What a great idea—you *must* go, Nona. It's only money, and this is no time to worry about that—not after what you've just been through."

"No, it's not only money. It's the madness of going away together when we're supposed to be getting a divorce."

"But, don't you see, Nona, this might bring you back together again."

"If it were only that simple."

"Oh, Nona, for once in your life—"

"What?"

"Nothing."

"No, tell me: what were you going to say? 'For once in my life' what?"

"Nothing. I mean, I just hope that you make the right decision, that's all." And before Nona could respond Rosalind rushed on, "In fact, even before you said anything I was going to suggest that you two go away together. I was going to suggest it a long time ago."

"Oh, really? And why didn't you?"

"Oh, you know—I was afraid that, if it came from me, you'd be sure to reject the idea."

Nona was silent as the implications of this remark sank in.

"Anyway," Rosalind said, "if you think it's too much—if you don't want to give yourself a big present like that, then do it for him."

What was happening here? Had Rosalind been talking to Roy?

"Oh, Nona, I know you hate it when I butt into your affairs, but this time I can't help myself. I do so want a happy ending."

Nona had to laugh. "You've been reading too many best-sellers."

"Oh, go—go," said Tim. "It's a wonderful idea. Don't put it off, or half the magic will be lost. And besides, you want to be there before it gets too hot. Don't even think about it—just go. I'd be glad to lend you the money."

Go, *go,* her friends all said. We'll take care of Pip, we'll water the plants and get the mail, we'll sub for you—just *go.*

It looked as if everyone wanted a happy ending.

The AIDS test came back, and it was negative.

Vabbene, Nona decided. *A Venezia, allora.*

She had to see the breast surgeon one more time. When he had removed the bandage and examined the scar, he said, "Not bad." But whether he was referring to her healing or to his own handiwork, she couldn't tell. He said, "Now, with this kind of abnormality, even when it's benign, it's something that has to be watched. I want you in here every six months, so I can keep an eye on you. And don't get another mammogram until I tell you to. God knows, you've had enough radiation."

Just in case Nona was feeling too safe.

They were in the same room where he had first examined her, but this time he had not brought along a nurse. And Nona did not flirt with him. As people often do in this type of situation, she had promised that, if she survived, she was going to live her life differently.

chapter
thirteen

There is a kind of happiness that is not diminished but rather deepened and enriched by melancholy. That is the kind of happiness Roy and Nona discovered in Venice.

The sunstruck water, the brilliant façades and their mercurial reflections, the constant drone of the boat engines and the rhythmic slap of wavelet against stone, the primeval smells of seaweed and salt—all this contributed to their enchantment, their sense of sojourning in a dream. It was strange, how little they felt like talking. They had imagined themselves talking a lot, away from it all, as they were, together again after their long separation. But from the moment they stepped off the *vaporetto* that brought them to the landing-stage near their hotel, they were subdued. The entire city was like one of its own churches or museums: only louts chattered away. There is something of the vandal in every tourist, and before Venice, ancient, transcendent, and as fragile-seeming as, well, Venetian glass, it was possible to feel not only subdued but humbled, even apologetic.

Nona had been to Italy before, but never to Venice, and it might as well have been Roy's first trip, too. He had been too young and harried the last time to appreciate what he saw (not much, in those two days squeezed between Barcelona and

Florence). Then it had been the middle of summer, and the crowds surging down the narrow lanes had reminded him of an illustration in one of his children's books: the rats following the Pied Piper. Now, though earlier, it was undeniably summer. The sun was hot and the air humid and pungent, especially in the afternoons. A miasmic atmosphere, redolent of decay. That Venice was perishable, that it would one day be lost, perhaps sinking, like a pirate ship overloaded with loot—this was one of the melancholy strands woven into the spell. In the lobby of the hotel where Nona and Roy were staying, someone had left a pile of brochures calling attention to threats to the city from industry on the mainland. The text was translated into several languages and tactfully omitted any mention of the damage caused by over a million sightseers a year.

Though it was not the height of the season, the crowds were dense. And the cameras, the cameras! Roy and Nona seemed to be the only tourists without one. All these cameras mystified Nona. At any kiosk you could buy a stack of picture postcards depicting the very sights everyone was so busy snapping. Those pictures were of far better quality than anything most tourists would be taking home with them—and if it was reproductions they wanted, why didn't they buy one of those gorgeous coffee-table books? *Because,* Roy pointed out: postcards and books would contain no photos of the tourists themselves against the famous backdrops. But the charm of such photos had always eluded Nona. Wasn't half the thrill of traveling the illusion that *you* were *not* there?

Here is a photograph that Nona and Roy will never see. The photographer is one of their countrymen, a retired car dealer, from Indianapolis. He is sitting with his wife in a gondola whose bottom is cluttered with shopping bags. "Quick, quick!" she hisses, nudging him sharply. Later, back in their living room, showing slides to friends, the woman will say, "And this one we couldn't resist. Perfect strangers to us, but aren't they sweet? Two Lovers on a Bridge." It is Nona and

Roy, it is a small bridge, over the Rio degli Ognissanti, they are two dark silhouettes against a red sky—"It was sunset"— and they never notice their picture being taken, engrossed as they are in another picture, in the red water: fine example of Photorealism, changing to Impressionism with the approach of the gondola.

Two lovers. Clever, prescient Rosalind: the trip *was* turning into a honeymoon. But each time Roy and Nona made love they felt, mysteriously, not so much like newlyweds as like adulterers. The poignant and unsettling sense that these hours were stolen, that at the end of this rapturous week they would have to give each other up. Their love shared the same dreamy, fragile aspect as their surroundings. Added to the vulnerability they naturally felt as foreigners was this other, lovers' vulnerability, whose emblem might have been the tender swollen scar on Nona's left breast.

Every day, they left their hotel right after breakfast. They walked everywhere, sometimes getting lost—once or twice hopelessly, with guidebook, map, street signs, and natives all seeming to contradict one another. But this, too, was part of the spell, these endless detours down meandering *calli*, this turning and turning in the labyrinth, holding hands, growing weary, frustrated, and truly anxious—and then at last recognizing the back or side of some familiar structure.

It was while they were lost one time that they came upon a quiet little *campo* where Nona recognized a British expatriate writer, a woman, sitting at a sunny table outside a café. There was an empty coffee cup and a half-empty bottle of *acqua minerale* on the table, and a notebook, in which she was writing. In spite of the sun, she was wearing a heavy dark cape. Not young, not pretty, but wonderful to see. Dignified. Monumental, even, in her heavy dark cape. She glanced up and returned Nona's stare with a look of disdain. There could be no question, of course, of speaking to her. But her image would stay with Nona, even after other monuments of Venice had faded.

One morning midway in their stay, Roy and Nona happened to wake at the same time, just before dawn. Instead of going back to sleep, they got up, dressed, and went out. They walked for about fifteen minutes, arriving at the Piazza San Marco, which they had seen already several times, but never at this hour, and never as it was at this hour: empty except for the pigeons, quiet except for the pigeons' warbling. So now they knew what to do. They would get up and go out before dawn every morning from now on, while everyone else but a few natives, and even fewer tourists, slept. Every day began with this mist that rolled in from the lagoon and filled the streets and canals. Then the sun appeared, striking the marble columns and the zinc cupolas, and the mist went up to reveal that grand vista of temples, palaces, water, and sky. The sounds that broke the hush were distinct: the echoing footsteps of some other early riser, wooden shutters being thrown open against stone walls, the cry of a gull, and the pealing of many church bells, distant and near.

Walking back to their hotel, they would have their coffee and rolls before setting out again. They would not come back until late afternoon, when they usually tried to nap (he successfully, she unsuccessfully) before going out to dinner. They ate simply, and were always satisfied with their meals of pasta and grilled fish and wine. They went to bed early and slept well, though Nona, who suffered from insomnia whenever she traveled, needed her pills. Horses and lions pranced through their dreams. Cherubs appeared to them.

They had been lucky to get a decent hotel room at such short notice. Expensive, like everything else in that city, but Nona had stopped thinking about money. It seemed somehow fitting to pour gold into that treasure chest. Besides, Roy hated shopping as much as Nona did, and they avoided the stores completely. They had no desire to buy anything—most of the designer boutiques had branches in Manhattan, after all. They wanted no glassware, no lace, no leather goods or jewelry.

Except for some carnival masks for Roy's sisters' children, they would go home without a souvenir. This would arouse the suspicions of the customs agents, who would search every crease of their luggage, the pockets of the clothes they were wearing, and even the insides of their shoes.

Their windows gave on a garden, where numerous cats could be observed in the afternoon sun, sleeping or grooming themselves, getting rested and ready for their nights. The first roses were in bloom and could be smelled from the balcony.

Except to eat, they did not go out at night. They avoided the opera house—they were not in Venice for the music—but once they had an early picnic supper of bread and cheese on their balcony and went to hear a recital in one of the churches. Local musicians, playing Mozart and Schubert.

Background is important. It was here, with the most beautiful city in the world behind her, that Roy acknowledged that his wife was no longer a beautiful woman. Most dramatic was the change in her coloring. She was paler than ever, but she had stopped dying her hair, so there was no longer that striking Pre-Raphaelite contrast. It had been a while, of course, since Nona's hair was that rare reddish-gold shade, beloved of painters. But the coloring she used had been a close match and natural-looking enough to fool most people. So why had she stopped using it? Because she was tired of it, was all she said. And Roy thought: She doesn't want to be like her mother.

Nevertheless, Nona was as sensitive about aging as she had always been. Back in New York, a few days before they left for Italy, this happened: Nona had gone by herself to Connecticut, to visit friends who had just had a baby. At the train station, she approached a conductor to ask where Track 12 was. He had frowned at her and said, "You know, lady, *twelve*? Like, between *eleven* and *thirteen*?"

"That sort of thing would never have happened when I was young," Nona told Roy. "He would have taken off his cap and bowed and scraped and offered to escort me himself. But now

I get this rudeness from men all the time. 'Come on, lady, I don't got all day.' 'Okay, lady, I heard you the first time.'" But it wasn't only men, she said. Some women were worse. The contempt of the world for the older woman . . .

"I think you're reading too much into it," Roy had told her. But an excruciating memory had come back to him, from the days when he was single. He was having dinner with another woman—one of those very pretty women for whom he had cast out his net unsuccessfully. The banquette of a crowded restaurant; an older couple sitting to their right. When it was time to go, Roy pulled out the table for his date so that she could get up easily, and helped her with her coat. And the woman at the next table said to the man, "See how nice he is to her?" And the man said, "I'd be nice to you, too, if you looked like that."

There were more women than men among the tourists, they had noticed—at least among the Americans. There seemed to be numerous groups of women traveling together, on special tours, and their loud American voices echoed down the canals, complaining about the food, the prices, the stench, and the insolence of the gondoliers. Where were their men? Nona wondered. Were these spinsters, widows, divorcées? Similar in dress, manner, grooming, and, especially, shape, they might all have been kin, these women. In the churches and museums you saw them come and go, talking not of Tintoretto, or of Titian or Tiepolo, but of sickness, fractious children, real estate, plans for redecorating. Among the masterpieces of the Accademia, a swollen sandaled foot is put down: "I don't care how great they are, I still wouldn't want one in my living room: too depressing." In general they do seem depressed, these women. Venice is not for them: too precarious, too extreme. The filth of the canals appalls them. This constant trudging on stone and up and down bridges is so hard on the feet. They prefer Paris, where they went last year. London, where they could almost always make themselves understood.

Decrepit city: creaking, tottering, coming apart at the seams—who needs to be reminded? They may not have read Mann, but they have seen Death in Venice, in the form of a tall, rough, insolent gondolier. His strange warning cries haunt their sleep. Nona cannot bear to think of the restless nights of these women, every one of whom, she is convinced, would have lived her life differently, if given the chance. That there would be no such chance, that it was too late, too late—was this what they heard in those strange warning cries? And yet, when they returned home, with their souvenirs and rolls of film, they would remember that they had been happy. You should have been there, they would tell the men who had not wanted to accompany them. We had a great time. And a terrible silence would follow.

Oh, really, Nona, Roy chided her. Don't you think you're reading a little too much into things? It was her nature. Once, in the nave of a cathedral, she turned to see him some yards behind, caught in a perfect cone of multicolored light, and was seized by an absurd suspicion. Who was beaming love to her husband?

Drinking wine in the Campo di Santa Margherita, in the shadow of the red bell tower, with the illuminated Madonna at the top. Pigeons scavenging under the café tables. A small boy leaning away from his mother at an acute angle suddenly breaks free and comes hurtling toward them, sending all the birds into the air. One of them flies so close to Roy, its wing grazes his cheek.

"Are you cold, Roy?"

"What? Oh, no—not at all."

"What is it?"

"Nothing. Just—déjà vu."

"Ah."

And then, much too soon, of course, came their last day in Venice, their last night, and their last chance for a gondola ride—something they had been saving for the full moon.

Others had had the same idea: the canals resounded with laughter and snatches of conversation and music. Out on the lagoon it was quieter, and they were grateful that their gondolier was not one of those who felt obliged to serenade them with some Neapolitan torch song or Broadway theme. What was it about being in a boat that made one want to sing? Now Roy was humming *Soave sia il vento*, from *Così fan tutte*.

That sensuous glide over black satin, the rhythmic rise and fall, oar cleaving water with a sound like satin tearing. Man, woman, water, boat. Nona remembered. One other time here in Venice she had remembered: when she and Roy were passing through a market and she had distinguished, among the more powerful smells of mollusk and eel, that mixture of cloves, pepper, and cinnamon that had tantalized her in Tucson again and again.

He had gone back to Charlotte. Phoebe had included this news in her letter.

The gondolier, who had been silent since he and Roy had agreed on the fare, startled them by saying, in English, "And now that you are in the boat, why not go around the world, eh?" Odd words, they delivered Nona with a jolt way back to that summer she had spent on the commune. They had called it a commune, but it was really just eighteen hippies crashing in one big house and growing a few vegetables out back— none too successfully. One day, four of them, including Nona, went for a drive in the mountains. "Now that we're in the car," someone said, "we might as well go to California." As wild an idea as the gondolier's. And yet, they had done it. Turned that old Plymouth onto the highway, and gone.

That was youth, Nona thought.

Moving closer to Roy on the cushioned seat, she said, "So, tell me, now that we have to leave. Was this trip everything you wanted it to be?"

"Oh, yes." He took her hand and he kissed it. He kissed her cheek, her mouth, her eyes, her hair.

They were approaching the island of San Michele, with its thousands of moonlit tombs.

Nona felt a stir of tiny wings within, as if one of the city's many canaries had perched on a rib. She took a deep breath and began to sing.

chapter
fourteen

"Did you get a postcard? We got a postcard."

"Yes—after they were already back."

"Italian mail—"

"—takes forever."

"But they weren't gone very long."

"You spoke with him—?"

"Yesterday. He said it was heaven."

"Does this mean they're back together?"

"Will somebody please tell me—"

"Well, it's not entirely clear. I mean, he hasn't moved back in yet."

"I never understood—"

"But things look good?"

"I think so."

"Well, hallelujah."

"How did he sound?"

"We only talked a little while, but I'd say very optimistic."

"Will somebody please explain to me why they broke up in the first place?"

Silence.

"He never came right out and said—"

"—but we have our suspicions—"

"—which we will keep to ourselves."

Laughter.

Good Cop and Bad Cop had names, of course, and their names were Regina and Clare. The names of their husbands were Larry and George. The children of Regina and Larry— Melinda, Jody, Brad—and the children of Clare and George— Wanda, Mack—ranged in age from one and a half to thirteen. The two families lived about fifty miles apart, and Regina and Clare's parents lived almost exactly midway between them. It happened that the sisters' birthdays fell on consecutive days, and for years they had followed a tradition: on the Saturday of their birthday week they would all meet at the home of the sisters' parents. They would spend the day together, and then grandparents and grandchildren would have a cookout while the others went out to a restaurant.

At dinner, the talk was about family. From Roy and Nona they moved on to the question of home schooling. Two of them were for and two against—agreement unfortunately not occurring within the same marriage. But tonight no one was in the mood to argue. They were at one of the best steakhouses in the country. It was not the sort of treat they allowed themselves often. They ate much, drank just a little, skipped dessert because Mom had a big cake waiting for them back at the house. They each had a cup of coffee, split the check, and stepped out into the clear midwestern summer air. The wind off Lake Superior that night was a warm one.

Meanwhile, in another part of town, another couple who had also been out returned home to find a stranger in their kitchen. He had come in through a window just minutes before. Now he stood facing them in his black turtleneck and black ski mask, clutching an empty white pillowcase. The owner of that house was a former Marine, a former state prison guard, now head of security at the local college. Calmly he measured the intruder: his scrawny build, his shallow breathing, the way he clutched the pillowcase with both hands to his chest: weak, terrified, unarmed. A kid, some local punk, probably just out of high school. Calmly nudging his wife to one side, the man reached into his jacket. ("I just wanted to scare the pants off him," he would say later.) Before he even saw the gun, the kid dropped his pillowcase and ran. In the street a car was waiting, his girlfriend at the wheel. She had been in agony for the past few minutes, having seen the man and his wife coming home. "I didn't want the punk to get away," was how the man would explain why he ran out to his own car and took off after them. It is possible that he was also influenced by the movie he and his wife had just seen, which included some spectacular chase scenes.

Like something in a movie was precisely how several people would describe what happened next. "He's got a gun, he's got a gun!" shouted the boy, and his girlfriend, panicking in turn, pulled onto the highway with her foot on the gas. As the car plunged into traffic, it was hit by a jeep, which bumped it right over the median. All together seventeen vehicles were involved in the accident, bringing an extraordinary range of injuries into the emergency room that night. In the car bearing Regina, Clare, Larry, and George, no one survived.

PIP, LYING ON THE BEDROOM floor, raised his head and beat his tail the first dozen times Nona appeared, but after that he ignored her. She was pacing the apartment from one end to the other. It was just past eleven on a sweltering night. Only the bedroom had an air conditioner, and so Nona passed from cold to hot to cold again. Once, she was interrupted in her pacing by Rosalind, who had been calling almost every day since they both returned from Minnesota. Rosalind had insisted on going, though Nona at first tried to dissuade her. Rosalind didn't know Roy's family, after all; she had met them only once, at her daughter's wedding. But in the end Nona had been grateful for her mother's presence: composed, compassionate, and unobtrusively helpful, in the midst of all that suffering.

Blow followed blow: right after the funeral services, Roy's mother had collapsed and been placed in a hospital for observation. Nona flew back to New York alone. That had been a week ago. Now Roy's mother was home but could not leave her bed. Roy had left for New York earlier that day. He should have been there hours ago, but his connecting flight had been forced to return to the airport after one of the jet's engines failed. Now at last he had made it and was on his way in a cab.

He was coming for just a few days, he'd said, before going right back home. That had struck Nona: he called it "home."

Tonight, on the phone, her mother had said, "He's shattered. I'm sure he feels alienated from everyone. You just have to hang in there and do what you can." But Nona knew that she was pitilessly inadequate to this task. The size of his grief and her inability to get her arms around it were a torment to her. In her own grief she had turned to Tim. Tim had been generous, though he himself was forlorn: Andrew had left him. Tim had escaped to his country house for a few weeks. He invited Nona to join him any time she wished. Meanwhile, like Rosalind, he was calling every day.

Before she left for Venice Tim and Nona had had a talk. "All my writer friends say a book is finished when the editor takes it away from you," Tim said. "But what if you don't have an editor?" He had suggested that she let him read the manuscript while she was away, and when she returned he tried to persuade her to take the next step. He knew people in publishing; he could show it to them.

The afterglow of Venice, the reconciliation with Roy, the finished book—it was into this happiness that the bomb had dropped.

She was in the bedroom when Roy arrived. The air conditioner was on high; not even the dog had heard the front door open. He did not touch her, he did not go to her and kiss her—she noted it sadly. He sank down onto a chair and muttered something she did not catch, but when she asked him to repeat it, he said, "No, no—let's make some coffee," and stood up again.

"I can't believe how hot it is here," he said. Nona poured the coffee over ice cubes.

"It's been this way all week," she told him. One of the worst heat waves the city had ever known.

How long before one stopped feeling absurd, complaining about the weather; before it no longer seemed monstrous, wanting to go to the country, or worrying about the fate of one's manuscript.

As they sat drinking their coffee, Nona observed the change in the shape of Roy's face. It was longer, narrower. When she asked him whether he wanted something to eat, he said he'd eaten on the plane and it was enough. The lines running from his nose to the corners of his mouth—those were new, and may have been only fatigue. There was a thumbprint on the right lens of his glasses. He had not shaved today. A thousand years ago, in a gondola, he had kissed her cheek, her mouth, her hair.

"Nona, are you okay?" She nodded, though her heart was breaking. "Nona, we have to talk."

She thought she knew what he was going to say; her mother had already tried to prepare her.

"I'm going to take all the children."

"All?"

She had thought he would say he wanted one of the children—or perhaps two—Clare's boy and girl. But all five? Not even Rosalind had foreseen it. "But that is impossible, Roy. Where will we put them?"

A look of pity crossed his face. "You're panicking," he said. "I understand. And I'm sorry, truly sorry."

"But why would you take all of them? What about their other relatives? What about your parents?"

"My parents are old, Nona. And after what's happened they'll never be the same. Of course they'll help in any way they can, but the kids don't belong with them. Children shouldn't be raised by sad old people. The others, well, they've got families of their own. Sure, they'd be willing to take one or the other to raise with their own kids, but I can't see splitting the brothers and sisters up. Remember, they've lost both parents. They need each other."

"But why *all?*"

"Because no one can possibly want them as much as I do." After a pause he added: "It's the only thing in the world that could even begin to console me. And it's what Regina and Clare would have wanted—for me and for them."

"But you haven't thought it through, Roy. Five children, for God's sake, when you've never had to take care of one. You have no idea—"

"Sometimes you know what the right thing is without having to think about it. I'm sorry, Nona. I know this isn't easy for you."

He was a different man. A completely different man. It could happen, just like that. You could be loved and needed and cared for, and then something could happen and change everything and you could be abandoned. Sometimes Nona wondered how anyone survived.

"But—in practical terms, Roy," she persisted. "How will you support them? And what about your career?"

"I don't know. These are things I still have to work out. It's true, I may have to change my whole life. I'm prepared to do that. It may be better to move out of New York, to be near my parents—I don't know yet. But I've made the important decision, and nothing's going to change that. Everything else will have to be dealt with as it comes. A lot depends on you, Nona."

"Me?"

"Yes, of course. You don't think I want to lose you, do you? I want us all to be together."

"It isn't fair, Roy."

"I know."

"You decided everything without me."

"I know, I know."

"What will you do—raise them all on your own?"

"If I have to. But of course I would try to find someone else as soon as possible."

"Oh, Roy."

"I'm sorry. I know this must sound horribly brutal to you."

"I think you'd better leave now, Roy."

"You've made up your mind?"

"I just have to be alone."

THIS TIME WHEN NONA appeared at the bedroom door, Pip scrambled to his feet: she had his leash in her hand. They had been going for much shorter walks these days, because of the weather, but Nona tried to take him out more often than usual.

Saturday night, and the streets were full of laughing girls and scary-looking boys and scattered trash. A deathliness over all, despite the bustle. No breeze. Who would imagine air could be so solid. A young woman sat on the pavement with her back up against a lamppost. More than half naked. Sores. Scratching. She cooed hopefully at Pip, but he walked right past her, like Nona, eyes straight ahead, heartless.

As Pip hunched in the gutter, a man yelled from a stoop, "You better be planning to clean that up, lady."

Oh, to be one of those scary-looking boys. Then she would make him eat it.

It was after two when they got home. Too late, alas, to call Tim. "I must, I must—" Pacing again. Whatever it was, she must do it quickly, or explode. She kicked off her shoes and sat down on the rug in the middle of the bedroom floor, folding her legs into lotus position. Not long ago it had been too uncomfortable for her to sit like this. Now she did it every day and had found that, for whatever mysterious reason, it did have a calming and head-clearing effect. She inhaled a deep breath. Breathing was the key to quieting the mind—she had heard this often enough. One of the purposes of the yogic contortions was to teach you how to breathe when air passages were constricted. Training, supposedly, for difficult and panic-inducing situations. It was control of the breath that enabled the yogi to remain serene no matter what was happening. So Nona breathed, as smoothly and as deeply as possible, trying to match the length of the exhalations with the length of the inhalations, as she had been taught.

It can never be too hot for yoga, it was said, and Nona, in her shorts and thin T-shirt, was too cold. She got up, went to turn off the air conditioner, and returned to the rug, to lotus position. Inhale. Exhale. She closed her eyes.

Years ago, when they had talked about having children, she remembered Roy telling her that he believed that any woman could be a good mother just by following her instincts. Of course, he had not meant women like that lost soul sitting out there under the street lamp. But most women. And most people, Nona was sure, would agree with him. She thought of her immigrant students, the majority of whom, when asked on a test to finish a sentence beginning "Because she is a woman," wrote "she can cook." In Nona's high school, the students had been divided into three groups, each working toward a different kind of diploma: academic, clerical, or general. The girls in the last group, which was made up of the worst students, the ones seen as least likely to succeed, took child care. Why only them? Nona had wondered. Why didn't every girl have to take child care, since just about every one of them, no matter what diploma she got, would go on to be a mother? She, for example, was as nervous holding a baby as any boy. And now she wondered why everyone, male and female, didn't have to study something about being a parent somewhere along the way. Because, from what she could tell, this relying on instinct had spelled doom for innumerable children.

When she was in college and needed extra money, Nona had signed up with the school's baby-sitting service. No experience necessary, no training, and only women need apply. (Was it like that still? Could men join that service now if they wanted to? Would any want to? Did the men still have maid service, while the women were expected to clean their own rooms?) For a time Nona had been called regularly to sit for a little girl, very beautiful, very tall for her age, daughter of unusually tall and attractive parents. An only child in a penthouse filled with Pop Art. She hated everything about the place, that child: how high above the street it was, the modern furniture, the art. One day Nona unwittingly confirmed one of the girl's worst fears: yes, she would grow up to be tall and thin like her parents. The girl began to cry.

"But your parents are gorgeous," Nona said.

"I don't want to look gorgeous." Sobbing, head buried in her arms. "I want to look like you."

Nona had seen a copy of *Vogue* in another room of the apartment, and now she ran to fetch it.

"Just look at this," she said to the girl. "You see all these women? They're all *very* tall and thin." The girl lifted her head eagerly to look as Nona turned the pages. Then she began to cry again. "And they're all *hideous!*"

Her loneliness, her beauty, her strange indifference toward her parents, whom she appeared neither to love nor to hate, what her father made light of as her "crush" on Nona ("I'll die if you don't come tomorrow!")—it was all too much for Nona. After a while, she made excuses. Told the parents to find someone else. ("But she's asking for *you,*" the mother said imperiously over the phone, her daughter howling somewhere in the background.) No, not for twice the money. And then, how hard Nona had worked to forget her. What had become of the little princess, with her endless legs and her long blond hair? Nona could no longer recall her name. A model herself, perhaps. As beautiful and as unhappy as ever.

That had not been the only child to develop an intense relationship to Nona, who believed that she must be doing something wrong. None of the other baby-sitters she knew was experiencing this kind of drama. All this caused Nona much anxiety. Not to mention those kids who hated her on sight, who shrank from her, and whose mothers never called her back—what was that all about? What had she done?

For her last baby-sitting job she was asked to keep a girl company for a whole day while her parents went out of town to a wedding. A girl who, at twelve, had already put away childish things and was into serious books and conversation. She had been very curious about Nona and had drawn her out. "Tell me about your family." "And how did that make you feel?" (Nona could guess what this one had grown up to be.) To her undying shame Nona had found herself pouring her heart out to her charge, who had shaken her head gently and said, "It sounds like you've got a lot to deal with." That night the girl's mother had called the dorm: vexed, perplexed. "This may sound strange but—is everything all right? My daughter seems to be excessively concerned about you."

And so Nona quit the baby-sitting service and joined a typing pool.

How Roy had laughed at these stories. "That was a long time ago," he said. "You have to have a little faith in yourself. Look how well you get on with my sisters' kids." True. It was something of a family joke, how, during visits, the children paid more attention to Nona than to their uncle. But that was an old story. Children were drawn to the eccentric, the flighty—everyone knew that.

(Here Nona eased her legs out of lotus position and lay down, crossing her arms under her head.)

Wanda, Jody, Mack, Melinda, Brad. None of these were names Nona herself would have chosen. "Mack" seemed to her particularly unfortunate. Quickly she calculated how old she had been when each of them was born. So, say they really had been her children: she would have had the first, Brad, when she was twenty-seven and the baby Wanda just a year and a half ago. Five children in thirteen years: not so unreasonable. Families of seven had been common enough when she was growing up. And one thing she knew for sure: Roy would have no trouble finding a mother for those children. Plenty of women who'd leap at the chance. Maybe some woman who would insist that they have one more: one of their own.

Wanda and Jody, who was five, and Mack (six) had been asleep when the accident happened, and Nona was haunted by what she'd been told about Jody, who had come downstairs the next day to a house full of distraught adults and, wriggling free of all the arms that tried to hold her, went from room to room: "Mommy? Daddy?"

It could happen. You could kiss your mother and father good night, go to sleep, and wake up an orphan. You could be celebrating your birthday at a restaurant and on the way home a car could come flying through the air and land on top of yours, crushing you. Nona would never forget the sound Roy had made when his father called to break the news: like a man being mutilated. Arriving at his parents' house, walking into the kitchen: a postcard of the Grand Canal on the refrigerator door!

Everyone had been moved to see how the children formed their own tight little cluster, with the elder ones, who understood what had befallen them, seeming to protect the younger, who did not. Poor Melinda: though she was not the eldest, it was inevitable that most of the burden would fall on her: she was the eldest girl. (It was Melinda who had finally gotten Jody to stop running through the house calling for her parents.)

But wait. (Here Nona opened her eyes and sat up.) The way

the children had clung to one another. Roy was absolutely right. It would be so much better to keep them together. They had all suffered the same calamity. Only they would understand, and they would be able to help one another. And Nona remembered how, after her parents had broken up, she had been sent to live with her aunts. She remembered how unhappy she had been, how she had always felt that she didn't belong anywhere and how, kind though people were, nobody could ever really make her feel at home. Those desolate days, when she would have given her right arm for a brother or a sister. And would she want such a fate for poor Melinda and the others? No. No, no. It wasn't fair. It must be prevented. Roy was right.

Looking at the clock, Nona saw that it was now too late even to call her mother in California. But she and Rosalind had already spoken, and Nona knew what her mother would say. Before hanging up tonight, she had told Nona, "I promise to do anything I possibly can to help."

The air in the room had become warm and moist, but Nona did not want to turn on the air conditioner—an old and very noisy machine. She got up and went to fix herself a glass of ice water. She drank it slowly, holding the cold glass to her forehead between sips.

There would be no question of sleep tonight. She could always take a pill, of course, but she did not want to. She had no desire to sleep tonight.

Instead, she undressed and took a long cool shower. Then, with one towel wrapped around her wet hair and another around her waist, she went and sat down at her desk, as if she were going to work. She even turned on the desk lamp. When they saw each other in Minnesota, her mother had surprised her by asking about the book—it was the first time either of them had mentioned it in almost a year. "You must be very happy to have that finally behind you," Rosalind said. But Nona did not feel happy now. She felt bereft. She sat, aching,

observing her reflection in the window: bare breasts and tur-
baned head: odalisque with a laptop. She thought of the
woman she had seen sitting outside the café, in that square, in
Venice. Superb in the sunlight, in her iron chair.

That is my trouble, Nona thought, getting up. No dignity.

Now Pip, who had been sleeping in the corner, got up, too,
and shook himself. Yawning, he reached forward with his
front paws, tail high in the air, chest low to the floor, and
stretched—the position known to yogis as Down Dog. Then
he stretched in the opposite direction, straightening his front
legs and extending his back legs out behind him: Up Dog. It
was said that at the creation of the world Vishnu assumed
each of the asanas—Dog, Lion, Fish, Peacock, Eagle, Cobra,
and so on—and lo, each animal was born.

Pip gazed expectantly at Nona, gently wagging his tail.

Pip, whom Nona loved, and who hated children.

Nona slipped into the loose cotton pants and tank top she
often wore to yoga practice. When she opened the back door,
Pip raced out into the yard ahead of her. The sound of many
air conditioners made a great roar, like a waterfall. That night
the temperature had never fallen below eighty. Now it was rising again. Nona's feet left dark prints on the flagstones. No
light in any window. The sky had just begun to pale.

Nona stood very straight with her feet together and brought
her palms together in front of her chest. Inhaling deeply, she
stretched her arms up and arched back from her waist.
Exhaling, she bent forward with straight legs, laid her chest on
her thighs and her head on her shins, and pressed her palms to
the ground on either side of her feet. Inhaling, she thrust her
right leg behind her and placed the knee on the ground, arching her back and neck, lifting her face to the sky. She thrust
her left leg back then and supported her weight evenly on her
hands and toes. Exhaling, she lowered first her knees, then her
chest, and finally her forehead to the ground. Inhaling, she
lowered her hips, pointed her toes, and arched her back and

neck, lifting her face to the sky. Exhaling, she curled her toes under and pushed her hips up so that her body formed an inverted V. Inhaling, she stepped her right foot forward between her hands, resting the left knee on the ground, arching her back and neck, lifting her face to the sky. Exhaling, she stepped her left foot forward to meet her right foot, straightened her legs, touching chest to thighs and head to shins, palms pressed to the ground. Inhaling, she straightened her body from the waist, stretching her arms forward and then up and back over her head. Exhaling, she returned to the same position she had started from, arms at her sides.

Surya Namaskar. The sequence of twelve positions used as a warm-up for yoga practice. Traditionally performed at dawn, facing the sun. There were said to be yogis who could do hundreds of rounds of Sun Salutation, without rest. Essential to move as fluidly as possible, flowing from each position to the next, coordinating the movements with the breath. Riding the breath, this was called. It sounded easy, when done well it looked very easy, but it was not easy at all. One round and Nona had broken a sweat. Soon there was not an inch of her body that was not soaking wet. She did not count the rounds as she did them. Certainly more than the five or six they usually did in class; more than she had ever done before. Every time she wanted to quit she summoned up a bit more breath and strength to persevere for another round. At last she stopped and stood waiting for her pulse and her breathing to return to normal.

Nona sank to the ground and lay flat on her back, palms facing up. *Savasana*: Corpse Pose.

Very dead she looked to the early riser who happened to glance out his bathroom window then, razor in hand.

She lay for a long time: still. She was tingling all over, which gave her a sensation of incredible lightness—as if she were no longer on the ground but suspended a few feet above it. As the sweat evaporated, she felt naked and cool, the way she imagined it must feel to shed a skin. When she finally stood up, she looked down and saw the full imprint of her body on the flagstones.

Hazy sunlight filled the backyard now. A garbage truck broke the quiet with a loud squealing roar, like a dinosaur. Someone's baby woke and began to cry. The man who had been watching Nona finished shaving.

Nona looked through the window into her bedroom, where she had left the lamp on, illuminating her desk and her empty chair.

Yes. I was happy then.

Pip stood at the door; he wanted to go back inside now. A sharp pain assailed Nona when she saw him, but she took a deep breath and quelled it.

That was what her mother must do for her: she must adopt Pip.

Nona went through the apartment, turning out all the lights. She got out of her wet clothes and took another shower, this one very quick. She dried herself and put on her blue-and-white bathrobe. She went into the kitchen and fed Pip. She went into the bedroom and lay down on the bed to wait until it would be late enough to call her husband.

She slept.